10

The Home Front

David Wickenden

Published by David Wickenden, 2022.

THE HOME FRONT

First edition. November 15, 2022.

ISBN: 978-1-9992791-6-5

Written by David Wickenden.

Also by David Wickenden

Laura Amour Thriller

Deadly Harvest

Standalone

In Defense of Innocence

Homegrown

For Heaven's Sake

The Home Front

Watch for more at davewickenden.wixsite.com/dave-wickenden.

Dedication

As I hammer the last nails into this story, I, like the rest of the world am watching the cowardly, brutal attack by a madman against the Ukrainian people. The horrors we are seeing are unbelievable, but are nothing compared to the brave, determined people who are living through this injustice. My heart goes out to these freedom-fighters and their courage reminds me of Donald, my antagonist in this story. Honest, loyal, and someone who would not run from a fight he believes in.

I dedicate this story to the people of Ukraine.

Acknowledgements

First and foremost, this, like all my other novels, would never have happened without the support and encouragement of my better-half, Gina. While I bang on the keys, she makes sure our home doesn't fall apart and ensures no one starves. Of course, with a second-generation Italian wife, who knows how to cook, you can understand my battle of the bulge. I would have it no other way.

I wanted this story to be perfect, so enlisted the services of Robert (Robin) Carson, who had come highly recommended from a fellow writer and friend, Scott Overton. He helped tighten the manuscript and brought so much to the overall story. As it turned out, this would become the most enjoyable process of writing this novel. I have learned so much from Robin and enjoyed our interactions. I look forward to working with him in the future and count him as a friend.

FIRST THEY CAME...

First they came for the Communists
And I did not speak out
Because I was not a Communist
Then they came for the Socialists
And I did not speak out
Because I was not a Socialist
Then they came for the trade unionists
And I did not speak out
Because I was not a trade unionist
Then they came for the Jews
And I did not speak out
Because I was not a Jew
Then they came for me
And there was no one left
To speak out for me

Martin Niemöller (1892 – 1984)
Lutheran Pastor and Dachau prisoner

"GET IT ALL ON RECORD now — get the films — get the witnesses — because somewhere down the road of history some bastard will get up and say that this never happened."

General Dwight Eisenhower,
Supreme Commander of the Allied Forces, 1945

Chapter One

Pancreatic cancer.

Well, damn. I didn't even know what the pancreas did. Liver and kidneys were easy enough to figure out, but I didn't even know where the damn thing was.

Just back from the bad-news doctor, and looking around my tiny apartment, past the American flag draped on the wood paneling and hanging limp in the still air, my eyes went to the old black and white of my wedding picture. My Maggie would know about the pancreas, having served as a nurse in England during the war and then back here at St. Mary's until she retired. She had helped me and a few of the fellows from my platoon deal with what we encountered at Dachau. Although the smells and visions would stay with me forever, she taught me how to live with them. She would rock me, her arms around my sobbing frame as I struggled to make sense of whatever could possess people to treat others like that.

I wish she was here to hold me now.

God, I miss her. Even fifteen years later, not a day goes by that I wish it was me rather than her that died that horrible day. But a '62 Dodge running a red light at over 40 miles an hour took that choice away from me.

I'll admit I'm scared. When the doctor made my diagnosis clear, I felt that familiar coldness in my chest drop to my balls. Being ninety-five-years-old, it had been a long while since I felt anything down there. I mean, what in hell am I scared of? It's not like I'm going to live much longer, anyway. Something would definitely help me check out, eventually.

I pushed the button on my automatic lift chair that my kids bought me a couple of years back. God bless them. They might not visit as much as I like, but they still take care of their old man. If they hadn't gifted it to me, I'm sure they would have found me dead in my old chair. Between bum knees and the loss of strength in my arms, I probably would have starved right there.

I shuffled across the room toward the table where another gift from the kids lay. I made sure I took small steps and had a firm grip on my walker, just like the nurse at the VA Medical Center taught me, so I wouldn't trip and go ass over teakettle. Might bust a hip or my neck, like the hollow bones of a robin.

Exchanging the walker for a kitchen chair, I sat, then ran a liver-spotted hand over my liver-spotted skull and pushed the strands of my comb-over back in place. I dragged my tablet towards me. When the kids bought it, I thought they were nuts. What did I know about such fancy gizmos? But I admit, after they showed me how I could move around on it, it was fun.

I could travel the world right from the comfort of my own home. I streamed all the old dusters and war movies rather than watch that crazy superhero crap or reality bullshit that's on every channel. People want to see real heroes? They should have been with me when we stormed Omaha Beach while the Nazis threw everything they had at us. Explosions were so intense, most of us couldn't hear for hours after the attack. Bodies were everywhere: brothers, childhood friends and buddies from small towns you never heard of.

Once the tablet powered up, I pulled up my browser and typed *pancreatic cancer* into the search box. In seconds, I had over 540,000 hits. Who the hell puts all that on the Internet? I tapped the image button and clicked on a picture that gave me a peek where the sucker hid—right up against the small intestines.

I read a summary of the cancer and understood where the pain in my stomach and back was coming from. Looking at the wrinkled skin of my arm, I had to admit it was a shade of sick yellow.

I'm sure the doctor, some kid that looked like she'd just graduated from high school, let alone the medical program at the University of Pennsylvania, told me all this. But my mind went south at the words: *terminal cancer*.

She'd rambled on for a good ten minutes while I sat there with my mouth open like some damn idiot. It wasn't until she reached over and shook my arm, did I acknowledge her.

"How... How long?" I remember asking.

"Because it's so advanced and has spread to both your lymph nodes and liver, I am guessing between six to seven months," she said, trying to hold back emotions evident in her misty eyes.

Even through my fear, I could see that the announcement affected her as well. No way in hell I could ever do her job. Hell, I went through the battle for Europe and another stint in Korea, but I could never sit there and tell someone they were going to die.

"Had me a long life, Doc," I said, struggling to stand. She jumped up and helped pull me from the chair, ensuring I had a firm grip on my walker. "Lost my wife and a lot of friends along the way. It'll be nice to meet them again."

"There are treatments that might prolong—" she tried to say, but I shook my head, cutting her off.

"I don't think so, Doc. I will not piss away what little inheritance I have for my family just so I can lose what little hair I have left and shit liquid for a couple days at a time just to gain a few hours." Glancing at her, I shook my head. "Not worth it."

"Here's a prescription for pain. You will need it as this progresses."

I looked her in the eye and could see she was being bluntly honest. I took the paper, folded it, and slipped into my wallet. Dropping the wallet into my back pocket, I nodded to her and shuffled for the door. She met me there to open it for me. As I walked down the hall, I could feel her eyes on me the entire way.

I guess the doctor would cut me some slack if I concerned myself with my own feelings rather than hers. I sighed and tucked the memory of the office visit away as I looked up from the tablet, scanned the apartment again, and wondered how I'd break the news to Richard and Gail.

Both my kids were retired and enjoying their time off, although Richard was on call for his son, Tyler, when there were questions about the store. I felt proud that Tyler agreed to continue the family tradition and not sell my old store to one of the bigger companies. He was the third generation to own Wilson's Groceries. After returning from my Korean stint, Maggie made me promise I would stop looking for wars to fight and settle down. Using the money they cashiered me from the military with, we purchased a small butchery from an old Italian who was kind enough to teach me the ropes of running a business before he retired. After years of sacrifice and hard work, I was able to expand the business by buying the entire block. Gambling every cent we owned, I razed the older buildings and put up a single large building that would house a fully stocked grocery store.

As they grew older, both my kids worked in the store; and while Gail followed her mother into nursing, Richard stayed on. Now Tyler carries the family name.

My news would probably screw up their retirement for the six months the doctor told me I had left. At least when Maggie went, it was fast. Although the pain of her loss almost shattered me, I didn't have to watch her die slowly while she withered in agony. I would spare my kids that pain.

When I stood and shuffled over to our family pictures on the sideboard, I noticed the one other photograph that sat proudly on my wall—me receiving the Bronze Star from none other than President Eisenhower, himself. Maggie had been so proud, but that turned into a coldness that was biting when she learned *why* I was awarded the medal! With a young wife and one toddler at home, I'd left my relatively safe Korean foxhole, run a hundred yards through enemy fire and not only recaptured one of our machine-gun positions, but also ended up killing a Chinese general. Even though we might have been overrun if someone hadn't secured that position, my dear Maggie didn't think it should have been me. She didn't talk to me for a week.

Passing the picture, I scooped up our wedding photo, and after sticking it in the front pouch of the walker, moved back to my chair in the living room. Settled, I grasped the frame with fingers that had stealthily become knobby and arthritic and looked at the only woman I have ever loved.

"Hey kiddo, going to be together again soon. You owe me a couple of dances," I said as my tired, dark-blue eyes began to tear up. "Not sure what I should do about telling the kids about the cancer. Tell them the news or keep it to myself? I don't want either one of them to be sitting here for the next while holding my hand, waiting for me to go. That would just extend the pain. I know Gail took care of dying people all the time, but I also know she changed departments in her last years because it was haunting her. Having her watch me die will hurt her all the more."

I traced my finger across Maggie's incredible smile and down her dark, flowing hair, my heart aching.

"Thanks, sweetheart," I said, lifting her image to my lips. The glass was cold. "I'll spare them the pain."

Chapter Two

My little apartment was cozy, but I made a couple of trips from it each week just to stay mobile and keep my sanity. By the way, Maggie and I owned the whole building. After Maggie was gone, I moved from the largest of the four apartments, which we had called home, into a smaller one on the ground floor. We'd paid off the building years ago, and added income never hurt. It would be a nice inheritance for Richard and Gail. They could keep it as an investment or get rid of it after I was gone. I wouldn't be around to argue either way.

One trip I made every week was for groceries, although I generally ordered on-line during winter months. Today was another and even more important trip for me, though—an afternoon at the Legion.

Wayne, the driver for the Veteran Affairs organization, pulled up to the curb and ran around the handi-transit van to slide open the door and help me to my seat. The big Black man had spent two tours in Iraq and still was dealing with losing a few good friends there. He and I really hit it off, especially once he heard of my past service.

"Dude," he said as he folded my walker, stored, and secured it with a bungee cord. "You really have to let me put racing flames or stripes on your ride."

"Can't be without it for as long as it would take you, Wayne," I said with a grunt. We had been here before, so I figured he was just jawing.

"Come on, man," he said, putting the transmission into gear. "You don't live forever."

I choked on my reply, realizing he knew nothing about my condition. "How much time would you need and how much would it set me back?"

His eyes flashed through the rear-view mirror to look at me. "For you, I can get it done in one night. And I have a loaner for you. As for price, you've already paid the price, man."

"Appreciate it, My Man," I said, trying to duplicate his slow, Cajun drawl.

He chuckled out loud, checking his mirrors before pulling into traffic. Keeping his attention on the road, he asked, "Meeting with the regulars today, Donald?"

"Whoever can make it will be there. We haven't seen Benny in a few weeks, but there's been no notice from the VA and nothing in the obits."

"I saw him," Wayne said. "He'll be back soon. Needed a new pacemaker, is all."

"Good to hear."

Benny was a close friend who had driven across half of Europe as a tank man. It would be good to see him back at our weekly meetings.

We pulled up to the Legion Hall and Wayne said, "You better get inside Donald. That sky looks like it's ready to dump its load." He pointed at dark clouds being pushed by a fresh wind that had come up since he'd picked me up.

"Thanks, Bud. See you in a couple of hours."

"I'll be here at fourteen hundred, as per normal. If it's raining, I'll meet you at the door with the umbrella."

He ran around the van, pulled the door, and opened my walker, holding it for me as I slid out. His powerful arms were a reassuring presence.

"You're the best, Bud." I said, really meaning it. All of us old vets in the area relied on this selfless soldier who put our welfare before his own.

I hit the silver handicap button beside the entrance, gave Wayne a wave as he pulled away while the door opened enough to accept the walker, then entered the dark but familiar interior. I stood there, letting my eyes adjust to the dimness before pushing toward a long table where most of my living friends sat.

As I navigated the walker between narrow aisles of chairs, a few heads turned in my direction to throw several salutations my way. Pictures of the past littered the room. I knew the Legion had my photo accepting my medal, but there were also reminders of the devastation left behind both in Europe and in the East. Recently, more and more photos show our boys and girls in Afghanistan and Iraq. They were welcome brothers-in-arms.

"Donny-boy, glad you could make it!" yelled Frank, voice raspy because of the packs of cigarettes I remembered that ran to two and three a day after he came back from the war. Other than the rough voice and the nicotine-stained fingers that looked like the current president's skin tone, cigarettes had never put their hurt on Frank. Part of me wanted to shake him to his senses, especially after hearing my own prognosis; but it was his life, his choice. I had to respect that. He was over ninety, after all.

He had flown one of the twin-engines, a P38-Lightning, against the Japanese in the latter part of the war. The massive horsepower of that gorgeous plane (that the Japanese called, "Two planes, one pilot") was more than an equal to the Japanese Zero, and Frank and his squadron had helped to alter the balance of South Pacific air warfare, allowing our ships a relief from the continuous onslaught of suicide bombers.

Decker kicked a chair out of the way to allow my walker. "What'd the doc have to say, Donald?"

I had decided to tell my Legion platoon members, because we never had secrets.

I was one of the first to know that Frank's daughter had come out of the closet and talked him out of expressing his rage. He now had two grandchildren who he adored, raised by not one but two daughters who adored him.

Across from me was Rita, whose husband, Nevil, died from a heart attack years ago while attempting his third Boston Marathon at seventy-two. She had been a WAC, a member of the Women's Army Corp. In those days, she had been an air controller, and her voice was sometimes the last voice our pilots heard before they crashed into the unforgiving depths of the English Channel. But she also coached a lot of beat-up aircraft home to land safely. She blew me a kiss, which I made the motion of catching and dumping into my mouth. We had played this teasing charade for almost two decades now.

"Let me wet my whistle first," I said waving at the bartender, a new guy I'd never seen before.

"What do you want, Old Timer?"

I stared at him, anger rising at his truthful but ignorant reminder of my age. I swallowed at the offense, but would have a better comeback the next time he mouthed off.

"Two drafts."

Leaning forward, I put my hand to my mouth, so my voice didn't cross the room. "Where's The Kid?" I asked. The Kid had been here for years, and although he was in his forties, he was still The Kid to this crowd.

"Sorry to be the bearer of bad news, but The Kid overdosed on fentanyl two nights ago."

I stared at Decker in shock. "What a bloody waste," I said, shaking my head.

I couldn't really criticize. After Dachau, I had used the morphine in our med packs to push back the horrors that had followed me from that place. I didn't know what had been chasing The Kid, but it was too bad he'd never found someone like Maggie to help fight the demons. Even though those demons were a mental health issue, it all still made me sick, and his death's added weight pushed me down further.

As ignorant as the new guy was, he did manage to get my two-beer order right, and I sipped at the froth, enjoying the coolness in my throat. I wiped froth from my upper lip and found everyone looking at me with intense attention.

Taking gulp of draft and a deep breath to help my courage, I said in a rush. "Terminal pancreatic cancer. Six to seven months."

There wasn't a single soul except me whose mouth hadn't fallen open in shock. No one said anything for a time, which allowed me to finish my first tall glass of beer in peace.

"Dammit, Donald," Rita said, tears falling freely, cutting me in two. "Is there no treatment they can give you? I mean it's 2020. New cures are being found every day."

I shook my head, having a hard time to keep it together, especially with her open emotions.

"Nope. It's spread to both my liver and lymph nodes. The doc was absolute and honest."

"But what will you do?"

I chuckled as graveyard humor bubbled up. "I guess, I'll die."

"Damn," Frank said, hitting the table with the palm of his hand. "It's not fair."

"Fair or not, I figured you guys needed to know. I'm not telling my kids, so keep a lid on it."

Rita reached out and touched my hand. "Why not, sugar?"

"Trust me, I have my reasons. I hope you'll respect that."

She nodded her head, her hand dragging across the table away from mine.

"So, what are you planning on doing for your last months on earth?" Decker asked around the froth of his beer.

"What do you mean?" I asked, confused because Decker's well aware of my limited mobility and other health issues.

"Are you just going to wait around to die, or are you going to make a statement?"

"What do you think I can do in six months?" He was pissing me off with his innuendos.

He shrugged and stood up. We all watched him cross to the bar and grab the remote that sat on the hardwood surface. The new bartender gave him a dirty look, which he ignored and pointed the remote towards the big screen mounted on the wall.

The idiot bartender had the channel on Much Music, as if anyone in the Legion would give a shit about modern hip-hop, rap or boy bands of the '90s. I could more readily relate to the harder rock that came out of the Middle East theaters. I actually enjoyed Five Finger Death Punch and Soldier Harm. Those guys had seen the horror of war and told their story in song.

Decker flicked to CNN, and what came up on the screen made me see red and gave me a reason *not* to lie down and die.

Chapter Three

CNN's flashing "Breaking News" disappeared to show a synagogue spouting heavy black smoke. As the members pushed through the double doors of the front entrance, two rows of black-clad neo-Nazis, with red shields held across their chests, greeted them, arms raised in the infamous Nazi salute. Pushed forward by panicking people behind them as they sought safety from the flames and smoke, those nearest the Nazis leaned away from the new threat.

The film was obviously from a phone camera because the frame never stopped shaking, but the picture was clear. The group fleeing their place of worship seemed to flatten itself across the shield wall rather than offer an opportunity to violence.

The group of neo-Nazis was chanting, and although the sound was garbled at first, it became clearer. "Blood and Soil!" and "We won't be replaced by Jews!" The ugly *Hakenkreuz*, the swastika, was prominent on their shields and on the flags they carried.

The camera broke to an anchor desk with a talking head who made a perfect show of expressing shock and pain for the victims as he said, "We have more footage from four more synagogues and one mosque that were torched in similar acts of domestic terrorism."

Seeing those black uniforms that had symbolized everything my friends and I fought against pulled me back over seventy years. German steel tore apart our buddies from the shores of Normandy to deep in Germany. We were told to eradicate these Nazi vermin by FDR himself. Freedom from tyranny, oppression and standing up for the little guy were the catch phrases.

My hand shook as I brought my second glass of draft to my lips, and I instinctively knew that those horrible images from the past would visit me again tonight. It was like the black-clad goons had resurrected the past in real life. In our time.

"We have unconfirmed reports that the Nazi Movement of America, the NMA, has taken credit for these acts of violence and promises more to come in the next few days in unnamed cities across the United States and Canada."

"The bastards!" I muttered, slamming my glass down, spilling beer over my hand and across the table.

Eyes flew to me and the mess I'd made. I just shook my head to apologize because I didn't trust my voice. I was fuming inside. How dare they flaunt that evil symbol at loyal American citizens and so blatantly express their hatred for a people who had never done them any wrong? That kind of arrogance started the war in the first place.

"Getting a little rowdy, Pops," the bartender said as he wiped up the spilled beer. "Keep it up and I'll have to cut you off."

"And you might be out of a job by the end of the day," Decker said, straightening up in his chair. "You forget that this is a Legion? Donald fought in two wars, so jack-offs like you didn't have to. Show some respect."

The man stood there like he would say something else but spun on his heel and strode back to the bar, his hooded eyes showing he wasn't happy.

"Thanks, Decker, but you should have just ignored the guy," I said, wiping my wet hands on my pant leg.

"Bull-roar," Rita said, baring her teeth. "Dexter said it before I could. People today do not understand what we've done or why. Too busy with their phones in their faces and their heads up their asses."

I couldn't help chuckling at the words of the toughest woman I had ever had the pleasure of knowing. Living and managing hundreds of men as they followed her lead to their targets in Europe, many who would never return, had hardened her like a diamond. When needed, she could shine brighter than a supernova.

"So why so upset about the news story, Donald?" Frank asked, his eyes flashing from me to the screen.

"It's that goddamn swastika!" I growled. "We lost a lot of people to stamp that hatred out. How can our damn government allow it to resurface? Worse, to allow it to operate so openly, and right in our own town. Those shits have no business in Lancaster!"

"That's the Constitution. Freedom of Speech and Assembly is part of the First Amendment," Frank said. "You know that."

"After what we had to endure and what they put the entire world through, there should have been an amendment to the Constitution to exterminate every one of those bastards!" I said, anger causing me to come close to losing my dentures.

I could feel my face burning and hear my heartbeat in my ears. I had to calm down or I would have something else to worry about. Tapping my chest pocket to ensure my nitro was handy, I took a couple of ragged breaths while my friends looked on with worried expressions. I resettled my glasses on my nose.

Once I got my breathing under control and the thumping in my head subsided, I said, "Look, I understand the Constitution and I support it. I despise all the hatred and White-supremacist bullshit that this asshole in Washington is riling up. All this is his fault. But there has to be a line. To me, that line was crossed in the '40s. And we did as asked and stomped those evil bastards to death. We cannot allow them to rise again. Especially here in our own country."

I slumped back in my chair, sipping what remained of my glass of draft, trying to remain calm. I refused to look at the big screen, knowing it would only get me more upset. For the thousandth time, I wished Maggie was here to just hold me. Her cold logic always spoke to the root of any problem without being blindsided by emotion.

I remember back when she was helping me get over the worst of the nightmares, she told me, "They're dead, Donald. Nothing you do will bring them back. You avenged them by forcing the Nazi officers and their men to dig the mass burials of the corpses left behind. You could have killed the Nazis without a thought, but it would have made you a monster, like them. The Army avenged them by putting each and every one of them on trial to answer for their crimes—and the world stood behind those actions."

She pulled away from our embrace and looked me square in the eye. "Your job is complete. You were successful, but now you have to move on, otherwise *they've* won. The fascists will claim you as another victim without having fired a bullet. Decide. Will you triumph, or will they?"

"Okay, Donald," Decker said, bringing me back to the moment, his elbows propped on the table with his glass in front of him, so I could only see his eyes. "What are you thinking of doing? Joining an opposition organization, like Antifa?"

"Who are they?" I stammered, not recalling hearing the term.

"They're a group that grew after the Charlottesville riots in Virginia in 2017. Since then, they have attended every extreme-right rally to disrupt, if not shut down, right-wing rhetoric. They have no issue about getting their hands dirty."

"Oh yeah," said Rita with a snort. "I can just see Donald mixing it up with a bunch of neo-Nazis with clubs. He'd be dead in seconds, or they'd use him as a stomping rug." I could tell the direction the topic had turned had pissed her off. She downed an entire glass of beer in one swallow. Damn, who the hell would pour her home? Wouldn't be me. Last time, she tried to get frisky and ended up falling asleep with her dress around her ears. Neither of us ever talked about that."

"Well, maybe I'll look them up," I said defiantly, not wanting any of them to thinking I'd lost my nerve.

"Oh shit," Decker said, running his hand over his short-cropped white curls. "That's the same expression he had when he saved my bacon in Korea. It was back in 19...."

"Not again," said Frank with a tired groan. "Are you really going to tell that story again? Enough already."

Decker's head drooped in a pout. What the others didn't know was that that was the most exciting night of Decker's life. I helped, and he would have been dead if I hadn't come to his rescue; but life hadn't been kind to this big-hearted man.

We might never have met had the U.S. Military not been forced to stop the segregation of its own troops. "Colored" troops never mixed with White until the Communists—the Commies—cleverly figured this out during the Korean conflict. Once they promised to treat any surrendering Black soldier better than the Americans treated their own because of the color of their skin, the American military had no choice but to face up to its own racist policies or face full-scale surrendering of US territory. Decker had been one of those Black soldiers that had been integrated with our company, and he and I hit off from the start.

Orphaned as a child, he grew up on the harsh streets of New York, escaping to what he thought was a better life by enlisting in another war we were not allowed to win. After the war, his luck didn't improve. He jumped from job to job until I found him living in the back alley of my grocery. I gave him the job of stocking shelves at night, which he did without complaint until his retirement.

As harrowing his wartime battle had been, it would continue to be the highlight of the man's life and he was always ready to tell the story to whoever opened the topic. If they didn't, he was not beneath offering his own intro.

When he finally looked up and sought my eyes, I gave him a quick wink to let him know our bond was strong.

Rita put her hand on my arm and gave me a squeeze. "I hope you're not thinking about doing something dangerous. You might have six months, but none of us ever really know when our time's up. I don't want to lose you too soon." She swiped at a tear forming at the corner of her eye before it could escape and, to cover her slip of emotions, yelled at the bartender, "Can we get another round here?"

I didn't know what I could do, if anything. I would have to give it some thought. One thing I knew was that I had some great friends. I would miss them.

Chapter Four

The shadows in the apartment welcomed me back with a warm embrace. I was feeling the effects of that last draft Rita had bought to replace the one I spilled. Normally, I never had over two. Not like the old days of drinking all night and then putting in a twelve-hour shift in the store.

I bumped through the apartment, the walker hitting anything that wasn't tucked in. I paused long enough to retrieve my tablet from its charge cord on the bookcase. Once I reached my recliner, I pushed the tablet's *On* button and settled myself in while the tablet booted up.

When the home screen appeared, I adjusted my glasses, mashed the icon for news, and looked and listened to the ongoing reports of the attacks on the mosque and synagogues. Every time the camera flashed over those hateful black uniforms, my stomach clenched, and I had to remind myself that I needed to think rationally if I was to find a solution. If this was to be my last kick-at-the-can, I needed it to mean something.

Two hours later, my bladder forced my eyes open, and I realized I had nodded off. It was an occupational hazard at my age. My glasses were askew, but my tablet had fortunately wedged itself between my thigh and the chair and not fallen onto the hardwood floor. Even with the rubberized cover, with the treatment I give the tablet, it was only a matter of time before the screen shattered.

Struggling out of my chair, I started the race to the bathroom. Freddy always laughed at my frantic bath-runs. After multiple bouts of bladder cancer, his doctor had fitted him with a urostomy bag after removing his bladder. While the rest of us dealt with waking up four or five times a night, he slept like a baby. Of course, he never let us forget it. Fortunately, this time, I won the race. My plastic mattress guard was a reminder that I didn't win them all. I had swallowed my pride years ago by wearing an adult diaper when I traveled long distances. They served their purpose, but I still hated the damn things.

Back in my chair, while finishing the leftovers from the meals-on-wheels offering of roast turkey, potato, and veggies, I researched Antifa. I had to admit, these guys were not into turning the other cheek. After neo-Nazis had beaten a bunch of them in Charlottesville for their opposition to the Right to Rule demonstration, Antifa members began arming themselves like the white supremacists. Masks over their faces to hide their identity, hardwood sticks, and shields cut from metal garbage cans.

But this resistance to fascists was nothing new. Under different names, Antifa rose to oppose the rise of Nazi Germany throughout Europe in the 1930s, but still fought for the same thing, Members saw themselves, as they did today, as the only entity to stand against hate-ideology and racism, because governments did nothing. In fact, even here at home, this president not only turns a blind eye to the actions of ultra-Right groups, but also displays his own racism to encourage those actions.

Regardless of their techniques, there was no doubting the results. There was nowhere the fascists could assemble now that didn't find healthy opposition. The organization had a quick response team that was ready to travel to any location in the US at a moment's notice. Tapped into the universities and colleges across the nation afforded them huge backing by younger, intellectual Americans—the same people who ignored fascist violence and who openly carried weapons that included firearms to their protests, but then complained about Antifa tactics.

It seemed neo-Nazis didn't like their own tactics being turned on them.

The more I read, the more I realized that this was not just an American issue. The rise and growth of fascism was a worldwide problem. It was huge in Europe, including Germany where the Nazis had been defeated; and although neo-fascists held to the old steady cadence to get rid of the Jews, now it included Muslims, Hindus, Africans and all other non-Whites.

And as the White-supremacist movement grew, so did Antifa's resistance, as it had mid-century. Equally important was that the mid-century Antifa movements went dark after we defeated the fascists in the late 1940s. Dormant, but not dead. It was like they knew it was only a matter of time before the serpent could rise again.

In my day, the belief was that if we cut the head off that serpent, the head being Hitler, the monster would wither and die. But we were wrong, and Nazis had returned, but now with the backing of a popular movement that was sweeping the globe.

GERMANY 1945

Jed's hand rose to indicate a halt, and we all dropped to one knee, waiting and watching. From my location, halfway through the line, I couldn't see what had caught his attention, but saw his frantic hand signals calling for the Lieutenant to come forward. While Epstein frog-walked forward, I kept one eye on them and the other on the surrounding forest. Leafless birches and poplars covered the hillside and visibility was good. But if it was good for us, it would be equally good for an enemy outpost.

We no longer cursed freezing cold and deep snow that plagued our 7th Army as we marched towards Germany. The April air was warmer and foretold summer heat, but nights could still be chilly.

A barrage of shots cracked the spring air, and we tensed up, not knowing if we were under attack or not. There were no nearby cries, or that dreaded thumping of metal impacting flesh, but my urge to urinate was strong and I could smell the acrid sweat of fear oozing from my pores.

It was always like this prior to seeing action. It was the waiting. The tension. But all that didn't matter if the Nazis surprised us. Once the fighting started, I would fall into training and adrenalin, operating without thought. Afterward, the nerves would return, and I would be fortunate to keep my stomach where it was supposed to be.

Lieutenant Epstein had field glasses tight to his face. He was the son of a baker in New York City who brought some of his family's delights to life for us with the meager ingredients we could pick up along the way. While other platoons ate bread-in-a-can from their rations, Epstein would bake us fresh bagels in our little field oven, and even challah *on one special occasion. He was sharp as a knife and always made sure his men's needs were satisfied before he looked after himself. To protect him from himself, several of us made sure he had ample to eat by sharing our own portions. We couldn't afford him getting sick.*

The lieutenant waved us into a huddle and spoke quietly but directly. Seemed a group of Nazis was executing prisoners, so we would mount a surprise attack while their attention was diverted. Charlie Bennett and Tommy DeLucca ran crouched over, while lugging the heavy Browning M1919A6 machine gun and the boxes of linked shells. They would set up to cover our flank and keep German heads down while we advanced.

The rest of us spread out across the top of the hill, keeping under cover. For the first time, I spied the enemy. They were lined up in front of several rail cars. Guards were screaming at another line of prisoners to move faster. These poor souls stumbled forward, some pausing as they saw their fellow prisoners lying lifeless in the bottom of a freshly dug ditch. Pushed roughly in place by the black-garbed soldiers, they stood timidly, hands bound behind them.

At a command, the rank of Germans raised their rifles, and I looked frantically to my left to see if the Lieutenant would order us to shoot, but no command came before the multiple cracks of German gunfire echoed across the shallow valley. As the breeze pushed back the dense cloud of gun smoke, I watched in horror as a Nazi officer calmly walked along the lip of the trench, firing single shots from his service revolver into the heads of any men still alive.

This wasn't war, this was murder.

The officer paid for his sins just as he signaled for the next batch of victims to be brought forward. He stood by, patiently loading more bullets into the clip of his Luger. Our signal to attack came from a single blast from Dillon Fox's MC1 sniper rifle. Down range, the officer's head disappeared in a halo of crimson mist, his body falling among his victims. Four more shots rang out in rapid succession. I watched as the closest Germans in the firing squad fell backwards, their chests taking the full impact of Dillon's high-powered .30-caliber shells.

I hadn't even taken the safety off my M1 Garand, yet Dillon had five kills in as many seconds. Damn, that boy could shoot. He had grown up on a reservation with his Apache mother and hunting was all that had kept his family from starving.

As one, our platoon advanced towards the remaining Germans who stood shell-shocked at the suddenness of the violence that had caught up to them. Before we were halfway down the grade, four of them had tossed their rifles to the ground and stood with their hands behind their heads in a sign of surrender.

Dillon's rifle reached out again, firing beyond the scene as two guards that had been leading the victims from the railcar to the trench made a run for it. Both flew forward in ungraceful tumbles to lie still along the rail bed.

The locomotive built up steam, but a couple of bullets clanged across the driver's compartment. The engineer dumped his tanks.

We closed in on the train, keeping a nervous eye on the remaining Germans who shuffled in fear, eyes glued to the ground. The last bunch of prisoners stood swaying, waiting to be told what to do. Their clothing, tattered rags, hung from their emaciated bodies. They were scarecrows shortchanged on straw. The men had a black or red triangle sown on their striped prisoner uniforms.

"Any of you speak English?" I asked loudly, as Keith Webster, a former teacher, and I walked among them. We gestured for them to sit in the limited shade of the leafless trees. It was like guiding scared children who expected a slap from an abusing adult.

A voice from inside the rail car reached me. "I speak English."

Rifles at the ready, we approached the open door on the railcar. It was still half-full of prisoners, apparently all men, standing in a tight group. Even though there was more space for them, they were so indoctrinated that they stood clustered together in the same position Germans had packed them in. One man had his hand up, like a child waiting to be recognized by the teacher.

"Can you tell these people that we are Americans?" I said. "We're here to free them."

In a slow, tortured rasp, the man repeated my words in a melodic sounding language that I would later find to be Romanian. News of their rescue didn't seem to faze the men, as they looked at us in a mix of bewilderment and fear. A few broke down, silent tears shining across waxen cheekbones. Slowly, with gentle coaxing, we led these tortured souls out of the railcar to sit or lie on the dry leaves.

A commotion on the other side of the trees flared our anxiety and my fingers grew stiff, clutching my weapon. I signaled to Webster that I would check it out and rounded the last rail car. Hunched over, our men in army green uniforms, all holding hankies over their faces, were relinquishing their last meal onto the rail bed. In hindsight, that should have been enough of a warning, but I moved forward, not understanding what was happening.

The stench reached out to me and stopped me at the lip of another trench. A line of shovels stood guard on the disturbed soil. The pit was full, with a topping of white dust that reminded me of icing sugar, but was anything but sweet. Beneath the white dousing lay a collage of bodies tangled together in a dance of death. Limbs stuck up from that pile of destroyed humanity. Long, slender arms and legs of women intermingled with short, stubby flesh of preadolescents and infants. Gaping mouths screamed a testimony to the madness that had slaughtered these innocent children and their mothers.

My vision blurred. My mind caught up with what we had uncovered on a routine patrol that had become anything but routine.

The next thing I remember was being dragged away from the bloody remains of the last four Nazi guards who had served on the firing squad. My rifle was torn from my hands, the stiff, razor-sharp blade of my bayonet slick with the blood of monsters.

The Lieutenant was screaming over the radio seeking help with the situation while my own buddies now wore the disturbed and bewildered expressions of those we had liberated.

Chapter Five

The first cup of coffee, after I awoke from the familiar dream, settled in my gut like battery acid and I forced myself to swallow some dry toast to calm things down. My trembling hands were also an issue with morning coffee, but I was used to the side-effects of that horrible episode, even though there were others much worse than what had visited me during the night. I wondered why the urge to pee every ten minutes never materialized when these memories visited me. I'd have welcomed the urges for a change.

According to the news feed on my tablet, the investigation into the multiple arsons was leading nowhere. One detective announced that all four fires had been started with similar ignition devices and that they were highly sophisticated. Forensic evidence had been collected and the officials were awaiting a report from the CIS labs. That black-clad Nazis were outside of each place of worship every time the fires broke out was troubling, but so far, police could find no evidence that linked them to the arsons.

One reporter asked if there were any video surveillance recordings that might help identify the culprits of the crimes, but the detective acknowledged that someone had previously sabotaged the cameras in the synagogues and at the mosque.

Talking heads on CNN and Fox had a hundred-and-one comparisons of other hate crimes across the US and even a few overseas. But once they started comparing different attacks, you knew they didn't have a clue about what was really happening.

With a sigh, I closed the browser and sat in thought while my second cup of coffee grew cold. I hadn't figured out anything before I heard footsteps outside my apartment door. A curt rap on the steel door had me shuffling my walker to the entrance. I checked the door's peephole and saw that it was Rita. I slid the security chain open and swung the door to be greeted by her enormous smile.

"Buy a girl a coffee?" she said in her best Betty Boop imitation.

"You're in luck, girlfriend. I have a pot on the stove."

I placed a steaming mug in front of her and sat myself across the table. I had known Rita since after my stint in Korea. Coming home, I found the need for the company of others who knew what I had gone through. I joined the Legion and met Rita that same year.

The years hadn't been kind to the tough old girl. Sagging skin and moist eyes had replaced her once-flawless features, but there was still the familiar warmness in her expression. There had been a day when she would have turned heads when entering a room, men wondering if they had a chance at having her on their arm, while the women were afraid it might happen. Neither had to worry. She had her heart fixed on Nevil from the moment they met during the war at the Co-op Dance Hall in Darlington, near Croft Aerodrome. He had been a RAF Hurricane pilot and was quite dashing.

She had convinced him to immigrate, and Maggy and I had attended their wedding. They had a wonderful life until his death, which shocked everyone because he was in such great physical shape. Or so we'd thought.

"What brings you by?"

"To be honest, I've come to check on you," she said over her coffee mug. "Between that horrible news from the doctor and your reaction to that news story, I've been worried sick."

"There's no nee—"

"Don't give me that, Donald!" she said, slamming the table. "You're one of my oldest friends. The rest of the gang is there for you, just like you've been there for them over the years. You're always doing this. It's like you're scared to ask for help. Yet you're the first to give a helping hand to the rest of us."

I spread my hands to calm her. "Look, Rita, I'm ninety-five. I was going to check out sooner or later. I am at peace with that. It's been a great life, Rita. No regrets." I took her hand and felt the velvet skin of age and gave her a light squeeze. "I would have preferred going with less warning and probably less pain, but it's the cards they dealt me."

"And you're still not going to tell your family?"

Her eyes implored me to consider it, but I shook my head. "Listen to me," I said, letting go of her hand. "The last thing I want is for Gail to come running over here to play Florence Nightingale. She'd have me tied to the bed and be fretting over me. I won't allow that. I don't want her to watch me die. She's seen too many folks fight their last, and it affected her badly. As for Richard, he's busy enough helping his son settle into the business."

"Shouldn't that be their choice, Donald?"

"Not for this." I held her gaze so that she knew I'd made my mind up.

"Fine, but you had better at least visit them before things get worse. Give them a last set of memories to hold on to." She held my eyes to let me know how important she thought this was. I finally gave her a nod.

She lifted the coffee and sipped it at her small victory.

Inwardly, I smiled. With both of us widowed, she had been trying to fill the void that Nevil had left behind. I knew that if I opened the door, she'd move in with me in a second. We had even talked about it a few times over the years, but I could not give up the solitude that I've become accustomed to. After all these years, solitude was an old friend that sheltered me like a warm blanket. I still visited my friends and enjoyed the company of others, but my apartment was where I could live within my memories of Maggie.

Rita was lonely, and she was looking for a companion to share the long days and longer nights. It wasn't sexual, of course. That train had departed long ago. It was about having someone to talk to or just to be around. She had always been social and being alone wore on her. She and Nevil could not have children, so she held her friends dear.

"And what about this Nazi thing?"

I shrugged. "I don't know if there's anything I can do, but I want to try. If no one says anything, they'll continue to grow like they did in Germany back in the '30s."

"But—"

"Listen. I know I'm an old, worn-out warrior. It's not like I can kick the shit out of these cowardly assholes. Maybe thirty years ago, but now... You'd be locking me up in an Alzheimer's ward, if I thought I could do that." I gave her a reassuring smile. "But I want to see if there is a way for me to do something. Anything."

"I'm scared for you. They seem so violent," she said, biting her lip.

Patting her hand, I said, "I told you. I won't fight them. But maybe what I saw in the war might be important. Eyewitness stuff to make people remember how evil that ideology was and would be today. Maybe just a letter to the editor or even the governor."

She stared hard at me as if to find out whether I was being candid. I knew my reaction yesterday had been over the roof and that worked against me.

"Will you let me help you?" she asked, still holding my eyes.

"Rita, there's no need. I'm just going to be talking to politicians and reporters. Most of this will be from right here at this table," I said, tapping the wooden surface for emphasis.

"You stubborn old fool. You just can't let any of us give you a helping hand. Can you?"

There was hurt in her eye, and it pained me.

"Look, if there is something I need help with, I promise to call you first. Okay?"

Lips pursed, she nodded.

I DID NOT KNOW WHAT I could do to make a difference with the political issue. I thought it might help if I just spoke out about the events happening across the country. The actions of the Antifa group seemed pretty radical. But at least they were a threat to the right-wing spectrum. But even some moderate Republicans were calling Antifa a terrorist group, although they were only using the same tactics as their far-right opponents.

I did a quick search for the local branch of the group and saw that they had an office in the industrial complex across town. Making a note of the address, I called Wayne to see if I could arrange a ride later today.

"You in luck, Donald," he said. "One of my regulars passed during the night and needed a different ride than what I offer."

"Doesn't *that* make me feel great?"

"I know it sounds cold, but it's going to help you out," he said, his voice humbler, having realized how it sounded. "I'll see you at two," he threw in quickly before hanging up.

Won't be that much longer before my own passing would open up a ride for someone else. No sense getting pissed off with Wayne. It was just life; neither right nor wrong. With so many seniors around, the services we could tap into were often overwhelmed, so I was lucky to have someone like Wayne looking out for me.

I fretted around the apartment until my ride came, then a short ride through town and Wayne stopped in front of a row of small office buildings. I had called ahead to ensure there was someone I could talk to about the organization. But before he got me out of the van, Wayne eyed the sign on the door and turned around in his seat. "You sure you want to get involved with these people? They're pretty radical."

"I'm looking for answers. I figure the best way to get them is to talk to the people at the root of the issue."

He looked at me, trying to fathom my intent, but I wasn't willing to go there. Although we got along, I knew little about his background except that he had served overseas. I did not know his political loyalty, so thought it safer to keep my thoughts my own.

Seeing he would not get an answer, he sighed heavily before he said, "I'll wait for you, Donald. Not worth me running back into town. I'd only have to turn around to come back for you."

Accepting his help to gain my walker, I squeezed his arm in appreciation. "I'll try to keep it short."

I shuffled into the building's entrance and was welcomed by a cheerful smile from the receptionist. Now I may be old, but I'm still a man who can appreciate a pretty woman, and this young lady was a looker. Long, brown hair with red highlights on either side of her face enhanced the clearest blue eyes I had ever seen, and I wondered if they were lenses. The friendliness of her smile reached those eyes as she said, "You must be Mr. Wilson."

"Yes, Ma'am," I said, returning her smile.

"I'm Amanda. Steve, our Chapter President is waiting for you. Can I get you a coffee or bottled water?"

"Water would be nice."

She led me to an office at the end of the hallway and ushered me into the room while introducing me to her boss. As I shook hands with the man, she grabbed a bottle of water from a bar fridge in a corner and placed it on the table where Steve had guided me. Then she backed out of the office with another smile.

The room wasn't large, but it seemed smaller with so many photos of counter-protests that had involved the group. A number of the photos featured masked members, shields and sticks at the ready, confronting the now-familiar black and red flags with a swastika on white.

"Welcome Mr. Wilson. I admit we don't get a lot of visits from the public, so it intrigued me when you requested this meeting. How can I help you?"

I studied the man as I thought about how I would word my response. He was anywhere between twenty-five and thirty, thin but with wider shoulders that spoke to either good genes or a routine of weightlifting. Sandy-blond hair was cut short and neat. There was a tattoo poking out from his short-sleeved shirt, but I couldn't make it out.

"Well, I might be barking up the wrong tree, but I found out about your organization through the Internet. I'm hoping that there is something I can do to help your cause of fighting neo-Nazis, in particular, those that recently attacked the Jewish synagogues here in Lancaster."

A bemused smile ran across the man's face, and I knew he was seeing a tired old man, half-crippled and possibly suffering from dementia. I felt my face heat up as the familiar temper sought control over me. To shut it down, I leaned over, staring at my feet rather than at the smug smile.

"I understand you might not see me cracking heads with the best of your crew, but I have a long history of fighting Nazis," I said in a quiet voice that forced him to pay attention.

From my pocket, I pulled out my World War II Service Victory Medal and slid it across the table to him, the red, blue, and yellow ribbon trailing behind. "I received that after we beat the Nazis, and I saw firsthand what those sick bastards are capable of." I raise my eyes to lock on him. "My company was the first to reach Dachau, and I witnessed what they had done in the camps."

His eyes came off the medal, and widened at my words.

"I understand the whole First Amendment thing, but the entire world went to war to stop their evil. They cannot be allowed to rise again!"

"Mr. Wilson, that is exactly why Antifa exists. We oppose them every time they come together to spread their hatred. Our opponents are those who value the votes the White supremacists offer. Some politicians don't care about the Nazi message, or the damage and fear their modern storm-troopers produce. They only care about getting re-elected. They are truly godless."

I shook my head, feeling depression fall on my shoulders as the truth of his statement hit home. Where were the honest people we used to have leading this once-great country? Men like FDR and Ike. Didn't matter which party they were part of, they treated everyone with respect. Neither of them would have hesitated in crushing these organizations, especially having led our country through the war.

I had seen the rallies for the current president, and it made me sick how he would criticize and belittle anyone who had a different opinion to his. There's no integrity, no honor, and definitely no dignity in such a man. All he cares about is himself and his own vanity. If he wants to *Make America Great Again*, then to do so, he and other pretenders need to go away.

"We attend all their rallies to stop their rhetoric and displays of power, even if it means mixing it up with the police. I just can't see how you could help in that kind of fight."

"So, there's nothing I can do that would change anything?" I said, resigned to the brutal truth.

"I'm not sure what would be effective. We certainly wouldn't want you getting hurt at one of the rallies. It might cause some resentment towards the Nazis, but not enough to shut them down. All it would do is cause you a lot of suffering for nothing, I'm afraid."

"Okay, Steve." I said rising. "I'm sorry for wasting your time."

"It wasn't a waste of time, Mr. Wilson. It was an honor and a reminder that there are patriots who still remember the horrors fascists represent." He walked around the table and handed my medal back to me.

Dropping it back into my shirt pocket, I centered myself over the walker and shuffled towards the door.

"If anything comes up," he said, trying to give me hope, "I *will* call you. We have your number."

I nodded, not believing him. I didn't need his false hope or pity.

Chapter Six

To say it pissed me off would have been an understatement. The Antifa guy, Steve, saw me as an old man that had nothing left to offer. Even they expected me just to sit back and wait for death to claim me. Damn young people didn't appreciate that seniors have a lot of experience and skills that they could tap into. I remember his expression was like he was humoring the old coot. But there had to be more than busting heads and showing up to right-wing rallies. I had real-life stories that I could educate people to see the harm these extreme-right groups threaten.

But he just dismissed me.

He got to me, though, because I brooded and felt sorry for myself that night, wishing I was a younger man so I could be part of that anti-fascist movement. On my tablet, I surfed the Internet, but my feeds kept coming back to the news clip of that frightened group of Jewish worshipers as they escaped their burning building only to come up against the more horrifying situation of a wall of neo-Nazis. Most of them were too young to have lived through that horrible time in Europe; but from the expressions on a few of the older ones, it was plain that they remembered. It would be like having stepped back in time for them. I know it because I felt the same for me. I might not have suffered like these people, but I'd borne witness and had to live with that horror ever since.

If age was the common denominator, then I certainly had more in common with those old Jewish survivors. I might have better luck speaking with them. At least, I wouldn't get laughed at. So, I pulled out my tablet for a search.

I COULDN'T GET A RIDE until the next day, because others had booked Wayne solid. But he was there the following morning, bright and early, and dropped me off at Beit Israel Synagogue. The building was a massive complex with the synagogue between two adjacent buildings connected to it with covered, passageways. The synagogue itself was a beautiful three-story block building with a high tower topped with a Star of David. Wayne pulled up to the handicap loading zone and helped me up the path to the building's entrance. Once I was safely inside, he left for his next appointment, promising to return in two hours for the return trip. I couldn't do without the service of Wayne and the VA's transportation, but I sure missed having the independence of my own vehicle.

Rabbi Lehrer introduced himself to me in the mezzanine that led across a walkway to one of the other buildings. His smile was gentle and welcoming. His hair was turning gray at the sides, but his goatee was still dark brown. Wearing a beautifully embroidered yarmulka on his head and a casual sports jacket that hung from his thin frame, he gestured towards the hallway.

"I'm sorry," he said, his hands clenched together in front of him. "Had I known you used a walker, I could have directed you to a closer entrance. Our offices are in the other section."

"No issue, Rabbi," I said, keeping up with him easily. "I need it for balance mostly. I can still walk a fair distance."

"After our conversation yesterday, I took the initiative and invited a few of our survivors to speak with you. Perhaps among all of us, we might come up with ideas on how to deal with this disturbing situation."

That caught me off guard. Didn't know how I would react to meeting these survivors. I mean, it was over seventy years; but for me, those years and the horrors we'd encountered were as vivid as yesterday. I couldn't imagine what it might be for those who survived. What if one of them had been liberated by my companions and me? What would I say to them? Too late to turn back, I followed the rabbi down the hallway, my mind in turmoil with terrible memories.

I was half-expecting to see the gaunt, malnourished ghosts that I had helped to liberate so many years ago and that haunted my dreams, but three men and one woman who all had to be near my age greeted me. Warm, welcoming smiles held none of the empty expressions I remembered.

Two of the men were short and thin, while the third stood over six feet and was barrel-chested, although he stood slightly slumped over with age. The woman was short and fleshy, eyes almost disappearing into the folds of her face; but her brilliant smile told much of her personality.

She immediately took my hand in hers, and her forwardness startled me. "The rabbi tells me you were once a soldier who helped liberate Dachau," she said with genuine emotion. "Welcome, friend. My name is Sarah."

"My name is Donald. That was a long time ago."

She studied my face before saying, "I don't think it was long enough. You, too, still struggle with those memories, nu?"

My face must have reflected surprise at her words, because two of the men chuckled, while the tall man just shook his head before he said, "You'll have to forgive Sarah, Donald. She can read people better than anyone. Never play cards with her. I am Saul."

I shook the man's hand.

"And this is Jacob and Uri," he said, introducing the other two men.

"I'm sorry for laughing, Donald, but Sarah's first impressions never grow old."

I nodded, realizing there was nothing mocking in their attitude. They were amused more with Sarah than with my reaction.

The rabbi swept his arm towards the board table. "Please, everyone, sit."

We settled around the table, and uncomfortable with all the attention shifting to me, I began, "Sarah is right, of course. I have struggled with those memories all these years; but after what happened the other day, they've become worse." I placed my hands on the table to gather my thoughts. "Listen," I said, struggling to put my frustrations into coherent thoughts. "Almost the entire world fought to eradicate the Nazis. The losses to your people and so many others were a testament to how evil they truly were. They cannot be allowed to rise again, otherwise all the men and women who fought and died will be for nothing. And the countless murders those evil people committed will be swept away as if they never happened, allowing history to repeat itself. While I'm still breathing, that's something I cannot allow to happen."

Continuing, I said, "For years, when I've heard the term neo-Nazi, I attributed it to young skinheads, stupid, rebellious kids; but now I realize they are only the surface of so much more. I might just be an old man, but I want to do *something* that will make a difference while I still can."

I covered my mouth and looked away as I struggled to contain emotions that were tearing me in two, but my hands shook, and they all saw it.

"Unfortunately, unless the police can identify the arsonists, there is not much any of us can do," Saul said gently.

"As for the Nazis, the Constitution protects them," said Rabbi Lehrer. "The only way we can take action is if they cross the line and break the law."

"Then maybe the Constitution needs to be challenged," I said turning back heatedly, betraying my growing frustration.

"We would like nothing more, but with the current political atmosphere and the world-wide growth of anti-Semitism, now is not that time. This government prefers a divided country."

I stared at my hands, feeling totally useless. Maybe there was nothing I could do except wait for the end. The weight of years seemed to push against me, and I felt suddenly exhausted.

"Donald," said Sarah, grief darkening her features. "This is what being Jewish has *always* been like. The world needs someone to blame, and we have always been the scapegoat for the world's problems. I know it's not what you wanted to hear, but we only stay strong by staying together and educating people every chance we get."

"And maybe education is something you might help with, Donald," Saul said seemingly staring at nothing as an idea germinated. His eyes cut towards me. "Would you be interested in being interviewed about what you saw and did during the war? Coming from a non-Jew, it would hold much weight."

"But haven't others done that already? There are plenty of historical documentaries and books written about the Holocaust already."

"Yes, there are, but they are usually through the lens of a historian or from the perspective of the survivors. But coming from a person who was an eyewitness, and then tying it in with what you're seeing today could paint a strong, emotional picture."

It was something. I wasn't sure I felt comfortable about—being in front of a camera! But at least I would be doing something positive.

And just like that, the weight on me disappeared, and I felt alive. It must have shown in my face, because although I said nothing, the others broke out in big smiles.

"I didn't need Sarah to do her magical reading that time," Uri said with a chuckle.

TO SAY I WAS NERVOUS in the TV studio would be an understatement; however, the crew that the rabbi and the others brought together was amazing at making me feel comfortable. They gave me a list of questions ahead of time, so I had ample opportunity to rehearse my answers so that I wouldn't be caught off guard. And the makeup lady's quiet chatter did a lot to calm my nerves. It was like she knew just what to say.

The interviewer was a younger, but experienced interviewer by the name of Jeremy Lister who drove down from New York. He was wonderfully patient and genuinely interested in my observations about my time in the army. By the time they began taping the interview, he had me feeling like we were having a conversation rather than a staged recounting.

We spoke of my time in the army as a very young man and all the horror I had witnessed. I described the unbelievable cruelty we saw when we entered the Dachau camp and encountered the emaciated prisoners. And how General Eisenhower ordered in the U.S. Signal Corps to record the atrocities of the Nazi regime, so that no one could argue the fact.

There were a couple of times Jeremy had to stop our interview as powerful emotions overwhelmed me, and I broke down and wept uncontrollably.

As Jeremy brought me to the present and what had spurred me to come forward, that pain became anger that I struggled to control. I expressed my shock at the arsons of last week and the confrontation with the neo-Nazis at the synagogue. I explained how I felt that the government had failed the veterans who defeated the Nazis by allowing this evil threat to resurface under the guise of the Constitution. I pleaded with both political parties to unite against this vile organization. And I reminded viewers of the investigations and punishments handed out for this evil at the Nuremberg trials.

And I concluded with, "I call on every living World War II veteran who fought and lost friends and comrades in the war against that evil Nazi empire to contact both your State and Federal representatives. They need to remember and honor our sacrifices and stop this growing menace from ever rising again. If it means changing the Constitution, then that's what has to happen."

Chapter Seven

I slept well that night, well, other than my usual regular trips to the washroom, but I was able to fall back to sleep without the ugly nightmares that had resurfaced after so many years. I woke refreshed and felt positive that my efforts at yesterday's interview might make some kind of difference. They had told me that once the editing was complete, I would have an opportunity to preview the interview before they used it.

Jeremy Lister, my interviewer, had good contacts in the media and wanted to see if he could drum up enough interest to get an independent exposé of the Nazi organizations off the ground. He felt it would enhance my message rather than just a twenty-second sound bite on the news.

Taking my cereal bowl to the sink, I rinsed it and my coffee cup and set them to dry on the drainboard. Looking through the curtains over the sink, clear blue sky and sunshine reflected my mood and called to me so I figured that I'd head to the park.

Gathering my coat and hat, I thumped my walker out to the street and stopped to inhale fresh air. The coolness of the breeze still had a hint of winter, but the sun's warmth more than compensated. By the time I made it into the park, I was sweating. Parking my old butt on my usual bench allowed me to regain my labored breath and clean my glasses.

The enormous fountain had been turned on again after it had remained silent all winter, and I appreciated the optimism of the town workers, who seemed to hope that we'd turned the seasonal corner once and for all.

Winter is hard on old coots. Most of the season, I was house-bound except for the odd trip to the Legion to touch base with the gang to make sure we're all still alive. I had my groceries delivered, as a hip-shattering slip on ice-covered sidewalks could prove as fatal as the ever-present threat of pneumonia to old lungs.

Now, with my cancer diagnosis, I couldn't say which way out was the favorite. No way I was getting out alive either way.

Having caught my breath, I got up and headed around the fountain, making for the duck pond. Mallards and pintails littered the pond, and their feathers and the milky-gray of duck-crap littered the edges of it. Signs warning people not to feed bread to the birds circled the man-made lake near coin-operated food dispensers with suitable feed for aquatic fowl. A troop of four children stood around one such station, hands held ready as a woman, probably their mother, pressed coins into the slots. Behind the group, a cluster of birds waited impatiently. Laughter and excitement had me grinning as I took in the scene.

Back in the day, I'd bring home dried-up bread and wrinkled produce from the store for Maggie and the kids. We didn't know about the harm we brought to the birds with food like that, but the genuine excitement was the same for the kids. The memory made me smile. I found another bench, sat, and allowed the sun to warm me while I enjoyed the children's encounter with their new, feathered friends.

When next I knew it, I was being gently shaken by the shoulder. My lids snapped open, and I found the children long gone. I looked up, squinting into the sun at a silhouette of a man.

"Just making sure you're okay, sir," said a gentle voice. "I noticed you'd been sitting here awhile." He held a small dog on a leash who was more interested in sniffing the leg of my bench than anything else.

"Thank you," I murmured, embarrassed that I had fallen to sleep in public. "Guess the walk and the sun did a number on me."

"Can't blame you for that. The day's beautiful and park is peaceful. Enjoy." He gave a tug on the leash and he and the dog continued on their way.

I stood, leaning on the walker, figuring I'd had enough excitement for the day. The wind had died down, and I had to open the top of my coat. It felt good to be warm again. I shuffled towards home, taking care to plant one foot securely on the path before moving the other. I took my time. Ever since my first hip replacement twenty years ago, safety was my second name. Besides, at my age, nothing was that urgent, and not even my diagnosis could change that.

As I shuffled to the crosswalk, I pressed the button for a walk light and leaned heavily on the walker. My stomach rumbled at the thought of food and my mind went to the remaining leftovers in the fridge.

When the light changed, I started across. On the far side of the intersection, two young men were walking towards my apartment building. One suddenly stopped and, from the pouch on his gray hoody, pulled out a can of spray paint. Looking both up and down the street, he quickly painted a large black swastika over the red brick of the building. *MY* building!

I stopped in the middle of the intersection, not believing what I was seeing. "Hey!" I yelled as loud as I could, but even to my ears, it sounded like a dry cough.

The guy didn't even look up as he continued to retrace the evil symbol so that it stood out even more on the wall.

Then I was doing exactly what I told myself never to do. I rushed forward to stop the man. The walker moved forward and quickly outpaced my shuffling gait. I was leaning forward, my feet not moving quite quick enough; and before I knew it, I was falling. The pavement rose up and caught my chin and elbows. The walker rolled on and when it hit the curb, it fell over with a clatter. The air went out of me as I gasped at the pain.

I heard the slam of car doors and the patter of running feet.

"Easy, old fellow," said a voice over me. "You took one hell of a tumble."

"Stop him," I cried.

"Oh my God, is he all right?" a woman's concerned voice asked.

"Stop who?" the man asked.

I tried to point at the man with his spray can, but when I twisted my neck, he was nowhere in sight. Only that blasphemous symbol remained.

"Do you think you can stand? We need to get you off the street," the young man, maybe in his twenties, said.

When I nodded, he helped me sit up. The woman had retrieved my walker and was holding it steady. The man stuck his arms through mine and locked his wrists around my chest. With the strength of youth, he smoothly lifted me to my feet, only tentatively letting go once I wrapped my hands on the arms of the walker. Both he and the woman walked me to the curb, one on each side of me, like worried parents with an infant taking its first steps.

Some impatient driver honked his horn in irritation, causing the three of us to twist around. The young man raised a middle finger.

"Don't worry about him," the young guy said to the woman. "The jerk can wait." He looked at me, "Are you going to be all right? Is there anyone you want me to call?"

"I'm okay. I'm just upset that asshole got away!"

"Who?"

I pointed at the still wet and dripping swastika. "He was painting it in broad daylight."

"I better move my car," the woman said. "I'm glad you're okay."

"Thank you for stopping," I said, squeezing her arm. She turned away, got into a little pickup truck, gave the honking motorist her own middle finger, and drove off.

The young man took a couple of steps toward the swastika, looked at it for a moment, and said, "No sense getting injured chasing after a scumbag. Let the police do their job."

I didn't bother to argue. He was too young to understand. The man watched the traffic and then jogged to a blue

Civic with the flashers on. He drove off with a wave as I shuffled to the entrance of my building, only stopping to glare at the hated emblem.

Back in my apartment, with a shaky hand I dialed 911 after I sat down. I could still feel the stickiness of blood on my chin. The dispatcher took my information but said that vandalism wasn't a priority, and it might be days before they could free up someone to take a statement. "You can use our on-line reporting portal if you have access to a computer," she said.

"Never mind. Obvious it's not important enough!" I said, hanging up the phone in frustration.

In the washroom mirror, I examined the scrape on my chin and rinsed the area with a face cloth, turning water red as I re-broke the skin. I cleaned the area as best I could and used the damp cloth to blot the last of the seeping blood. Inside, I thanked the Fates that all I got from the tumble was a scraped chin and not a broken hip.

Back in the kitchen, I bent into the refrigerator, but nothing appealed as my mind kept churning at the blatant disrespect of the idiot with the spray can. I was too upset to eat.

Finally, knowing I'd get no rest until I completed the job, I gathered cleaning supplies and left my apartment again. Minutes later, I stood in front of that poisonous talisman and attacked it with hot soapy water, a spray bottle full of solvent and a stiff floor brush. It was hard work, especially on brick, and I managed only one of the four arms of the symbol before calling it a day. If it took me a month of Sundays, I would tear that image off my home.

Chapter Eight

Cleaning the brick walls of the building of the hateful image took longer than I thought. With very little of my muscle tone left, I could only work a little at a time, taking many breaks. Overhead work was the worst. Having been away from any real exercise for over two decades left me panting and sweating in minutes. Even holding the brush was difficult as my hands cramped.

To make matters worse, once I stripped the swastika off the wall, the contrast between scrubbed surface and dirty brick left a faint but distinct duplicate of the same insignia. It would take a few more days to stretch each arm to become a blob of clean masonry.

Finally complete, I took my cleaning tools one last time up to my apartment, hoping I'd never have that job again. I certainly wouldn't have to put up with the annoying beeping of horns from the odd vehicle passing by to either applaud and encourage my efforts or deride my stance. The first I didn't need; the second, well, I just didn't give a shit what they thought.

During my breaks, I tried internet searches followed by phone calls to find some political leader to speak to about the issue. A polite and professional woman at the Governor's office seemed to be sympathetic until she launched into what sounded to my ears as a pre-written spiel about how busy the

Governor was and that it might take months to see him—if ever—and how I might find contacting my local representative a lot faster.

The woman who answered my call at the local office of my congressional representative was a lot more personable. When I explained what I was calling about, she was honest in her advice.

"Don't get me wrong," she said. "I fully agree with your sentiments, but the Constitution protects them in expressing their opinion, no matter how vile it might sound to the rest of us. This country is founded on the idea."

"But this country, heck, the whole *world* fought against the fascists. Our leaders promised us they would never rise again."

"I'd don't know what to tell you, Mr. Wilson. You must remember the McCarthy years. They tried to shut down anyone even suspected of being a Communist, and the courts eventually overturned every charge. People have the right to believe what they want. Even something as disgusting as fascism."

"It's not fair. I lost a lot of friends during the war...."

"I'm sorry, Mr. Wilson. Please believe that."

I closed my eyes in frustration, my hand cramping on the phone.

"It's not your fault," I murmured. She was still trying to comfort me as I ended the connection.

I sat in my chair for a long time staring at nothing, a sense of helplessness covering me like a thick blanket. No matter how old you get, in your mind's eye, you always see yourself as you were in your prime; and I found I had to keep reminding myself of my current limitations. What I could do even a decade ago was now impossible for me today. With the cancer beginning to add to my physical issues, I felt like life was telling me I had nothing else to contribute, and it was that idea that was eating me up. If I was useless, then what was the point.

My eyes dragged to the cabinet that held my big-screen television. Deep in the right-hand drawer, behind a false back, was my old service .45 automatic. I could picture the M1911-A1, with its sleek lines and real checkered walnut hand grips.

It had been ages since I held the piece, and even longer since I last fired it. The pistol had been a symbol of bravery under fire, so a part of me baulked at even contemplating using that faithful symbol to end my impotency. I was feeling sorry for myself, and I knew it. The fact of the matter was, I just didn't care.

In the end, it was the pressure of my bladder that pulled my mind off the pistol. By the time I stumbled in a mad race for the bathroom, just barely making it, the rumbling of my stomach overpowered my earlier depression.

Returning with a plate of cold cuts and cheese, I settled in, my tablet balanced on the chair's arm. While I nibbled, I surfed news sites but saw nothing of interest. The fool in Washington was alienating more of our staunchest allies and making wildly inappropriate comments over social media. Why someone didn't take his God-damn phone away was beyond me! It was obvious that he had no discipline and even fewer morals. Thinking about all the magnificent sacrifices young men and women had made for this country and all the achievements we can accomplish when we work together, it sickened me that one man could unravel all that good through a tweet.

In frustration, I swiped at the screen so I wouldn't have to see him make a mockery out of the highest office in the country.

I searched for news of Nazi organizations in the state and found that a chapter was located right here in my own town. It surprised me for a moment, but then I considered the fact that there also was a local Antifa in the area. The latter had probably established themselves to counter the former.

And it had been here in town that the attacks had taken place in the synagogues. Not in some big urban setting but in small-town America. That realization was unsettling. Nor was it the Federal building in Oklahoma City. This had been an act of domestic terrorism at the neighborhood level. And the people of this branch more than likely had been the ones involved.

I copied down the address and checked the on-line map as to their location. I wasn't sure it would help to request a meeting, but like any reconnaissance, it paid to know as much about the enemy as possible. And that was how I was looking at them now: the enemy. They were the same evil bastards I fought seventy-six years ago.

As lunch settled into my stomach, the now-familiar ache of my cancer radiated in my intestines. It was like I had sipped battery acid with pain coming in waves, rising and ebbing. I gasped out loud as each wave crashed through my abdomen.

It was getting worse, and I knew the doctor had been right about the need for the painkillers. I hated the idea of popping pills and had stubbornly gritted my teeth in the past, but the pain was quickly becoming more than I could bear. Was it also a sign of how fast the cancer was spreading? Probably.

I'd be lying if I said it didn't scare me. The idea of this thing growing in me was terrifying. I got up and shuffled to the tray on a side table where I kept bills and important papers that had to be dealt with. I panted, which seem to help to contain the worst of the agony. My hands shook as I rifled through the collection of papers until I found the prescription the doctor had given me.

Using my tablet, I took a photograph of the script and sent it by email to my pharmacist. Technology is a blessing for someone with mobility problems like mine. They would deliver the medicine by the end of the day, paid for by the credit card I had on file with the pharmacy.

Until then, I would avoid eating anything more.

Chapter Nine

The pills made my next meal a lot more tolerable. The ache was still there, but much more manageable. I even slept most of the night. The pharmacist had emailed me that I should take the pills regularly rather than only when the pain was bad. I wasn't about to argue.

Wayne was booked up solid, so I called for a regular cab. I had to get out of the apartment and decided to do a drive-by of the local Nazi offices, the so-called NMA, the "Nazi Movement of America."

For the trip, I pulled out my old uniform, the yellow thunderbird centered on a red shoulder patch. I pinned both medals on the left chest. The old suit hung on my bony frame, and I felt like a twelve-year-old wearing his dad's clothes.

A blast of a horn signaled that my ride had arrived. Reaching the street, I settled into the rear seat of the cab, my folded walker across my knees. Twenty minutes later, after paying the driver, I stood across the street from an older, two-story brick building, on an ordinary street in an ordinary part of town.

There was no sign on the building signifying that there was even an office within. No swastikas graced the windows. I was wondering if the address I'd found on the internet had been wrong or outdated. Maybe they had moved locations.

Frustrated, I sat on the bench of the walker and stared at the structure. With no sign of my enemy, I felt ridiculous sitting on the street in full regalia. I was getting an eye-full, from each vehicle that passed me like I was an exotic creature on display at the zoo. The public gives vets our one day a year, but then it was business as usual. The public no longer remembers or cares for what we did so many years ago.

I pulled out my cellphone to recall the cab to bring me back home, when I spotted two men walking towards the building along the sidewalk opposite where I sat. A familiar gray hoody pulled my eye, and I glared at the young man, who looked like he was maybe twenty years of age. The hood shadowed his head and he'd stuffed both hands within the folds of the sweater's front pockets. I wondered if the spray can was tucked inside.

His companion was a larger man with short-cropped, dark hair and a long, unkempt beard. He was wearing jeans and a light blue windbreaker.

I don't remember standing, but whether it me rising or my uniform that caught the man's eye, he almost tripped on his own feet as he stumbled to a stop. The punk in the hoody kept walking and only stopped a few feet further on when he realized his companion was no longer beside him.

As the shadowed face within that hood looked first at his friend and then over at me, I raised my finger and pointed it at him.

"What your problem, old man?" the hooded man yelled across at me, his voice harsh.

"You," I called back, "are my problem."

The two men looked at each other in confusion. It was obvious he didn't know me from Adam.

The punk looked like he would explode. His body was rigid with constrained anger. He stepped forward toward me, but his companion grabbed him by the arm and said something in a low voice that I couldn't hear. The two glared at each other and I could see the younger man was ready to ignore the larger man.

Finally, the bigger man, after checking for traffic, crossed the street towards me.

"What's this all about, Pops?"

"That son-of-a-bitch painted a swastika on my building. Took me over a week to clean if off."

The man looked at me as if I had just slapped him. The surprise looked genuine.

"How did you know to look for him here?" he asked.

I nodded at the building across the street. "Is that not the office of the local NMA Nazi bastards?"

"That's pretty harsh. We have the same right to express our beliefs as everyone else in this country," he said, his chest rising as if he asserted that right.

"I know what you people really stand for," I spat back. "I've seen it up front at Dachau and remember Nazis only as evil, cowardly bastards. When I was with the 45th Infantry, when we liberated Dachau, we saw what your kind are capable of. I'm not scared of you people. I killed plenty of Nazi vermin when I was overseas."

He stared at me, taking in my uniform with a studious glare. His eyes traveled over the two large medals on my chest. He might not know what they stood for, but their weight and size would at least suggest they were important.

"Well," he said. "The Constitution allows you to voice your own opinions as it does me. And while we might disagree, I would be very careful when dealing with our young friend across the street. He has a habit to be..." He paused for effect. "Quite volatile."

"If he wants to have a go at a ninety-five-year-old," I said, "tell him to have at it. It would give me the excuse to have him arrested and put in a cage where he really belongs."

The man's lips pressed tightly together, and he huffed. He leaned over me in an almost companionable manner. "Trust me," he said in a hard tone. "He doesn't care about the law or the police. If he comes for you, it won't be just to slap you upside your head."

His cold, hard eyes bored into mine, and I saw that he was being brutally honest. I don't think he was warning me out of the kindness of heart, but just telling me the way it would work out. Of course, from his perspective, any confrontation with a medal-winning veteran would bring attention to his organization, and not the good kind.

He spun on his heel and marched back across the street. Grabbing the younger man by the arm, he steered him to a door between the two business fronts and they disappeared inside.

Tension bled out of me, and I sat down hard on my walker, only now recognizing the old body tremors that always followed a hard battle. It was fear and adrenalin slipping away. I sat there for more than a few minutes, regaining my composure. Finally, I reached for my cell and dialed the number of the cab company. They told me that my ride would be by shortly.

I had mixed feelings about the day's events. Yes, I had confronted my old foe, but nothing came of it. There was no solution. I had changed nothing.

I stayed sitting, not knowing just how long it would take my ride to get here. Movement across the street caught my attention and I focused as the young punk in the gray hoody emerged from the building. He stopped and stared at me. With his face in shadows, I couldn't see those eyes, but I could feel his hatred and maleficence.

If looks could kill...

It was his turn to point his finger at me, and then he drew it across his throat in a gesture that needed no explanation.

I recalled what his companion had said about this one's volatility. But at ninety-five with six months to live, I just didn't give a damn. I pointed my own finger at him. Then I twisted my wrist, lowering my index finger and raising the middle one.

His reaction was instant, and it gratified me. I had shocked him, and he stepped back as if I had fired a shot at him. With a curse, he came at me in a steady stride. I could feel his hatred and rage.

It wasn't a death wish, but I knew that if he did kill me, I wouldn't have to worry about dying a little each day as cancer ate through me. And if the cops did their job, they would put this bastard away for a very long time. Not a big win, but one that I could accept.

As he closed on where I sat on my walker, I could make out his features. Dark hair swept down to his hate-filled eyes. Other than rage, the boy seemed normal, handsome even. His skin was pale, probably from hiding in his hoody all the time. But evil feared light, and he seemed to embody that mantra.

He was three paces away when his clenched fist rose over me. I knew I was in trouble. There was no way I could defend myself, let alone combat one so young and energized.

I rose to my feet, wanting to meet him on equal terms; and for a second, I saw confusion replace the hatred. He was not used to having someone stand up to him. It unsettled him, but only for a second. His eyes hardened, and the fist began its descent.

It was then that a police siren ripped across the quiet street, startling both of us.

A cruiser pulled to the curb not ten feet away, both doors flung open.

The punk took off running without looking back as I sank back onto my walker with no more strength in my legs.

Chapter Ten

I sat on a hard chair in the police station, having given my statement to one of the two officers who'd pulled up in the squad car. The younger of the two had given chase to the Nazi punk while his partner questioned me, but the kid got away.

"While I appreciate your frustration, Mr. Wilson," said the older officer, his hands clasped together sitting at the battered desk between us. "Confronting that guy was, although brave, also very foolish. At your age, he could easily have crippled you or even killed you had we not been there to stop him from assaulting you."

I stared hard at him, not liking what he was saying, although deep down I knew he was right.

"Even if he just knocked you to the ground, you might have broken a hip or cracked your skull on the sidewalk."

"I tried calling the police the other day," I said hotly, "but they treated my complaint like it was a joke. Someone has to stand up to these bullies."

He nodded and rubbed his eyes. "The system isn't perfect, and I'll apologize for that. I'll pass your case up the ladder. Hopefully, next time, they'll treat your complaint with more respect." He reached into a chest pocket of his uniform and pulled out a business card, and taking a pen off the desk, wrote something on the back of it. "This is my email and cell-phone number. Rather than you taking on this fellow by yourself, call me if he shows up again."

I took the card and read his name, "Sergeant Wade Simmons." I nodded to him and slowly rose to my feet.

"Let me give you a lift home, Mr. Wilson."

"I can grab a cab. You've already helped me enough today."

He stood and pulled the uniform cap over his balding skull. "Nah. Taking you home is the least I can do to say thank you for your service."

Fifteen minutes later, I watched as the cruiser pulled away from the curb. With a sigh, I entered my building.

Exhaustion dragged at my heels. My little adventure had taken the wind out of my tattered sails. I settled into my chair, listening to the apartment's companionable silence, and promptly fell asleep.

GERMANY 1945

We had been marching all morning, scouts out before us. It was like a stroll along a country lane. Birds fluttered nervously as we moved forward, searching for the enemy, our own movements unconsciously as skittish as the birds.

The scouts were about one hundred yards ahead of us when we got the signal to halt. We all went down on one knee, searching the tall grass and trees for signs of threat. One of the scouts ran, bent low, moving back towards the main group. He slid to the Lieutenant's side to give his report.

"Looks like a German camp, Boss," John, the lead scout, whispered harshly. "There's a rail track leading into the camp, and from what I can see, the train is half in and half out of the camp. No sign of soldiers. There's barbed wire on all the walls."

"Good work," said Epstein. "Take us in, but watch your corners."

As John scurried ahead, Lieutenant Epstein sent word down the line to be ready for action. Each of us checked that we had a round in the chamber and slammed the clip against our helmets to ensure all the extra rounds sat ready to load smoothly.

Looking up, I saw Epstein staring at me. He put both hands forward and motioned me to take it easy. I knew he worried that I would lose it again if we found more Nazis.

I swallowed hard and nodded. I would try to do him proud. No way I wanted him in trouble because I couldn't control myself.

With a swing of his hand, we rose together in a half-crouch, our carbines swinging back and forth over our fields of fire, looking for any threats. In two staggered columns, we moved forward. My heart was pounding in my temples, and I couldn't swallow if I had wanted to.

We came to a set of rail tracks and turned towards a length of cars that sat unmoving. The Lieutenant gave hand signals for the columns to split and move down either side of the cars. Stepping behind me, Epstein fell into line.

The silence of the late morning was shattered by gunfire further ahead of us. We all froze, searching for the cause.

"Let's move," Epstein hissed.

We ran, but that was when we came alongside the open cargo door of the railcar. A wave of nauseous fumes enveloped us before we could cover our mouths. My breakfast rose without warning, and I was spewing canned eggs and ham across my shoes. Others were also getting sick.

Turing toward the rail car, I saw bodies piled like cordwood, three feet deep. Some corpses had shifted and had fallen out of the car looking like a frozen waterfall of bent and broken people.

More shots rang out and the Lieutenant, no longer worrying about stealth, yelled at us to keep moving. We had to support the scouts who were in some kind of one-sided firefight.

Every car we passed had rows and rows of bodies, some naked, some in tattered and torn striped uniforms. All were little more than scarecrows, heads too large for their scrawny bodies.

The tramp of boots was broken by dwindling gunfire and the retching of soldiers vomiting as they advanced. We could see a huge white cross on a building's roof beyond the wall. With the train gate open, there was no need to scale the wall.

Rounding a cement partition, we entered a large compound. A last shot explained what had transpired. John, with his .45 extended, shot a German point blank in the back of the head, where he had fallen. The scouts, having found the murdered prisoners, had entered the hospital and dragged all the sick and wounded German patients out to the courtyard. Like I did days earlier, they lost control and killed each man to avenge the murdered prisoners. Bodies lay scattered across the yard, their blood fresh and bright.

As our presence became known to the scouts, their rage dissipated suddenly, and their weapons dropped as they looked around in terror at the carnage they had caused.

Epstein groaned beside me and put a shaking hand over his eyes.

A high steel fence covered with barbed wire blocked the far end of the courtyard. Beyond that, a river of humanity poured out of the building. Hundreds, if not thousands, of prisoners rushed the fence. I thought for sure that their combined weight and numbers would crush the fence. They cheered us in a multitude of languages, tears of joy covering ragged, sunken cheeks.

One man climbed a set of stairs to peer over the crowd. He yelled and pointed, then yelled in German to the rest, "American troops at the main gate! The Germans have surrendered the camp!" At least, that's what I was told he yelled, since I speak no German.

Our cheers joined those of the prisoners, tension melting off us as we grabbed canteens and smokes.

"Stand ready," Epstein yelled. "Let's make sure this is legit." He grabbed my shoulder, swinging me around. "Donald, grab two others and circle around to the main gates and find out what is happening over there. And stay sharp!"

"Will do, Lieutenant!"

I grabbed two other guys, and we hoofed it back out the train gate, steering wide around the open doors of the cars with their horrible cargo. I made it the length of the train in one tightly held breath. We stopped to breathe, as my two companions had done the same as I had.

We cut through some birches and came to a road that ran across the front of the prison. A large group of American soldiers stood firing warning shots into the air as they tried to herd a group of prisoners back into the prison.

A small group of black-uniformed Nazis were being guarded near the rear of the loose formation, defeat and fear clear in their cowering postures. As we neared, I noticed the outfit was the 42nd Division.

A couple of these fellows turned at our arrival. "Private Wilson, of the 45th Thunderbirds," I said. "We made entry through the rail line in the southwest corner."

"Was that you doing the shooting?" asked a captain pushing up his helmet.

"Yes sir," I said, not explaining further.

"Good job. The SS Commander surrendered the prison minutes ago. Let your people know."

"Thanks, Captain." We turned around and began to run back to our people to inform the Lieutenant of the surrender.

Prisoners still pressed the against the steel fence. Whenever the breeze swung our way, we could smell their unwashed and starved bodies—and they were almost as bad as the corpses behind us. Many of the men passed rations through the fence to the starving men inside.

We stayed behind as the 42nd left for Munich. There was still a war going on.

Later that day, under the weapons of our men, we forced the German prisoners and any able citizen from the town of Dachau to dig vast graves for the dead. It would take three days.

General Eisenhower sent word that he was on his way to see for himself the conditions within the camp. No one in the modern world had ever encountered this level of evil before. Even though I was actually there, I still could not grasp the enormity of the situation. But I was to learn firsthand.

The Red Cross set up a small city and began processing the camp's prisoners, who were a mixture of political and ethnic prisoners, each represented by a different colored inverted triangle. Red for a political criminal, pink for a homosexual, purple for a Jehovah's Witness, and, of course, two triangles—one facing up over the other facing down to make a yellow star of David for the Jews.

Every morning after, we would have new bodies to bury as those who had survived to finally be liberated gave up the fight and succumbed to their injuries, neglect, or disease. These deaths were the ones that hurt me the worst. To have overcome the hardship and inhumanity of a concentration camp only to die once free seemed to me such a sad waste.

Their only possible consolation, if there was any at all, was that they'd died free.

Chapter Eleven

Wayne picked me up for my weekly Legion visit. I'd missed last week's excursion because of the paint cleanup, and I was looking forward to seeing the others. Although I enjoyed solitude, I still looked for any chance to escape the apartment, especially after a longer-than-usual winter.

As I pushed my way into the Legion hall, I was pleased to see Benny Lowe and his wife, Edith, at our regular table. The Lowes gave me a wave as I made my way across to them. I offered my hand to Benny, who took it without hesitation.

"Heard you wore out another pacemaker," I said, pumping his hand. "Pretty bad when I have to hear about it from Wayne."

Benny's gaze lowered at my comment.

"Don't worry, Donald," Rita said. "I've already torn a strip off of both of them."

I patted Benny's hand. "Good to see you're okay."

"Me too, and thanks."

Benny and Edith were the only couple in our group. They had married at nineteen, the night before Benny shipped out to war. Part of the 2nd Armored Division, he had sat the first year of the war doing nothing but training in Morocco. It wasn't until the spring of 1943 did they see any action, when his division made amphibious landings during the invasion of Sicily. But this was all just to prepare him and his men for the main event, which was the knock-down fight with the superior German armor in the Battle of the Rhine. Fighting had been so intense that Benny had three tanks destroyed from under him. Each time, after a couple hours' rest and a hot meal, his crew had been given a replacement tank and pushed back into the fray.

As with most of us, he still had nightmares about watching soldiers burn to death, both allied and enemy, when the tanks were hit and caught fire. We heard more about this from Edith rather than Benny, as he rarely spoke about his time overseas.

Originally from rural Texas, he had confided once. "After traveling and seeing so much of the world from the turret of a M36 tank destroyer, there was no way I was going back to run my old man's seed store."

Now he took care of his wife as she slowly descended into the hell of dementia. I figured he'd worn out that pacemaker and was worried that she'd outlive him and have no one to watch over her. He'd confided to us that some days he didn't think she remembered his name yet clung to him like he was a life raft. It was heartbreaking to watch.

Before I could even settle in my chair, a young woman with green hair and a ring in her nose approached. She wore a black shirt proclaiming a Trivium album with a screaming demon skull centered on the front. The identical picture was tattooed on her forearm, I noticed. *Must really love the band.*

"What can I get you?" she asked in a no-nonsense manner.

"Two drafts, please."

She smiled as she glanced around the table, removed an empty glass and returned to the bar.

To the group, I asked, "What happened to that miserable guy from a couple of weeks ago?"

Frank smirked and pointed this thumb towards Rita. "Your guardian angel brought his attitude issue up to the Legion executive committee and they let him go. Frankly, I like the alternative," he said, raising his eyes to the woman returning with my beer.

"Yeah, like you'd remember what to do with that." This got a round of chuckles. Even Frank snorted. The woman, not realizing that she was the center of attention, left the drinks and walked back to the bar.

I took a sip of my draft, savoring the flavor.

"We missed you last week, Donald," Decker said. "Wasn't the cancer thing, was it?"

I shook my head and explained about the punk painting a swastika on my building and, since it was on brick, how it had taken the full week to wipe out the hated symbol. I could feel Rita's stare, so I didn't bother including my encounter with the Nazi bastard outside their headquarters.

Benny shook his head in disgust. "I don't see what these young people get from painting graffiti on buildings. Or why *that* symbol? Most are too young to even understand what it means."

"I think it's because of all the broken marriages," said Rita, making a conversational divergence. "No one stays married these days, and the kids are the ones who suffer."

"Hell," Frank huffed. "There are a lot of kids raised by single parents and most end up fine."

"I think it's because we live in a 'me' world," I said. "Everyone is out for themselves. You guys remember, when someone built a house, the whole community would pitch in. Women would make lunches and lemonade, and the house got built in a week. People don't do that anymore."

"You got that right," Decker said. "Even personally, I don't know how many painting parties I went to over the years, or fences I helped to build."

"Damn," Benny said. "Painting parties. I haven't heard that term in a long time."

The conversation ebbed as we all remembered earlier times. I finished my first glass and pushed it to the center of the table. The movement brought Decker out of his thoughts, and he looked towards me.

"Getting back to that Nazi thing," he said, cuddling his glass to his chest. "Did you decide what you're planning on doing?"

I caught Rita throwing him a harsh look, her lips locked in a hard line.

"I already have done something," I said, sitting back in my chair. I knew my admission would surprise the group, but the expressions across the table were quite comical, Rita's more so. They all exchanged glances before returning their attention to me.

"Well...?" Rita asked, annoyed at my holding back.

"Antifa was a bust," I said. "And so was the Governor's office and our local state official. No one gave a crap."

"Or they know nothing will get accomplished under this president," Benny said.

"He's no president!" Frank spat.

"Regardless," Rita said. "I think Benny might be right. It's the right-wing crazies that are backing the president and his people."

"So," I continued, getting back to Decker's question, "I went and spoke with the victims. Jewish people at the synagogue. I met some camp survivors. It was very moving." I pulled on the draft. "Together, we agreed to document my experiences during the war, especially liberating Dachau."

"That's a fantastic idea," Frank said.

I nodded, glad to have his support. "And I had an actual TV interview, lights, camera and makeup and all, down at the Channel 10 studios. We ended the interview by appealing to veterans who had lost friends and family to the Nazis to call for a constitutional amendment to stop this new neo-Nazi hatred."

Decker slapped the table surface with a grin. "You didn't?"

I nodded, feeling good.

"That's about three hundred thousand veterans calling their representatives," Rita said. "You should think about sending out a newsletter through the Legion with the date and times the documentary will be airing. And then follow it up with another asking for their support with publicity."

"That's not a bad idea. Of course, I'd have to contact Jeremy Lister, my interviewer, and the others. I wouldn't think it be a problem, but it's their show."

Benny leaned forward, a look of concern on his face. "Donald, thank you for that kind of support. It means a lot to Edith and me, especially since we lost relatives in those camps. But you might wish to reconsider."

"What? Why...?"

He reached over and placed his hand on my arm. "Because too many times in the past, those who have stood up for Jews have paid the price. Once this airs, you might find a target on your back."

Chapter Twelve

I groaned aloud at the now familiar pain in my gut and reached for the small plastic pill bottle on the table beside my chair. I struggled in frustration with its child-proof top and was ready to kick the manufacturer in the ass when the pill bottle opened with a jerk, spilling pills all over my lap. They should have called the lid an "old-hands-that-shake-proof" top. I grabbed the closest pill and popped it into my mouth. By the time I had collected all the pills and secured them in the bottle, my pain was receding. It never went away now: there were only highs and lows depending how long since the last pill.

I'd had my uniform altered and pressed as Jeremy had advised when he shot the interview. Now it looked like I would have to get it taken in again. In the two months since I spoke with the filmmaker, I'd shed more weight because of the damn cancer, and at 95, I didn't have any extra to lose. Fortunately, I had been using the same service for three generations, and Sergio Aillo was always willing to send someone to my home for the measurements. I made the arrangements with the surprised tailor, hearing that unspoken question hovering over the hesitation on the phone.

To appease Rita, I let her write an article for the Legion newsletter that spoke to the interview with Jeremy and when and where it would air. She did an excellent job, and glowed when I told her as much. The newsletter had gone out at the beginning of the month, and already lots of vets I knew had received it; so, it was a good guess that veterans across the country would have been made aware of the broadcast. The questions would be would they watch it, and would they act on my request?

I'd have to wait all the same, so there was no sense worrying about it. We would know in two nights. For the broadcast itself, they invited me to the synagogue for dinner and a viewing. Jeremy had also organized a press conference following the airing, promising that this would give the story a real national—and possibly even international—push.

I had to admit, at least to myself, that I was getting anxious for my interview to air. It would give me peace before I faced my maker. I just prayed that I would make it until I could see if it brought results. My ever-increasing pain levels were a sure sign that the cancer was taking firm hold and running amok.

Pulling myself out of my chair, I put together a meal, finding that my appetite had returned, as had my sense of taste. As promised, the little vial of medical marijuana oil that a not-to-be-named friend had recommended (and supplied) was making a difference. It helped with the pain and allowed me to sleep better in between my usual nightly bathroom breaks. Who would ever believe that at my age, I would do drugs? Ha! My Maggie must be laughing her ass off.

With the plate balanced on my walker, I worked my way back to my chair and turned on the television to get the evening news. The lead story was again about the firebombing of the synagogues. Police had released a photo of an "individual of interest" who may have been the individual responsible for the fires. When the photo came on the screen, I almost spilled my dinner into my lap.

It was him! The swastika-painting Nazi who I flipped the bird at! The photo was grainy, but not enough that I couldn't recognize the same hateful sneer that he gave me as he planned to strike me down.

A police officer appeared on camera. "We are asking for the public's help in identifying this person of interest. We currently regard him as dangerous, and we request you do not approach him, but contact Lancaster County Crime Stoppers immediately. This could lead to a cash award."

As the newscast turned to the next story, I considered how lucky I'd been in my encounter with the Nazi. If he was capable of firebombing not one but four houses of worship filled with innocent people, he definitely wouldn't have spared me. He was a savage.

I found the business card that Sergeant Wade Simmons had given me and called him. He answered after the second ring.

"Simmons."

"Sergeant Simmons. You might not remember me, but my name is Donald Wilson. I'm the old guy that you and your partner helped out of a fix I was in with a dirt-bag Nazi, a little over a month ago."

"Of course, Mr. Wilson. How can I help you?"

"I just saw the news and the photo of the suspect the police believe might be responsible for the fires."

"And...?"

"It was him. The same guy that tried to attack me," I said.

"Are you certain?"

"Definitely."

"Okay, thanks for the information. I'll make sure it gets to the investigators. They might want to interview you in light of this. Might be FBI by then, though, since there's federal laws involved."

"Not a problem. Any time."

"You haven't encountered him since, have you?"

"No. And I've stayed away from the NMA headquarters, as you advised."

"Good to hear. Thank you again, Mr. Wilson."

I hung up the phone and sat a while pondering whether the police might watch those headquarters to see if he showed up. It's what I would do if I hadn't made the promise to stay clear of the place.

AS SIMMONS HAD SUGGESTED, I got a call the next morning to ask if a couple of investigators could come by to ask me some questions. Coffee had just finished perking when there was a sharp rap at the door. After checking the peephole and seeing two women holding up open badge wallets, I opened the door.

"Mr. Wilson, I'm FBI Special Agent Monica Gilpin and this is my partner, Special Agent Jennifer Pointer. Thank you for seeing us at such short notice."

"Not a problem. I've made fresh coffee. You'll have a cup?"

"That would be nice. Thank you," she said.

As I poured their coffee, I studied the pair of women. The one who identified herself as Special Agent Gilpin was in her thirties with short dark hair and light brown eyes. She stood taller than my five foot ten and looked like a long-distance runner. Her partner wasn't as tall, but her wide shoulders might have been from weight training. Special Agent Pointer wore her red hair in an Annie Lennox crew-cut, and her green eyes were unsettling, reminding me of a serpent ready to strike. Both wore conservative dress suits.

Once I had served coffee—black for both— and settled in my chair, I said, "Ask away."

"We read your statement about the confrontation a few weeks ago, but we'd prefer hearing about it from you," said Gilpin.

I walked them through my story from the point where I saw the hooded man painting a swastika on my building's wall, to where the chance appearance of police had saved my bacon that day in front of Nazi headquarters.

"And both times, the suspect was wearing a gray hoody?"

"Yes, and although I can't be certain, it looked exactly like the one he was wearing in the photo the police released."

The two women glanced each other in an unspoken communication. From an inside breast pocket of her jacket, Agent Pointer pulled out a small manila envelope. Without a word, she placed four photographs of different young men in front of me before looking expectantly at me. "Can you identify any of these people?"

Glancing down, something immediately pulled my eyes to one familiar face. The image might have made him a year or two younger, but there was no mistaking the face. I pointed at the third photo in the lineup. "That's him."

"Do you recognize any of the others?"

I studied each of the others but shook my head. "No, I haven't seen any of them. So, who is he?"

Once again, there was that silent communication between the special agents.

"You are extremely lucky that Constable Simmons and his partner happened by that day," said Gilpin, taking the lead again. "His name is Joseph Russell, and he's a very dangerous individual. He has ties with a neo-Nazi group called the *Atomwaffen* Division with strong connections to the Nazi Movement of America, the NMA. They're one of the most violent groups out there. The FBI has been tracking that group since it first came to our attention about three years ago. Russell is a suspect in a number of arsons and even a couple of murders. We think his involvement in the area is to bring attention to the march being planned here for the summer."

"Here in Lancaster?" I choked in shock.

"Yes. It's set for the second week of July."

"I can't believe the city is going to allow it," I said, taken aback. My hand covered my eyes as images of Charlottesville came to mind.

"The city is trying to have it stopped and has refused to issue a permit, but our sources have confirmed that the organizers plan to ignore any lack of permit."

"Wouldn't they be arrested if they attempt to march without permission?"

"Well," Agent Pointer said, "That's where it can get hairy. Do we attempt to arrest a fully armed group for a misdemeanor? A lot of innocent people could get hurt if the group resisted arrest."

I saw her point, but it was frustrating to think that they could break the law with such impunity.

"And what about him?" I asked, pointing at the photo. "He's bound to be there."

"Once we have eyes on him, he's as good as caught," Gilpin said. "We'll wait until after the march, and when his supporters have dispersed, we'll pick him up. That way, there's no risk to the public."

I nodded, but I didn't think it would be that easy with the guy. My gut was telling me that Joseph Russell would not go down without a fight.

Chapter Thirteen

A gleaming black limousine pulled up to the curb, and the rear window slid down revealing Sarah's bright smile.

"Donald, the man of the hour!" she cried out, her voice full of excitement.

The chauffeur came round the vehicle to open the door for me, taking my walker to the trunk. I dropped onto a plush leather seat to find Sarah's three other companions sitting across from us.

"The rabbi had said he was sending a car, but I never expected something so elaborate."

"Only the best for a friend," Saul said, reaching out to shake my hand. "And the rabbi tells us that thanks to you, the police have identified a suspect in the firebombing."

"News travels fast," I said, surprised that it had become common knowledge. The fact didn't sit right with me, but I pushed the feeling aside, not want to ruin the night's event.

Sarah put her hand on my arm. "You look so handsome in your uniform, Donald. So many medals and ribbons!"

I shifted in my seat and noticed Saul's smile at my discomfort at the attention.

"Is that the Bronze Star, Donald?" he said, trying to put me at ease.

I nodded.

"What does one have to do to earn an award like that?" Jacob asked.

"Something that in hindsight was pretty stupid," I murmured, remembering that night on a rain-soaked mountain in Korea where I ran across the dead-man's zone to retake an overrun machine-gun position. I had saved Decker's life and stopped the rollover of our flank by the Chinese regiment. To this day, I still don't remember making a conscious decision to run that gauntlet. I had just acted.

The group chuckled, and it relieved me that none of them pressed any further.

At the synagogue, Rabbi Lehrer and Jeremy met us as we exited the vehicle. For poor Saul, getting out of the car was an ordeal because of his tall frame. He reminded me of a praying mantis extracting itself from its ootheca shell. As he looked up, it was his turn to feel self-conscious; but he must have been used to it because he strode forward to greet our hosts.

I thanked the driver for helping me with my walker, our group moved inside, and we took an elevator to the second floor. Doors opened to a grand lobby where people stood mingling. It was like they were attending the opera, with the men wearing formal suits and even a couple of tuxedos, while the women seemed pulled from the pages of a fashion magazine.

The entire group began applauding and parted to allow my group to enter a large assembly hall. I looked at my companions in surprise. I thought it was just to be the few of us and found myself overwhelmed. There had to be a couple of hundred people here. Camera flashes bombarded me from every direction, and I teetered on my walker. Jeremy's hand closed around my arm, giving me support.

"There is a lot of gratitude in this room for you, my friend," he said in my ear.

"Ah ... I wasn't expecting ... all this," I stammered, glad I gripped the bars on my walker, because I was shaking like a leaf.

"But, my friend, this is a tremendous opportunity to get your message pushed right across the country. We have the major networks here tonight; and after they see the documentary, they'll also be seeing the growing neo-Nazi movement from a whole new prospective—from someone who sacrificed much to help to put a stop to fascism."

He led me to the table where Sarah and the others had taken their seats.

"A good crowd, Donald, *nu*?" Sarah said as I sat beside her.

I nodded, looking around the room, feeling like I was sitting in a fishbowl.

"Donald," Jeremy said. "Let me introduce you to the light of my life, Miriam."

A petite woman with dark hair and wide-brim glasses extended a hand with a warm smile. "Donald—may I call you Donald? Jeremy has not stopped talking about you, so that it feels like I've known you forever. Even our little girls talk about you like you were their favorite uncle."

I took her hand and nodded. "I'd be hurt if you called me anything else. So happy to meet you." I glanced at Jeremy. "I can see why you've kept her hidden from me. Scared of the old guy, sweeping the girl away."

"Eh ... yes, my friend." Looking at this wife. "You see, everyone loves him."

Dinner was a formal affair, and I was glad I had thought to take my painkillers in advance. The last thing I needed was to have pain flare up just when I was expected to interact with this crowd. I wanted nothing to interfere with the message we were sending out tonight. As it was, my nerves kept me from eating much, and I pushed the food around my plate waiting for the main event.

As dessert dishes were still being gathered, Jeremy wasted no time. He walked to a microphone that was set to one side of a gigantic screen. "Ladies and gentlemen, thank you for coming. The broadcast will start shortly, but let me provide a little context.

"As you all know, several synagogues have been firebombed here in Lancaster with lines of men in black SS costumes standing outside as congregants fled. Days after the fire-bombing attacks, Mr. Donald Wilson, who wanted to do something about this new Nazi threat, approached Rabbi Lehrer. You see, in the Second World War, Mr. Wilson fought against Nazis, and it was his regiment that was responsible for liberating the infamous Dachau concentration camp."

There was a collective gasp at the admission, and I felt all eyes turn to me.

"Tonight, you will hear his story and a plea from a soldier who, seventy-plus years ago, sacrificed so much for his fellow veterans and his country."

He gestured toward the screen, and on cue, it lit up, and the documentary began. For the next hour, the only noise in the room was that of either Jeremy's or my voice on screen as he led me through the events leading to the German surrender of the camp at Dachau. Even though I had seen the finished product weeks ago, my emotions were running high, and I wept during some of the more horrible memories. I wasn't alone. I watched many in the room mirror my wiping of swollen eyes. Although only a handful of survivors were here, many had lost relatives and friends to the horrors of the Final Solution or were moved by my story.

As my last plea to other veterans and Americans who felt the same way to make some noise echoed through the room, everyone in the room rose in a standing ovation for me. House lights brightened as Jeremy took the microphone and walked to my table, gesturing me to stand. He grabbed my hand and raised it over his head to even louder cheering.

"You have lit a fire here, my friend. It's going to grow high!" he said, hugging my shoulders.

"Thank you for giving an old man his last request, Jeremy," I said with genuine emotion. He looked at me strangely and I remembered he knew nothing of the cancer. I hoped he would leave it alone, and he did as he said a few words to his young wife, then left to speak with some others who were vying for his attention.

My new friends around the table all congratulated me and commended my determination to defeat a common enemy.

"Oh, Donald," Sarah said, hugging me. "I'm so glad you came into my life. You prove that there are people still willing to do what is right."

"Donald," Jeremy said, moving back to our table. "There are more than a few reporters waiting to interview you. Are you up to it?"

"Can I do it sitting down?"

"Of course, my friend."

"Then if they're willing to spread the story, let's not keep them waiting."

I excused myself from Saul, Sarah, and the others and followed Jeremy to a corner of the room where there was a small pack of reporters waiting, most with smartphones ready for photos and sound bites. Only one, an older Black woman, held an actual notebook and a pencil at the ready. She gave me a gentle smile as our eyes met. I warmed to her immediately.

There were the regular questions that dealt with my war years and how I won the star. I pointed out that the star had been from action in Korea, not fighting the Germans.

A broad-shouldered man with a ruddy complexion that suggested years of heavy drinking pushed ahead of the other reporters aggressively. He was from GoAmerica, one of those right-wing broadcasters that seemed a fan section for the president and his supporters. They were all about propaganda and nothing about the truth.

"You fought in both wars," he said. "Was that because you enjoyed fighting? Do you see this little crusade of yours as merely one last chance for a fight?"

The stupidity of his innuendo shocked even the other reporters and they stepped away from him as if they might catch something. Jeremy took a step forward, but I waved him down.

I looked down at my hands as I collected my words.

"I'm guessing you never served in the military?" I asked him.

"I covered the Paris Peace Accord," he snapped back, his tone indignant.

I chuckled aloud, which caused his face to turn a darker shade of red.

"Sir, I fought because my country asked me to, not because I enjoyed it. Only a psychopath could *enjoy* it. I was scared out of my wits every day I was in those conflicts, and I brought those horrible memories home with me.

"Yet you, like *your* president, feel you can overlook the sacrifices our men and women have made for this country and slander us the minute we say anything contradictory to your agenda. Just remember," I said, pausing for effect. "It was that sacrifice that gave you that particular right. A sacrifice that apparently you never made."

I kept my tone calm, which was an effort.

He stepped back as if I had slapped him. I'm sure I would have some tweets aimed at my back by tomorrow; but seeing that I didn't even use social media, tweets would be the proverbial water off my proverbial duck's back.

A smattering of applause among those around us startled the man, and he turned away abruptly in a huff.

The rest of the questions were more civil and respectful; and after fifteen minutes, I was alone with Jeremy, and we began to move back to the table where his wife waited patiently for him.

"You handled that jerk nicely. I was ready to throw him out physically."

I shook my head. "That would have distracted from the message. The news would have been all about a physical confrontation."

"One of our sponsors has a proposition for you, Donald," he said. "Give me a minute and I'll get him to join us." His wife shrugged and smiled as if to say, 'This is usual' as he walked off into the crowd, which was thinning out as people left the hall.

I sat, reached over the table and pulled a water decanter to me. Turning over a clean glass, I filled the glass, my throat dry from all the talking. I would pay for the water during the night, but at the moment, it was divine.

Jeremy returned with a small man who sported a full head of white hair that matched his goatee and eyebrows. A diamond stud sparkled in his right earlobe. At my age, everyone is young, but I was guessing he was in his mid-seventies. He waved at Miriam, who he seemed to know.

"Donald, please allow me to introduce you to Simon Krakow."

I took the man's hand, and he shook it with a genuine smile. "My friend, thank you for seeing me. You did a noble thing tonight. Thank you."

"I only did what I thought was right," I said, feeling self-conscious at all the non-stop compliments.

Simon and Jeremy sat down at the table while Miriam rose graciously and placed her hand on her husband's shoulder. The gesture so natural seemed to me so intimate. She smiled at us and said, "I'll let you boys talk. I'm going to mingle."

Simon began, "The thing is, today most people know what's the right thing to do, but rarely make the effort. Our society, for all its advancements, has become a closed group of individuals who seem not to want to be noticed, in case someone ridicules them for their beliefs."

I nodded. "Things have definitely changed over the years."

"Doing what's right is exactly the reason I wanted to talk to you tonight." He glanced at Jeremy before returning his attention to me. "Donald, I run a very successful entertainment conglomerate that has allowed me the opportunity to assist those trying to create a better world. Being Jewish, I also help my own. After I heard about the attacks on the synagogues and then heard your story, I'm pretty certain that all this will go viral. I want to help your message grow."

"What do you have in mind?"

"I'd like to have you and Jeremy travel, at my expense, to tell your story to several groups of like-minded supporters. Who knows, we might even help some to get off the fence."

I sneaked a glance at Jeremy, but the stunned look on his face told me he had known nothing of the offer.

"I'm not sure," I said hesitantly. "I'm no spring chicken, you know?"

He smiled at my little joke.

"I fully understand, and I promise we can accommodate you at your pace."

He was giving me a chance to go out fighting. I knew it was only so long before my cancer advanced to the point that I would be homebound; but damn, it would be great to make a difference before it was too late.

"I'll do it," I said. "I'll need a couple of days to talk to my family about this, and I'm guessing Jeremy and Miriam might want to discuss it, too. After Jeremy's interview airs, I'm sure my phone will be ringing first thing in the morning, if it hasn't already."

"They'll definitely be seeing it," said Jeremy, shaking his cell phone at me. "I have already heard that two of the networks are picking up the segment. We're going national, Donald."

"Any presidential tweets yet?"

The two men chuckled.

Simon handed me his card. "When you're ready, call me and I'll make sure my people are ready."

Chapter Fourteen

"What the heck were you thinking, Dad?" Gail's voice came out of the phone in a loud, demanding voice. "You're ninety-five-years-old. Why would you get involved?"

"Because I was there, damn it!" I told myself to ease up. She was upset because she worried about me, and I guess that was only natural. "Listen, you of all people know the nightmares I've struggled with all these years. Nightmares caused by the Nazis over seventy years ago. And now they're back! And they're here in our backyard. I had to say something!"

"But Dad—."

"Listen," I said in a softer tone. "If what I have done can help make people wake up to these assholes, then it will have been worth it. It's one of the last positive things I can do with my life. It's better than sitting in this apartment watching old movies I saw decades ago, waiting to die."

The silence on the other end of the line told me I had made the point, but probably also reminded her that my days were numbered. For the hundredth time, I thanked my stars I had not revealed news of the cancer. There would have been no talking to her or Richard.

"Gail," I said. "Doing this is important to me. You have to see that."

I heard her sigh in surrender.

"I know it is, Dad," she said in a hushed whisper. "For what it's worth, the documentary was extremely powerful and the message you sent will touch many people."

"Thank you, but I'd like to reach more."

I explained what Simon had proposed, and that almost set her off again.

"The man has a private jet and he's paying the entire shot. He's agreed that I will determine the pace of the trip because of my age, and even suggested hiring a nurse to travel with us to ensure my safety. Jeremy, the producer of the documentary and the interviewer, will travel with me, too."

"How long will you be gone?" she asked, worry still in her voice, but restrained.

"Might be a month or more. It'll depend on how I'm feeling. The last stop is Chicago, so maybe I can visit with you, Alex and kids, if you've got the room."

"Of course we have the room, Dad. The kids will jump for joy when they hear. We miss you something terrible, Dad."

"Then it's a date. I'll text you once I know when we'll be in Chicago so we can meet up."

"No," she said sternly. "You'll text me each day, so I know you're okay. Doesn't have to be much. Just a line or two. Promise?"

"Promise." And I smiled.

MY TALK WITH RICHARD was not as emotional. He was concerned about me, but understood why I got involved and was excited to hear about my trip.

"How do I get an all-inclusive trip around the country in a private jet?" he asked with a laugh.

I also called Rita, who was really impressed, and would be able to tell the others at the Legion.

"I'll be the first to admit that you were right," she said. "You wanted to make a difference, and you did it in such a big way! I've seen the program twice now, and I teared up both times when you described what you found inside the Dachau camp."

"I was fortunate to find the support I received from the Jewish community and that Jeremy got interested. That's what catapulted my story across the country. Now with Simon's help, we can keep the momentum going."

"I'm so proud of you, Donald."

"Thank you. Do me a favor and let everyone down at the Legion know I'll be out of town for a while. I don't want anyone thinking I'm dead or anything."

"Not a problem. I'd be happy to keep everyone up to date. Drop me a note once in a while so we know how you are doing."

"Sure thing."

"Have fun, Donald. You deserve this adventure."

After hanging up, I contacted the pharmacy to ensure I would have all my medication topped up, and then made sure that the steam-cleaners would pick up my uniform for pressing. I figured I'd be wearing it regularly over the next while.

Two days later, Wayne carried my suitcase and garment bag out to his handi-transit for the short drive to the Lancaster Airport. Jeremy would be flying from New York, and the little private jet would touch down long enough to pick me up before flying to the west coast.

"I caught the interview, Donald," Wayne said as he navigated through traffic. "Very impressive. I've known you for three years now and never knew that stuff about the concentration camp. No wonder you had problems after that. Made me wonder if I'm making too big a deal over my own experience."

"Bullshit! Don't make light of what you had to deal with. It affected you, and this is not a competition. What gets to one person may not bother another. We're all unique."

He grinned in the rear-view mirror and raised a hand in surrender. "I get your point."

"The issue I have with the situation," I told him, "is that the government is aware of PTSD but does so little to help those who fight the wars that their incompetence has caused. Personally, I don't think we should have been in any fight since 1945! There has been no global threat since then except the Communists, and that was a cold war. The rest have been for political or financial reasons, and I don't think any of that's worth one single human life."

I could hear the anger in my voice, and I forced myself to calm down. It wouldn't do to have a heart attack just before my trip.

"You won't hear me argue."

The rest of the ride was quiet, each of us thinking our own thoughts. As Wayne pulled up to the terminal, he said, "When you know when you're returning, text me the day and time and I'll schedule you a ride home."

I nodded. "Thank you, my friend."

Carrying my luggage, he led me to the check-in desk.

A young clerk smiled at me when I showed him my identification. "Mr. Wilson, we've been expecting you. Mr. Krakow's office called, and everything is arranged. Allow me to call a shuttle to carry your luggage. Don't worry about security—all that is taken care of. The jet should be in right away."

"Well, I can see you're in excellent hands, Donald. Have a glorious trip and remember to message me." Wayne shook my hand vigorously.

"Thanks Wayne. You be good, now."

He gave me a tight grin and left the terminal. Minutes later, a quick, electric cart whisked me along to a small boarding room overlooking the landing field. The steward transporting me pointed out a sleek business jet that had just touched down on the tarmac. "I think that might be your ride, Mr. Wilson."

"Beautiful aircraft," I said as I watched the white and blue machine brake.

Minutes later, the little plane had eased up to the loading door, and soon Jeremy jogged through the ramp doors into view.

"Donald," he said excitedly. "Ready to take on the world?"

"Just the fascists."

He laughed, grabbed my luggage, and led the way towards the adventure.

Chapter Fifteen

For the next few weeks, we skipped across the country meeting various groups to keep our message loud and strong. We'd started to make waves on both sides of the question. More and more tweets were aimed at Jeremy and me as the government began to feel definite pressure to halt the fascists' hateful rhetoric and marches.

Politicians of the political right kept up their demands to name Antifa a terrorist group while turning a deaf ear to similar calls to include the fascists and White supremacists, with the argument that if the far right disappeared, the far left would as well.

In every city, we faced one interview after another, from talk shows, to news outlets, for both television and radio. There was even an hour-long current-event documentary of our journey and the influence we were trying to awaken in regular Americans.

It was exhausting; but true to his word, Simon ensured I that I rest before advancing to each event. My pain pills were still holding back the bulk of the pain, but I was aware of it always being there, just under the numbness of the oxycodone. Mornings were the worst until the meds worked their magic. I would lie still until they cut the growing pain in my pelvis, back and ribs. Only then could I carefully rise and begin my day. But at least the marijuana oil was allowing me to sleep most of the night.

I had confided my condition to Emily, the nurse that Simon had hired to travel with us, and she monitored my pain therapy allowing me to concentrate on the campaign; but she watched me like a hawk and would shut down both Simon and Jeremy when she felt I needed a break.

We had arrived two days ago in the west-coast Portland, and I was scheduled to make a presentation to a mixed group of veterans and members of the Western Diversity organization. As we approached the community center where we were to speak, we met with a vast crowd and a heavy police presence. From our position in the vehicle, we could not make out what the disturbance was, so Jeremy left the car to find out what he could.

Minutes later, he returned with a worried expression.

"A group of neo-Nazis are blocking the entrance to the hall, Donald. It's an obvious ploy to keep you from speaking. The police are talking to them and hopefully they'll force them to move on."

"They should arrest the bunch of them," I said, now familiar anger rising in me.

"There's over thirty of them that I could see."

"I don't give a damn if there's a hundred. They have *no* right to do this!" My hands were shaking with rage. Yanking the car-door latch open, I struggled to get my walker out of the car.

"Donald," Jeremy cried, his hand on my shoulder. "C'mon! Let the police deal with it!"

Ignoring him, I unfolded the walker, pulled away from his hand, and lurched to my feet. I heard the door on the other side of the car open and he called out to me again, but I was already moving through the crowd.

"Excuse me. Let me through." Surprised expressions met me, but they fell back as they took in my dress uniform, with all its chest candy. As I moved forward, Jeremy caught up to me, face red with concern.

"Damn it, Donald, you're only going to get hurt! If they see you! It's going to get worse than it already is!"

"Good. It'll be great press," I said in a growl, pushing forward.

The crowd pulled aside at my harsh tone, and I saw four police officers with hands on the butts of their pistols, standing menacingly around a group of Nazis, while a fifth cop argued with the leader. None of the idiots were wearing black uniforms, but a few carried swastika flags over their shoulders.

Sensing me, the nearest police officer turned at my approach. He raised his hand to stop me from advancing.

"Hold it, sir." He stepped in front of me, blocking my path.

I shook my head. "I'm doing a presentation in that building," I said, pointing at the building across the street, "And I will not let those scum-bag idiots get in my way."

"They will not be in the way for much longer. We're getting them to leave, right now."

"You should put them behind bars."

"They haven't broken the law. Yet," he said, looking over his shoulder. "If they do, then we'll deal with it."

I glared at the group as they reluctantly allowed the officers to herd them away from the building's entrance. I felt more than saw Jeremy arrive at my side. An expression of annoyance met me when I turned to him.

"You can't be doing that, Donald. They train the police to deal with those people." He looked at the large lawman. "Thank you for your help, officer."

The man nodded and moved with his fellow officers to follow the retreating Nazis. We were moving across the street towards the entrance to the hall when someone grabbed me from behind and threw me to the ground. I hit the pavement hard, taking most of the impact on my left hip and shoulder. Pain flared in both places as I grunted. The walker fell and landed on me but fortunately, didn't hurt me further.

"Donald!" Jeremy's voice rang out before it turned into a cry of pain. I rolled in time to see him collapse to the ground, a thin framed man standing over him.

"Die, you fucking kike!" He kicked Jeremy viciously in the back and my friend let out a painful scream. People all around us held cameras at arm's length, filming the one-sided fight with no one trying to stop it.

The figure turned towards me, his hate-filled eyes narrowed. I was shocked to recognize Joseph Russell, the swastika painter, his head still covered in the same gray hoody from the last time I saw him. What the heck was *he* doing here, in Portland? What was he up to?

He stalked towards me, and I felt a tinge of fear in my gut. I tried to get up, but my shoulder refused to work. Pain blurred my vision. He bent over, grabbed my uniform tunic in tightly rolled fists and pulled me, so we were face to face. His teeth bared in a snarl.

"You're dead, old man," he said in a harsh growl. "You've made your last speech." He raised his hand over his head to punch me, but before his hand could come down, a huge Black man grabbed his arm and gave it a wrench that made my attacker scream. He dropped me unceremoniously to the pavement, my hip once again signaling that he'd messed me up pretty badly.

"Why don't you try picking on someone that can fight back, punk?" said my rescuer.

From beyond the crowd, I heard someone yelling, "Make way. Police!"

Russell's head snapped towards the report, his arm still held high by the big man who could have played center for Franklin and Marshall college's football team. Without warning, the smaller man twisted and kicked his opponent solidly in the groin. The man's face expressed the shock and pain that every guy dreaded, and he dropped his hold on Russell's arm.

"Next time you want to touch your betters, nigger, don't!"

Joseph twisted towards me, then his eyes caught an approaching police officer pushing through the surprised crowd.

"This ain't over, you old fool! I'm gonna bring you a *world* of pain."

Then he turned and lurched into a fast sprint, pushing and twisting his way through the crowd. In seconds, he was out of sight. The police officer, the same one I'd encountered earlier, broke into the circle of hand-held cameras to take in the scene. There was the big guy rolled into a ball, hands holding his privates, Jeremy unconscious on the pavement, and me lying on the ground, tangled in my walker. He rushed to me, but I pointed in the direction that Joseph had taken off in.

"Gray hoody. FBI is looking for that guy."

His eyes widened, and he ran after our attacker, pushing through the crowd like a bulldozer, looking to make the collar of his career.

Around me, cell phones fell as there was nothing left to video. Now that the action was over, these simpletons finally remembered to be human and attempted to help.

"Check that guy over there," I said, pointing at Jeremy. He wasn't moving, and I worried that he was really hurt. I felt guilt course through me because it was my temper that had put us in this spot. Had I not left the car and, instead, allowed the police to deal with the situation as Jeremy had implored, Russell would not have hurt him. That big fellow wouldn't be heaving his guts into the dust, and I wouldn't be lying in pain as helpless as an upended turtle.

LOOKING DOWN AT HIS clipboard, the doctor's eyes rose to peer at me over his glasses. "You've had a busy day, Mr. Wilson. You're old enough to know not to go picking fights, especially at your age and in your condition." The look on his face told me he was aware of the cancer. "It's a good thing this guy hadn't hit you, because as is, he's already done enough damage. You shoulder is dislocated. Easy fix, but it's going to hurt. However, your hip has a hairline crack that extends halfway across the iliac fossa—that's the big plate of the upper hip. Let me be straight with you—I'm afraid that given your age and weakness of your bones, you may never walk again. You're going to need a wheelchair moving forward."

I took in the information with a sigh. It might make things a little more difficult, but considering I was dying anyway, it would only be a short-term inconvenience.

"How about Jeremy and that big guy that got kicked in the jewels?"

The doctor chuckled at my choice of words. "The jewels are fine, but they'll be tender for a day or two. He was released hours ago. As for your friend, I'm not really at liberty to discuss his case with you. You can ask him yourself, though. He's in the next room and is waiting to visit. He's very concerned about your condition."

Minutes later, Jeremy moved slowly into my room. He was bent over like an old man. He gave me a lopsided smile between swollen lips to reveal a gap in his teeth. "Two teeth and bruised kidney. Doctor said I was lucky the kidney didn't burst."

"This is my fault, Jeremy," I said.

"How's that?"

"If I hadn't lost my temper and gotten out of the car, that asshole would never had gotten the chance to jump us. For that, I'm sorry."

My friend shook his head sadly. "The fault lies with that animal. Who is he, to you?"

"I had a run-in with him back home. When I first recognized him, it threw me for a loop. I couldn't understand why he would be here; but I think he must be following our tour, waiting for opportunities to strike."

"But what did you do to him to make want to hunt you down?"

Looking down at my hands before replying, I said, "He's one of the Nazi NMA leaders back in Lancaster, and I stood up to him. I think that it's the first time anyone has ever done that to him and I'm guessing it's eating him up inside. He's got an image to maintain, and bullies need to be in charge. If they're not, then they have no reason to carry on."

Glancing up, I added, "I think he's scared. He needs to beat me to feel vindicated."

THEY GAVE DILLON FOX and me the duty to escort General Eisenhower and his staff through the camp. Having heard of the horrors, he had to see for himself.

It pissed us off as the rest of our boys got to express their frustration and horror on the Germans that still held against the Allied forces, while we had to stay and babysit the brass instead of making someone pay.

To look at him, Eisenhower was just another guy. Average height and not much hair. Of course, a lot older than most of us. But that was where similarities ended. 'Ike' had a . . . a presence . . . *that you could actually feel. It was like he was a giant among men. He carried himself with such reserve, such confi-*

dence; yet he was still human, and I witnessed his reaction to all we showed him that day.

"The first thing we came across, General, was the train at the gates leading into the camp," I said to the man and his entourage. "There were forty cars, both flatbeds and boxcars, all full of dead prisoners. We smelled them long before we saw them. Most were semi-clothed, but a lot of them were naked. It was pretty nasty."

One headquarters man pulled a handkerchief from his pocket to cover his face as the wind turned and brought the stench from the prison towards us. Others quickly followed suit, but Ike did not.

Swallowing hard, the general, in his pressed uniform, walked forward as if this was a walk in the park. "Have we discovered how many prisoners are still alive, private?"

"Thirty-two thousand, General, but we're losing almost two hundred per day to typhus, exhaustion and malnutrition."

He stopped and stared at me. "Thirty-two..."

"They designed the camp to hold around ten thousand. From what the prisoners have been able to communicate, the Germans had been shipping thousands out each day ahead of the allied advance. They were either killing them outright or allowing them to starve on some side rail."

We walked under the arch, and I saw him notice the white slogans that were painted across each wall of the prison: Es gibt einen Wed zur Freiheit. Soine Meilensteine heissem:

Gehorsem, Sauberkeit, Nuschternheit, Fleiss

"It translates to, 'There is a road to freedom. Its milestones are: Obedience, Cleanliness, Sobriety, Industry'" I explained, to which he just shook his head.

"When we first got here, the first thing we did was try to feed these poor people, but we ended killing more than we helped. Not accustomed to solid food, even a piece of chocolate was enough to cause them to drop to the ground in agony. A lot of us are having a hard time dealing with this, sir. It's like we killed them with kindness." I was blinking hard to keep from losing it.

He said nothing but put his hand on my shoulder for support. To support me, that is.

Once I pulled my shit together, we moved on, his eyes moving from one pile of corpses to another. When we reached the barracks, the group hesitated, but then Ike demanded that we continue to witness the true barbarity of the Nazi regime. General Patton stuck his head into the building and then made a fast retreat behind the structure. We could all hear his retching, but no one thought less of the great man.

Dillon and I were completely empty. There was nothing left to throw up.

I watched as the General motioned a full bird-colonel to his side. "Bill, I'm putting you in charge of recording everything about this place. I want to invite members of the press here and will give you some people from the Signal Corps to help document what we're seeing. Some day, some idiot is going to say that this never happened, and we need to show the world what we were really fighting for."

"Yessir."

"I want to know two things. First, what was it like to live in this hellhole, and second, how much did the locals know about what was going on? We need to know if the German people are equally responsible."

"I'll get right on it, General."

Ike nodded and motioned for us to continue. We took him and his party to the crematorium, where they saw the hundreds of bodies that waited before the four coal-fired furnaces. Next were the showers, the execution rooms where the SS had administered deadly Zyklon-B gas, and there was more throwing up as their acrid smell touched each of us. By now, Ike's men were chain smoking, trying to get the taste out of their mouths.

"Some inmates, those we've been able to converse with, have been saying that the Germans performed medical experiments on hundreds of prisoners."

"What kind of experiments?" Patton asked in horror.

"The prisoners were exposed to malaria and given a variety of treatments. Most did not survive the cure. They exposed others to the elements; and when they were close to freezing to death, they put them together with other prisoners to determine if and how body heat could heal the body. They exposed others to high and low pressure to determine how to protect high altitude pilots."

"My God, how can one man do that to another?"

There were many piles of burnt bodies that the Germans had unsuccessfully tried to get rid of. Burned arms, legs, and torsos were tangled in heaps of charred railway ties. The smell of roasted flesh had even Ike turning pale.

"How much more, Private?"

"Just more of the same, General," I said, drawing hard on my cigarette, which was shaking like a leaf in my unsteady hand. "However, please, I won't show you the last building. It was a small blockhouse where they kept those who had broken the rules. It housed them until the Germans decided their fates."

"After all, we've seen, soldier, don't hold back now."

I nodded and swallowed hard as I bit my lip. "Well, Sir... they'd been there for quite a while... without food."

He put his hand on my shoulder to settle me. "Go ahead, son."

"We found they had eaten the dead." My eyes filled, and I choked out the last. "They'd become cannibals."

Chapter Sixteen

When Simon Krakow, who'd arranged my trip, heard about the incident, he flew immediately to Portland and brought company. They shoved open the hospital door to my room with enough energy to startle both Jeremy and me.

Jeremy had been sharing pictures his wife, Miriam had sent him. His children had made of drawings of him and me traveling across the country in a sleek jet. His kids reminded me of my own grandchildren. The drawings slipped off the bed, with the fast-opening door, causing Jeremy to jump for them

A massive brute of a man with high cheekbones and dark eyes and wearing a dark suit entered the room ahead of Simon. The man's eyes swept the entire room for threats. Seeing none, he stepped over to one side and assumed a relaxed, at-ease position. But it did not fool me. He looked like he was ready and capable of walking through a wall.

As Simon strode into the room, I saw another similarly built man standing outside the room before the closing door cut off my view.

Simon stood at the foot of the bed, and from the hard glint in his eyes, I could see he was livid.

"Donald," he said in a voice that sounded more like a growl. "Are you trying to be a bloody martyr?" His finger swung up and took aim at Jeremy. "And *you* were supposed to be looking after him! *Schmendrick!*

Jeremy's mouth dropped open.

"It wasn't Jeremy's fault," I countered, my own anger rising. I flinched at the pain in my hip that flared as I tried to sit up higher in the bed. "And I don't need any looking after. I've been doing that for a lot longer than you."

His mouth twisted into a lip-curling smile. "Yeah, I can see how well both of you are at doing at that." Then he let out a sigh, visibly relaxed, and shook his head. "So, what's the extent of your injuries?"

As Jeremy and I filled him in on what the doctor had told us, his shoulders slumped in defeat. "Well, that's it. There's no way we'll be able to continue the tour."

"Why the hell not? I can still talk from a wheelchair, Simon. It's not much different from what I was doing earlier. And now with this attack, I'm living proof that modern Nazis are just as brutal as the originals. I can use that in my speech, in fact. It'll add weight to the message."

Simon stared at me, and I could see he was fighting some kind of inner war with himself. I could tell he didn't want to put me in harm's way, so I decided to play my trump card.

"I have something to tell both you and Jeremy, but you're going to want to sit down for it," I said, my eyes flicking at the enormous man standing guard across from me. Simon moved hesitantly towards a chair beside Jeremy's, almost like he was afraid to hear what I had to say. He glanced at Jeremy, who shook his head in obvious bafflement.

"Simon, I know you're worried about me getting hurt on your watch, but this is my only opportunity to make a difference. Two months ago, my doctor back home diagnosed me with terminal, stage four, pancreatic cancer. The doctor has given me maybe six to seven months to live, and that clock has been ticking for two months already."

Both men looked stunned and exchanged a look before returning to gawk at me. "Don't look so shocked! You know how old I am, anyhow. So, you see, I've got nothing to lose. Even if Joseph Russell had *killed* me, it would have advanced the message ten-fold. The impact of that might have cleared the fog from an America that's been asleep to a menace that's become normal, because of assholes like this president and his pack of parasites."

"You used a name. Are you saying you *know* the bastard who attacked you?" Simon said, leaning forward.

I nodded. "Sure. His name is Joseph Russell. He's wanted by the FBI and is a particularly nasty piece of work. I admit, he caught me totally off guard the other day, because I didn't know he was here. He wasn't part of the group blocking the entrance to the hall. I think he was waiting to attack me when the opportunity offered itself."

I explained to them all my history with Russell and what I learned from the FBI agents. I watched as Simon shifted his gaze to the silent stranger across the room. The man merely nodded.

Simon leaned forward, his elbows on his knees, staring at his clenched hands as if in prayer. He nodded. "Okay, Donald," he said, looking up at me. "We'll continue the tour, but I need your promise that there'll be no more heroics."

I nodded. "Promise."

"This is Mack Knight," Simon said, indicating the man who stood silently against the wall. "He and his crew will be your new shadow. For your own safety, and for Jeremy's too, I must ask you to follow any direction or order that Mack or his men give you. So, as to yours and Jeremy's safety, his word is final. Is that clear?"

"Clear." I knew I had no choice if I was going to continue with the tour. It was that, or it was clear that Simon would have me on the next flight home.

He glanced over to Jeremy. "That goes for *you* as well. I need to ensure you are both safe."

"You won't hear any argument from me," Jeremy said with a tired smile.

"As for the cancer, what else do I need to know?"

I shook my head. "Emily, the nurse you hired, is aware of my condition and has put me on pain-management treatment, and I also have a supply of opiates that my oncologist prescribed." I was about to lie back in the bed when a thought occurred to me. "My family doesn't know about my condition. I want that kept quiet."

Simon huffed, shaking his head. "You're unbelievable, Donald. I'm glad you're on my side. I'd hate to have you as an enemy. There's no give in you."

I chuckled, "Hmmm. That's a nice way to call me a cranky, stubborn old fart."

Simon and Jeremy laughed and nodded. Even Mack smirked, one lip curling upward.

I SPENT ANOTHER THREE days in the hospital; but because I had my own private nurse attending to me, the hospital released me to her care. Instead of returning me to my hotel room though, our small convoy of three vehicles headed north, skirting the area of local protests and riots that were other signs of the decay and decline of the American way of life.

My heart ached as daily we watched our great country seem to fall apart, piece by piece. During the war, the entire country united; and I can say confidently that it was our greatest moment as a nation. But since, we've allowed hatred, bigotry, and greed to divide us rather than pulling us together to eliminate them. Were our people and our leaders blind to the fact that it was by working together that we had become one of the greatest countries in the world? But now, we're at risk of losing it all.

"We're headed to the airport," Mack said when I asked what was up. His voice was surprisingly gentle. "I convinced Simon to alter the tour schedule so that we make it harder for the opposition to plan any protests. We'll only release news of your presentations two days prior to each one, and we'll bounce back and forth between the coasts. Unless someone bankrolls them heavily, your Joseph Russell and his buddies will waste their time trying to follow us."

I nodded at the logic, but thank God Simon was picking up the tab. This would not be cheap! I felt a twinge of guilt, knowing the bulging budget was my fault. As well, because of my wheelchair, Simon had to arrange for a scissor lift for me at each airport, because my walking up even a few steps was now impossible. And of course, Mack and his six-man team must cost a ton as well.

Everything was ready by the time we reached the airport, and boarding was smooth. I was helped into a seat, buckled in, and within minutes, felt the thrust of the engines as the Learjet 45 XR jet rocketed down the runway. The way the craft angled, I was able to catch a spectacular glimpse of a sunlit Mt. Hood out the port-side window.

"Richmond, Virginia," Mack said to my questioning look. "That's where we're headed. Fairly large veteran pool and a sizable Jewish representation."

I nodded.

He stood, pulled his suit jacket off, and hung it neatly over the back of his chair. "Coffee? My treat," he said with a smile.

"That would be nice."

The machine in the tiny galley was one of the new gizmos with little cups of coffee brewed one cup at a time.

"So, what's your story, Mack?"

"Not much to tell. I'm mostly Navajo. Grew up in Arizona on the Colorado River Indian Reservation. Name's too long, too formal, too White, so we just called it the rez. Didn't see any future there, so I joined the army just before 911. I ended up in the 7th Special Forces Group, spent two tours in Afghanistan and one in Iraq. Once we saw what a shit-show it was there, a bunch of us decided to go out on our own, so we started this protection service. Pays a hell of a lot better than Uncle Sam."

He placed the steaming coffee on the pull-down table between us with a little bowl of sugar and pretend-sugar packets. His own, he cupped with both hands as if he was cold.

"You must have seen a hell of a lot of action."

He grunted and nodded. "I've seen my share. Shooting coyotes and groundhogs as a kid served me well. I took to soldiering pretty easy."

That admission didn't surprise me. He reminded me of a sleek jungle cat. Beautiful to behold, but you wouldn't want to meet him when he was hunting. He'd tear your throat out before you knew what had happened.

He looked at me. "And you saw your share during your time. I heard one of your presentations."

I held his eyes and saw similar ghosts in his gaze. I knew he was talking about more than just the action.

"I can only offer the same advice my wife gave me, and she was a nurse during the war." Staring him in the eye, I said, "Talk about it."

I sipped the hot bitter liquid, realizing I'd added no sugar. I hadn't added sugar since my doctor told me I was 'prediabetic' over five years ago. Considering my cancer, though, I reached over to the bowl and took two sugar packets and stirred them into the remains. Look back towards the huge warrior, I saw he was waiting for more from me.

"Look, Mack," I said. "The longer you keep whatever it is bottled up inside you, the longer it will eat at you. Think of it as a parasite: the longer you ignore it, the more it creates damage to your system. You expose it, it loses strength and allows you to recover. I've gone through this."

I reached out, grabbed his wrist, and looked squarely at him. "Find someone you trust and let it out. Or find a stranger, like a shrink. It's all confidential. Just open up."

He leaned back abruptly, pulling out of my grip. I prayed I hadn't been too forceful, that he'd retreat further into himself; but he gave me a weak smile.

"I'll give it some thought." He pulled on his coffee, draining the cup. "But now, I'd better get some shut-eye before we land." He patted my shoulder gently, "Thank you for the advice."

I nodded, and he walked over to one of the recliner seats and stretched himself out before pulling a blanket over his huge frame and instantly falling asleep.

Chapter Seventeen

We criss-crossed the country multiple times over the next few weeks, and everything went as per plan. Today, it was to be Houston, and were not sure of what kind of reception we would get, because of Texas's shift to conservative politics in the 1990s. Simon believed Houston was the best match for our message because it had developed a much more liberal attitude towards its different ethnic groups. It was also known for friendly acceptance for the LGBTQ community, a stance not as evident in other areas of the State.

We sat at the jet's little pull-down table discussing the results of the past events. For this trip, Simon had joined us. Mack and his men were watching a ball game near the back of the compartment.

More and more veterans finally seemed to be getting the news, and our message was stirring the pot. President Idiot in Washington was attacking me almost daily now, just like he did to everyone who disagreed with him, but I wasn't particularly worried about him or his supporters. As Simon reminded me, his rhetoric, as negative as it was, was keeping my message in the spotlight. I suggested we offer to hire him for promotional services, which had everyone rolling their eyes.

"Can someone let him know I don't even have a Twitter account?" I said as we watched the news after my last presentation.

"He's getting a lot of pressure from his own party," said Jeremy, "because of veterans; Republican veterans having been calling their representatives. And the steady increase of Jewish constituents who vote Republican who will never forget what the Nazis did. They have been very vocal since you started all this."

"You're making an impact, Donald." Simon said with a grin.

"Maybe, but while this president is still in power, I see nothing changing. Hell, there are still four states that don't even have hate crime legislation and refuse to even talk about it," I said, suddenly getting frustrated. "We fought for freedom for everyone, but those legislators, lawmakers, those who are supposed to represent the people, are the ones who decide who is more equal than others."

"You're preaching to the choir, Donald," Simon said. "Keep doing what you're doing. It's working."

I let it go as I felt the familiar burn in my stomach ramp up. As if she had me wired to a monitor, Emily, my nurse, entered the cabin with my pills. Her knowing eyes must have read pain in my features, because they dropped to where my hand pressed hard against my gut.

"Okay Donald, enough strategy talk. Time to get some rest."

She unlocked the wheels of my chair from their restraints on the floor and wheeled me away from the table. I could feel the other's eyes on me as we left the plane's common compartment for my tiny bedroom, but growing pain extinguished any sense of shame. The frequency of bouts of pain was multiplying as was the intensity of what felt like internal flames. There was no way I could ignore Emily's gentle prompting, and she knew it. She didn't need to argue for compliance. My own body did that for her.

"The pain is getting worse." It wasn't a question.

I nodded. "It's worse in my back now."

Wrapping a blood-pressure cuff around my arm, she pressed a button and it inflated. Reaching its peak, the little machine first displayed systolic pressure, followed by diastolic as pressure was released. My heart rate flashed in one corner of the display. My skin was becoming like parchment paper, and I was sure that I could have new bruising where the cuff circled my arm.

"Well, your heart is still working fine. BP is OK, too." She sat on the edge of the bed. "We talked about the evolution of the pain as your cancer progresses, Donald."

I nodded. "Not whining. Just answering your question."

After staring at me, she closed her eyes. "I still think you should be in a hospital."

"I know, but I need to make a difference while I can. I would be in the same pain lying in a hospital, except they'd have me doped so I high, I wouldn't know my own name."

I laid my hand on hers, touched by her compassion.

She offered me a sad smile and withdrew her hand from mine in order to hand me a pill and a glass of water. "Get some rest."

BY THE TIME WE ARRIVED in Houston, I was feeling more like my old self. The rest had done me wonders. We landed at George Bush International Airport north of the city, then taxied to a hangar south of the main terminals.

As the engines spun down, Mack's phone buzzed. After he listened for a moment, he undid his seatbelt and rose to lean over me to look out my window, which faced the hanger.

"We have an issue," he announced, clearly annoyed. "Somehow, the press found you're arriving, Donald, and there are several TV crews outside the gate."

Simon leaned to look out my window and take in a large portable antenna being raised behind an office building beside the hangar. He looked at Mack with confusion. "So what? They're our biggest allies."

"Yeah, it wouldn't be a problem—except we hadn't even announced the next presentation yet. That news was supposed to be released later this afternoon," he said with suppressed impatience. "If the media know, you can bet that other unwelcome parties might also be aware. I don't like the idea of walking into something that my people haven't scouted."

"So, what do we do?" Simon asked.

"Give me a minute." With that, Mack spun on his heel and made for the jet's cockpit. The rest of us sat there trying to get a look out the window, but there was little to see.

A few minutes later, as Mack came back, we heard the engines start up again.

"Okay, the pilot has requested permission to take us to another airport, William P. Hobby Airport, south of the city's core. Smaller airport. I'll arrange vehicles for us there, but I'm get my men to setup the media crews and anyone else waiting for us on a wild goose chase. With the tinted windows, they'll never be able to tell the vehicles are empty."

He called his men on the ground and filled them in on the plan. Minutes later, two black, full-sized Yukons left the hangar out to our little jet as our crew let down the boarding steps. The SUVs parked by the steps, waited a few minutes, and then traveled to the access road and out the gate. Seconds later, the media antenna began retracting. Mack's phone buzzed, and he listened with a smug expression.

"They took the bait. My guys will take them for a tour of Houston Memorial Park and maybe, if they're lucky, a trip to the zoo."

I chuckled at his sense of humor and the thought of the caravan of vehicles chasing each other for nothing.

In less than a half-hour, we were in the air again. We rose quickly, but nowhere as high as usual. We climbed to about 1000 feet and made a slow circle of the city's core. It was the first time I'd visited Houston, and its skyline was something beautiful to behold. Modern, stylish high-rises clustered around the downtown area, giving way to a park and the meandering Buffalo Bayou River that emptied into Houston's huge harbor.

It seemed the jet had just leveled out before its nose dipped into its landing at William P. Hobby Airport. This time, because of the speed of our change of plans, there was no special hanger for us. It took a little time to acquire a scissor lift to accommodate my wheelchair, but that gave Mack time to make other arrangements.

Our hotel canceled our accommodations without thought, and Mack arranged for a different location for us to call home for the next week. He wasn't taking any chances with our safety and stayed on the phone the entire time, making sure everything was in place.

"We're in luck," he said with a nod to Simon. "Because of the number of consular offices and foreign banking centers in Houston, there is no shortage of armored vehicle rentals. I've got three for us for a week. I've canceled the ones my men are using for their grand tour because the media will have their license numbers by now."

"Are you sure this is all necessary?" asked Jeremy. "It all seems over the top."

"It might be, but without knowing who got hold of our itinerary or how widespread it's gone, I can't take any chances that one of the White-supremacist or Nazi groups aren't planning on catching us with our pants down. They only have to get lucky once." He looked over at Simon. "I'd like to change the conference center we'd planned to use as well, but we can discuss that later."

"That's fine, Mack. You do what you feel is necessary."

Mack's phone chirped, and he read the text.

"Okay, we're set. Cars are waiting for us. We go through the terminal together. No one strays. Keep it tight. If anyone tries to stop us for any reason, my men will deal with it. But we all just keep moving."

In a harried rush, we sped through the terminal and were hastily, but gently, deposited into one of three dark Escalades that left the curb together just as the last doors slammed shut.

"Well, that was a lot of excitement for nothing," Jeremy said.

"If they were all like that, I'd be a lucky man," Mack said without taking his eyes off the traffic as we sped northward to the city's core.

Chapter Eighteen

It took only a few phone calls for Simon to find out who had leaked news of our trip to Houston. A quick search of histories on Simon's business-computer network found several offers to some of the major news networks to provide information in return for cash. A low-level public-relations manager assigned to contact the various organizations invited to my presentations and clearly unfamiliar with how easy it is to check histories on computers had decided he could cash in on the info. His only justification was that his wife was taking him to the cleaners in divorce proceedings. Now, he'd added to his problems because Simon fired him on the spot.

Three nights later, we were waiting in a holding room at Houston's George R. Brown Conference Center, named after a contractor who had helped build the city over the past half-century. They'd jam-packed the place with city officials, Houston's prominent movers and shakers, and lots of vets, old soldiers. Most veterans wore loose-fitting uniforms that hung on thin bodies. Most needed help to make it to their seats, either by leaning on steady, strong arms, or with walkers and wheelchairs. Reminded me of me.

The large hall was situated in the center of four other halls on the main level of the sprawling complex. For bigger events, collapsible walls on either side could open so that the space expanded from its 100,000 square feet to over 500,000 square feet for bookings like trade conventions. Circular tables for ten filled the room, their white tablecloths contrasting with black, stackable chairs. The hall had set a fair-sized stage at one end, with massive projection screens mounted in each corner of it. These would allow even those sitting farthest from the stage an unhindered view of our presentation—not that there'd be much to see after the replay of the documentary. It would be just me and my wheelchair.

Behind the main doors to the hall, a hum of voices sounded like a swarm of cicadas, rising and falling in the summer heat. Through a monitor, we could see the hall filling up.

Mack was always close by, issuing orders or checking on his men through radio-linked wrist-microphones and earpieces that the Secret Service had made famous in the movies. Mack wore a tailored black tuxedo like a second skin.

Mack spread out a team of twelve because of the size of the building and the number of guests. All were ex-special-forces, and Mack assured me that no ragtag group of fascists could match his people in an all-out fight.

Before long, Simon ducked in with a pleased look on his face. "These people that run this facility are top-notch. They've got everything to our specifications and in record time."

Jeremy stood up and buttoned his suit coat nervously.

I laughed at his jitters. "Come on, my friend. We've done this so many times, you can do it in your sleep. Relax! Go with it."

He nodded and looked at Simon.

"Everyone ready?" Simon asked. "I'll go out and make my introduction, and you follow when I announce your names. Just like always? OK?"

Behind me, Mack said, "Show-time. Eyes open, ladies."

Simon left the room, leaving the door ajar. We listened to him welcome veterans from the World War II, from Korea, from Vietnam and from our more recent conflicts, because this was as much their story as it was mine. The room exploded with applause when Simon thanked them for their sacrifices through the years on our behalf, and in the name of freedom. He also thanked all the other groups and dignitaries who had assembled to listen to my story and the message it contained.

When he finally announced Jeremy's and my names, we pushed through the door that led out to the stage. The huge audience met us with a standing ovation, applause echoing off the walls in a deafening roar. I wheeled my chair to the tape marks that showed my spot beside a small coffee table that held bottled water. Techies had set up a microphone so I could speak after the documentary. There was a chair beside me for Jeremy to use while the documentary ran.

Although my back was to him, I knew Mack stood behind me, his eyes covering the large gathering in the hall. Every once in a while, I would hear him whisper a question or make a reply to his men over his communicator.

Jeremy crossed to the right to a single podium. He gave a simple recollection of the circumstances of how the two of us met and how we developed the documentary. He also thanked Simon for the opportunity to push this important story across the nation and the urgency to create changes so that no American need feel unsafe.

Then lights dimmed and projection screens lit up. For perhaps the hundredth time, I sat through the discussion that Jeremy and I had had over my experiences during the advancement across Europe and the liberation of Dachau.

Then, maybe fifteen minutes into the film, a tremendous crash came from outside the hall, followed by multiple cracks of what could only be gunfire! Mack was demanding a situation report from his men, but I couldn't hear the reply because of his earpiece.

A pair of rear doors to the hall flung open to show a man in full, black-clad, Nazi SS regalia—holding an automatic rifle. He wore a red swastika armband and the visored cap of an officer. A figure from my past holding a very modern weapon.

I could see flames through the doors behind the gunman, and thick black smoke trailed into the room with him. He fired his rifle, spraying a lethal barrage of bullets just over the heads of the crowd, many bullets hitting the projector screens, causing sparks and glass to explode off the walls.

The crowd dove for the floor, pushing away from the madman with the gun. Tables and chairs crashed and muted cries of pain from those crushed or trampled grew louder. Elderly servicemen and women fell like mowed wheat in the panic of the crowd. I watched in horror as a man in a long-retired naval uniform went down in a tangle with his walker; and another vet in a wheelchair tipped backwards to land on his back, his extended legs not moving.

Mack wheeled me around so fast, I almost was flung out of my own chair, and he pushed me towards the back room out of the line of fire. My glasses had almost flown off, and I steadied them on my nose. I could hear more gunfire behind my back. Jeremy's muttering as he followed us changed into a painful groan. But when I turned to look for him, I could not see the stage because Mack's enormous frame was in the way.

The gunman's gun empty. He dropped a clip, rammed in another, and this time let fly directly into the crowd. As his second clip fell from its housing, his body stiffened as he took multiple hits from behind. I saw one of Mack's men advancing, his pistol leading the way.

One of the hall's security guards just stood helplessly, a revolver in his hand as his rent-a-cop training proved he wasn't ready for a full-out assault. His eyes flashed between injured patrons and attackers, until he finally turned and fled for the nearest exit.

High above the chaos, the remaining monitors continued the presentation with my crackling voice speaking of horrors, while Houston's finest scrambled away from this modern monster. Our message was now lost to the screams of our audience. The commotion and bedlam starkly contrasted the slow pace of the interview on the remaining screens that seemed like slow-motion strobe lights.

As we cleared the stage, Mack pushed me deep into the back room, then turned back to slam the door. Then he began to call his men for a report of what they were dealing with. As he listened, he pulled out a large-caliber pistol from a holster inside his carefully tailored tux and checked to ensure he had a round loaded.

On the monitor, the chaos in the hall continued. As I watched, another assailant appeared. This one, with a huge potbelly and in hunting camouflage, lumbered into the hall and lobbed a bottle into the room, fire extending from its neck. Before he could retreat to the lobby, an invisible force caught him, and he spun in place before collapsing into a tangle of legs.

His home-made Molotov cocktail spun its fiery arc before shattering on one of the overturned tables. Its breaking glass threw flames in a wide circle, igniting anything in their path. Like a silent horror movie, I watched the monitor as one woman's gown ignited, wrapping her in flames before climbing to engulf her. Others around her fled instead of trying to help extinguish the fire. There was a visible wave of people now pushing away from the growing fire, tripping over chairs, tables—and people.

With the door to our back room closed, the screams were muffled, but no less horrifying. The monitor showed the stage in the foreground, and I saw the prone form of Jeremy.

I yelled at Mack, "Jeremy's hit! I don't see Simon."

His head snapped to the image, and he growled, "Damn." From his waistband behind his back, he pulled a small but lethal looking Beretta and handed it to me. "PX4. Seventeen shots in the clip. I'm guessing you remember how to use one."

I nodded.

"Don't shoot me when I come back through that door," he added with a grim smile.

I pulled back the slider and loaded a round. "I'll try not."

He took a quick look at the monitor, looking for gunmen. At the door, he nodded and slipped out.

I held the pistol in both hands, ready to kill my first Nazi in over seventy years. Glancing at the monitor, I watched as Mack reached Jeremy and pulled him over his shoulders in a fireman's carry. He was yelling into his wrist mic as he made for the door.

The door burst open as his shoulders pushed through. As gently as he could, he laid my friend on the couch.

"He's alive, but the bullet is inside him, somewhere. Took one in the back. No exit wound."

Bells reverberated through the hall as the fire alarm finally set off. On the monitor, I watched as several sprinklers exploded in curtains of water, extinguishing and containing the fire in the room's center.

Mack was still talking to his men, calling each for a sitrep. When he received no answer, he ordered others to seek their missing comrades. Except for the fire alarms, there were no more gunshots. It seemed the attack was over.

Now we had to deal with the dead.

Chapter Nineteen

Although it seemed like hours to us, within minutes, emergency services descended on the complex. Fire fighters and paramedics began to move through the hall rendering first aid and transporting injured to area hospitals. Police shut down the entire building and apparently had set up a perimeter outside.

Mack called over the radio to demand paramedics for Jeremy and then called for two of his own crew to respond to the back room.

"Donald, you're going to have to hold up here for a while. You'll have guards, but I need to see to my team. I have two unaccounted for."

I nodded. "You do what you have to, Mack."

He whirled at a sound at the door, his hand grabbing at his pistol, but relaxed when he recognized Simon leaning against the door's frame, blood dripping from one arm. Mack guided him to a chair.

"It's okay," Simon said as his eyes went wide, seeing Jeremy sprawled on the couch. "Is he—"

"No, he's hit, but he's still alive," Mack said.

Movement on the monitor caught my eye. "Mack, paramedics."

He opened the door and ushered the two into the room. He pointed at Jeremy. "At least one bullet in the back. No exit wound."

Two medics rolled in a collapsible stretcher. The first medic, a young woman with cropped blonde hair, immediately started cutting away Jeremy's jacket, while the other, a thin young man, began opening their trauma bags.

"Mack," yelled a voice from the hall. "Coming in."

Our tall bodyguard stepped to the door and motioned two of his guys into the room. He walked them across the room and spoke to them in low tones. Both nodded.

"Donald," Mack said. "This is Ted and Joseph, and they'll stay with you while I sort out my team. I'll try not to be long." Not waiting for a reply, he turned and stalked out of the room, his expression grim.

Simon was grimacing in pain as he tried to pull off his jacket. I rolled my chair over and helped him take it off. Warm blood transferred to my hands immediately. His shirt sleeve stuck to his skin.

"Just leave it," said the blonde paramedic. "I'll just cut the shirt when I'm done here. It'll be less painful."

Simon's shoulders slumped in defeat. Lowing his head, he shook it. "They didn't care who they hurt... or how many."

"Not much different from the people I've been describing in my presentations. It's not just Jews tonight, though. It's anyone who disagrees with them or stands in their way."

The medics lifted Jeremy to the stretcher. While one secured him with straps, the other turned his attention to Simon. As promised, they easily cut away the bloody shirt at the shoulder to expose the wound. Most of the bleeding had already stopped, but the wound looked angry.

"Bullet. Went through cleanly," said the thin paramedic as he pressed pads over the entry and exit wounds. "I know it doesn't feel like it, but you were lucky. An inch to the right and it would have shattered bone. An inch to the left, it would have been in your chest and who knows what damage we'd be dealing with." He used a roll of gauze dressing to hold the bandages in place and tied them off. "Are you able to walk?"

Simon nodded. To me, he said, "I'll meet you back at the hotel, Donald."

I sat helplessly while they rolled Jeremy out of the room and across the hall to where my two friends would be loaded into an ambulance. On the monitor, my eyes took in the growing number of bodies that lay covered with blood-stained tablecloths. Now, never to rise. I realized that most of the crowd was no longer in the hall. Had they fled or had police moved them to a safer location?

A couple of police officers were taking photos of the scene from a variety of angles.

On the monitor, I could see Mack come in the rear doors of the hall, leading two strangers. The two men were both dressed in suits, and I figured them for detectives. One somehow managed to scribble in a notebook while he walked, while the other spoke with Mack. From their gestures, it was easy to see that Mack was walking them through the attack.

Minutes later, the three men entered our room and Mack introduced me to Detectives Spencer and Tillwood. The younger one, Tillwood, was the guy with the notebook, and he recorded my full name and birth date, then asked me to describe what I recalled of the attack. I filled him on what I saw, both from when I was in the room and afterwards, on the monitor.

"So, it was the heavy guy in the camouflage threw the Molotov?"

"Yes."

"And you saw him get shot? Did you see who shot him?"

"Yes, I watched him get shot. It spun him and then he hit the floor. I didn't see who shot him. There was just too much happening, especially once the fire spread. That woman..."

"It's okay, Mr. Wilson. They kind of thing would shake anybody up. We'll have to get a written statement from you, but that can wait until later. We have over eight hundred interviews that need to be done over the next week."

"We're staying at the Embassy Suites," Mack said. "But after this attack, I'm thinking we might have to consider moving. If we do, we'll let you know. It's Donald and his presentation that they were targeting."

"How can you be sure?" asked Detective Spencer.

"Donald and his group hired my team after an earlier attack by a guy named Joseph Russell. He's a neo-Nazi and part of the Atomwaffen Division of the NMA. And he's wanted by the FBI."

The two detectives exchanged glances. They looked over at me. "Would you be able to identify Russel if you saw him?"

"Definitely," I said.

"Security cameras caught the entire assault. There are the four suspects that your men took out, but there's three we have yet to identify. Maybe one of those is your perp."

"I'd be happy to have a look."

Minutes later, Mack guided my chair into the security office of the complex. Spencer moved a chair to give me room to pull my wheelchair up to a console that held a bank of video screens. He looked at Mack, "I've got to warn you, the video caught the death of one of your men."

I looked at Mack with surprise. We hadn't talked since he went looking for his crew.

"Dillon was wounded, but he'll be fine. He'll have another scar to boast about. They killed Scott when they crashed into the front entrance."

I'd never met Scott, but still it felt like someone had kicked me in the gut. I took a shuddering breath and blinked hard to catch the dampness that threatened to overwhelm me.

"Damn. I'm sorry Mack."

He put a hand on my shoulder. I think as much for his comfort as mine. "Let's see if we can catch the bastard." He nodded to the detective. "Let's do it."

The officer reached forward and hit the play button, the file already loaded. They pulled up the camera in the main lobby. It centered Scott in the picture, standing casually with hands clasped in front of him.

In the recording, Scott's head moves back and forth as people stroll by him. The last of the crowd flows past him entering the hall behind his back.

Then his face suddenly lights up and he raises his hand to shield his eyes. He tries to turn away from the flood of light when a white van crashes through the glass doors and hits him squarely. His body flies, and he hits a cement pillar with such speed that I don't even see him fall.

Even knowing it was coming, the footage of his death shocked me, and I gasped. The video blurred with rising dampness in my eyes that became a torrent. My hand shook, as I took off my glasses, wiped my eyes with the back of my trembling hand and covered my mouth to swallow the pain of seeing this man killed.

My stiff hands fumbled, but I managed to get my glasses back on and watch the rest.

The van continues until it hits the same pillar and comes to an abrupt stop. Driver and passenger doors open up, and two men scramble out. The rear door bursts open, and five or six men rush out of the back. All are armed, and one man, the guy in full SS regalia, clutches a wicked-looking assault rifle as they rush the hall doors.

Something hits the driver in the chest two times, and he collapses, while the passenger turns and tosses a package into the vehicle. When he turns, I see his face.

"That's him!" I said, pointing at the passenger. "That's Russell!"

The detective hit the button to freeze the video, but not before the vehicle's interior burst into flames. He backed the video up. With a mouse, he centered the cursor on Russell's image and zoomed in on the man, so his head filled the screen.

"You're sure?"

I nodded. "Definitely him."

He tapped another button, and the picture zoomed back out before he hit the play button.

On the screen, the lobby sprinklers open up and drench the hostiles in seconds. Another man with a rifle makes it to the entrance of the hall and enters. Another of the attackers falls as someone shoots him. The shooter is out of sight. The other attackers fire handguns at the shooter.

"That's where your guy gets shot in the arm." The detective hit another button, and a second screen lit up.

Another camera angle shows a long passageway that runs the width of the building to access the other conference halls. Mack's man Dillon stands beside one of the cement pillars firing at the attackers. Behind him, two more of Mack's men are running towards the shooting, handguns at the ready.

Dillon takes a bullet to the shoulder, and it spins him around. He staggers behind the pillar. The other two bodyguards fire rapidly before diving to cover.

As the men continue to fire, the overweight hostile wearing the camouflage lights the rag of his Mototov cocktail and ducks into the main room. The remaining men duck for cover as bits of concrete erupt from the pillar in front of the burning van.

Another camera scene picks up two of Houston's finest and a security guard as they slide-stop in classic shooting stances and fire at the terrorists. They have them in a lethal crossfire.

The monitor shows Russell crouching behind a large planter that stands next to an information desk. His mouth opens, and he yells something to his men; but like the gunfire that was clear in the video, his voice is silent. There's no sound. But then it becomes apparent what he was ordering as the last three attackers bolt for the entrance of the building and run past the camera.

The doors to the main hall fly open and men and women in expensive and stylish clothes run for their lives. But when they reach the burning vehicle, the curtain of water and the carnage, they stop and look frantically for safety. On the other screen, Mack's men wave them forward and they race towards what they hope is shelter.

"Did you recognize any of the other men?"

I took a deep breath and shook my head. "No. Only Russell."

I suddenly felt done in. Exhausted. I took off my glasses and massaged the bridge of my nose with my thumb and forefinger. I closed my eyes. All these people were dead or hurt because they came to hear me. For what little time I had left, I was going to have to live with that. I thought I was doing some good, one last fight; but in the end, I haven't made any positive difference. People were hurt because of me and what happened over seventy years ago. Even one person was too much, and I'd caused a slaughter.

It was over. I wanted nothing but to go home. To quietly meet my end, surrounded by all that was familiar. Where no one else would get hurt.

Chapter Twenty

As promised, Mack and his team moved us into yet another hotel. Because my face and my crusade was known throughout the country, Detective Spencer added a heavy police presence to our new lodging, but it didn't fool us. It might look like a goodwill gesture, but there was no way the Houston Police Department wanted any of the political fallout if Russell and his group were successful in a second attack.

Earlier, I had to field a frantic call from my daughter, Gail, followed by a worried, but less emotional one from son, Richard. Although relieved I was unhurt, both were very concerned about this second assault. I was planning to come home, but I begged off Gail's offer to come to Houston to fetch me by telling her I couldn't leave until we satisfied the police that I was no longer needed for the investigation. When I explained about the security detail that Simon had arranged and how they got me to safety, she calmed down some, but I know she was beside herself with worry.

My name was all over the networks as news of the attack spread across the country, if not the world. Russell was now on the FBI's most wanted list, and both they and Homeland Security were working with State officials to bring him to justice. Foreign national leaders were condemning the attack and offering prayers for the victims. Members of both Houses were stepping forward, calling for the capture of those responsible. Ironically, there were no presidential Tweets about the incident or me, so far. Cellphone pictures of the asshole in the SS uniform were circulating on social media and seemed to have finally raised disgust among regular folks.

Simon, who rejoined us in the morning with a sling on his arm after spending a night in hospital for observation, looked haggard, yet determined. Since returning, he had his phone glued to his head, as he used his vast network and influence to make things happen.

"Hell, Governor," he said into his phone, "we have a body count of twenty-seven so far, a bunch of them old men with medals, Texan World War II veterans—and you're making excuses? The people of your state as well as the rest of the country want to see results. Now! This Joseph Russell and his group make the Proud Boys look like a bunch of children crying for their mommies."

I was only hearing one side of the conversation, but Simon wasn't giving an inch.

"It's been over twelve hours. What have you done? Are the highways closed? The airlines? This was a terrorist attack against American citizens, and if I don't see something concrete in the next couple hours, I'm going to be asking these questions in the press! Maybe that will light a fire under your conservative ass! Now, I've got to go. I've got an interview with a network pool at 3:00, and what I tell them will be up to you!"

Simon ended the call and threw me a smile. "He's a *putz*, but that should get us some reaction."

Mack entered the room, his face grave. My heart did a lurch.

"Just got a call from the hospital," he said, then paused. "Jeremy died in surgery."

I closed my burning eyes and wondered if and when the carnage would end.

Why the hell couldn't it be me instead? I was months, if not days, from the end, anyhow. Jeremy was in the prime of his life. He had a wife and two young kids. My mind flashed to the first night our presentation aired and the petite yet happy lady, Jeremy had introduced me to. How would I face Miriam with this news? He had a heart of gold and always an encouraging smile. And he was so, so talented.

We had shared a lot these past months and had become friends. I would miss him. I'd miss him a lot.

What a goddamn waste!

My guts burned, and I must have let out a groan, because Simon called for Emily. But I didn't give a shit. At least I was *feeling* the pain. From the shooting, at least twenty-seven—no, twenty-eight!—people would feel nothing ever again. I could bear it for them. In memory... of my friend.

I waved Emily away, and she reluctantly retreated to the other room. I looked at Mack before bringing my attention back to Simon, now sitting staring at nothing. Jeremy's death had devastated him as well. No longer as tough as he was moments ago with the Governor.

"The body count is getting too high," I said, staring directly at him.

He sat up like a fighter getting his second wind. "What are you saying?"

"I'm saying they— *I* — have hurt too many people. I want no one else on my conscience."

"So, you're quitting?" he said, his tone suddenly hard with disgust. "You're ready to give up all the gains we've made and go back to your little apartment to die?" He jumped up and began pacing the room. "You *are* making a difference, Donald. A real difference. It's not just the Jewish community speaking up now. It's regular people, from all across America. After that last attack in Portland, the outcry by veterans' groups and ordinary people for change was a massive wave. After last night's slaughter, it'll be a tsunami."

He rounded on me. His complexion was dark, and his voice had become a growl. "If you leave now, then our momentum will die and all you've gained will be lost. Those people who died last night will have died for nothing, Donald. *Jeremy* will have died for nothing."

"You think I don't know that!" I spat back, sitting up straight and sending a blaze of pain through my cracked pelvis. "But how many have to die to stop this one son-of-a-bitch?" I swung my gaze to Mack. "When Mack handed me that gun last night, I was ready to kill me some Nazis. I could almost taste it, especially watching those innocent people dying while I hid in a back room." Wiping at the spittle at my mouth, I said, "I want to do more. I want to bring the fight *to* this cowardly motherfucker." I looked from one man to the other. "Show me how to do that, and I'll stay on; but even though I'm a dying old geezer, I need to hit back!"

All three of us were quiet for a couple of minutes. Finally, I looked up and said, "And if there are to be any other presentations, I need them *completely* protected from any kind of assault. I don't care if you have to bring in the National Guard, but the public has to be protected."

Simon raised his hands in surrender. "I agree we must do everything to protect those that stand by us." He huffed. "But after last night, I'm not sure just how many would even be willing to attend another of our presentations. I'll have to speak with my spin-doctors to find some ways to fix this. As for protection beyond Mack's team, I'm sure we can twist some political arms to ensure there's a heavy police presence. I'm not talking about uniforms, but counter-terrorists or SWAT."

Mack spoke for the first time. "Of course, this all stays within this room, but if we do plan on hitting back, how are we supposed to find the bugger if every law enforcement agency in the country can't?"

I smiled. "Because I know exactly where he'll be in two months' time."

Both men looked at me with surprise.

"Back home, in Lancaster."

"So where did you come up with *that*?" Simon said, skepticism deep in his voice.

"The FBI interviewed me after my first encounter with Russell. They thought he was in the area to help set up a massive rally, like the one in Charlottesville. The city is trying to put a stop to it, but it'll probably happen, regardless. Unless they find him in the meantime, it would be our best chance for some payback."

Simon stared at me, and I could see his mind working furiously. He looked over at Mack. "This goes way beyond the scope of our agreement. What are your thoughts?"

"I can't speak for the individuals on my team, but I owe it to Scott. I want a piece of this asshole."

Chapter Twenty-One

Over the next few days, while we waited for the Houston police to signal that we were no longer needed for their investigation, we looked at the problem of flushing out Russell. Although every resource, both federal and state, was being thrown into the hunt for Russell, they had found very little.

Someone called in a report of suspicious activity to Crime Stoppers of Houston the morning after the attack. Working on the tip, police attended and raided a small, run-down bungalow on the south side of the city in a neighborhood called Sunnyside. Regardless of its upbeat name, the area was considered one of the most dangerous in all of America.

Witnesses spoke of a dark-colored SUV that pulled up to the house later in the evening after the shooting. Two men went into the home assisting a third, who seemed to be injured. Within minutes of arriving, they had turned all the lights on in the house. An hour later, a barrage of gunfire shattered the neighborhood's quiet night, and one man was seen exiting the home. He fired up the SUV and left the area in a wheel-spinning roar.

We got all this news when Detective Spencer had us to his tiny office for some follow-up questions. With four of us and my wheelchair, we were packed in. Mack stood, and Simon took the wooden chair in front of the desk. I, of course, had my own seat.

"When our officers arrived," Spencer added, "they spied one man through the front window, lying face down in his own blood. They entered the building and found a second victim in an easy chair in the living room. The ME declared them both dead at the scene." He looked up from his notes to eye Simon, Mack and me. "It was an obvious shoot out. The guy on the floor had a pistol, recently fired, in his hand. We also dug out two slugs from the kitchen door frame, which is where the other shooter was located. Our ME believes the guy in the chair was already dead from previous wounds before our shooter made sure with a couple of taps to the guy's chest. We identified both as those who took part in the attack. Neither was Russell."

"Any sign that he'd been part of the shoot out?" Mack asked.

The Detective shook his head, his eyes red at the lack of sleep. "As if we'd get that lucky. But no, we did find evidence that he'd been there around the time of the shooting, and evidence that it might not have been a shoot-out at all, but a staged execution. But nothing to tie him to it directly, other than these two had been with him at the time of the attack."

"But why kill his own men?" I asked.

The older man shrugged. "Could have been a disagreement about hiding out or running. Or blame for the failed attack. At this point, it's all speculation."

Mack leaned back against the wall. "Harder to track one person, rather than a group, especially with one injured."

Spencer nodded. "We spotted the SUV in a shopping-center parking lot. Back seat was covered in blood. Russell's prints on the steering wheel. Whether he changed vehicles or met someone is anyone's guess."

Our meeting with Spencer had been the second day after the assault, and we were all becoming frustrated. Being locked away in a hotel room was getting us all antsy. Russell was the fugitive, but we were the ones locked up. It might have been plush, but it still felt like a jail cell.

As Simon has suggested, most American people were in an uproar concerning the attack, especially with the loss of the American veterans. In the past, Nazis had only gone after either non-Whites or the Jews. Most people turned a blind eye because it didn't threaten them or their way of life. They may have shaken their heads despairingly; but as a country, they shrugged their collective shoulders. The German people behaved the same way when Hitler segregated one group after another in the 1930s.

But today's neo-Nazis had not differentiated. They had targeted everyone. White, Black, Hispanic, young, old—anyone who listened to or supported my message was fair game for these animals.

Russell and his group had made a colossal mistake by leaving the winning strategies of their earlier brotherhood: fear and division. By attacking the Houston gathering, they gained the fear, but gave up the division—and it looked to be a fatal mistake.

America was waking up. They couldn't afford to sit on the fence like people had in Germany and Austria during the

1930s. Something had to be done so that history could not repeat itself.

AFTER ONE OF MY RESTS, I rolled my chair into the common area to find Mack and Simon sitting across from two familiar faces, Special Agents Monica Gilpin and Jennifer Pointer.

I rolled to the group and accepted a protein shake that Emily insisted I drink. I had fought her, being a meat-and-potatoes man, but the shake caused less pain in my stomach than meat and potatoes, so I relented.

"Ladies," I said in greeting, adjusting my glasses and running a hand to fix my few strands of hair. "Surprised, but happy to see you. Are you here about Russell?"

Agent Gilpin smiled. "In part, Mr. Wilson. We were following up with Mr. Krakow and the information that his... em... *past* employee sold to the media concerning the location of your last presentation."

"What about it?" I said, confused. "I thought Simon dealt with it."

Simon sat forward. "As you remember, the press met us at the gate at George Bush International Airport."

I nodded, waiting for him to elaborate.

"We had not released the media event yet and hadn't planned to until later in the day. But someone had advised certain networks the day before. Almost twenty-four hours before."

I looked around the table, feeling like an idiot. "I'm still not getting this."

Agent Gilpin lifted a hand. "When we investigated the release of the information, we of course determined who'd leaked it; but we also found out who the early release had been given to. There is one network, which for now will remain nameless, but I'm sure you can figure it out for yourself, that passed the information along to a third party. We'd investigated this network before because of their links to the far right. But this time, we have found electronic evidence. The reporter passed the release on to a leader of the Aryan Brotherhood at almost the same time they got it from the leak."

"So, they knew we'd be in Houston."

Mack nodded. "They had more than a twenty-four-hour window to gather a team here, waiting to attack. Even though we changed sites, it was nothing for them to shift to the new hall once we publicly announced the new location. The attack itself was a pretty basic frontal assault, all shock and awe, right out of some Blitzkrieg handbook. Not much planning required."

Agent Pointer's grin made her look downright evil. "Except they hadn't expected to deal with security composed of ex-Special Forces. Those Nazi losers practice on paper targets. It's a little different when the targets shoot back." She pulled her gaze to Mack. "The body count was high, but it would have been much, much worse if your people hadn't reacted so effectively."

Mack nodded, his lips tight.

"We picked up the reporter, who threw 'reporter's privilege' in our faces, until we reminded her that we were not after her source, but the consequences of her passing on the information to a third party—in this case, a White-supremacist group. We have charged her with aiding and abetting in a domestic terrorist attack."

We all exchanged a look of surprise.

"And to add insult to injury, but appropriately in my opinion, her network dropped her immediately. She won't be getting any of their high-priced corporate lawyers to bail her out."

"The other issue we'd like to speak about, Mr. Wilson," said Agent Gilpin, "Is protection. I'm sure you've heard of the witness protection plan, but what many do not know is that we also use it for high-target victims. We can make you disappear, so Russell and his people never find you."

I laughed and almost choked. "There's no way that little shit is going to get me to hide in a hole in the middle of nowhere while he's out running free! I ain't scared of the coward. I'm a ninety-five-year-old with nothing to lose. He's the one who's scared. He's come at me three times now, and he's failed each time. That's got to be eating away at him."

I took a pull at my protein shake to calm myself and squirmed to ease some of the pain in my pelvis.

"All we're saying—" said Agent Gilpin.

"Look, I appreciate the offer. I do. If I was a young buck with a lifetime ahead of me, I might consider it. But I'm nearing the end of my run and I'll take my chances. If he comes—*when* he comes—I'll meet him head-on, and he'll see what it's like to face a real man."

A harsh bark of laughter made me swing my head to Agent Pointer. "What the hell are you planning? And don't deny you're planning something. It's written across your face." She leaned back, green eyes narrowed, as she studied me.

I gave her a smirk. "Actually, unless Russell's picked up by one of the law-enforcement groups, the ball is entirely in his court. He has to come out of the shadows."

She leaned forward. "And there's only one thing that will get him to do that."

She pointed her finger at me, ignoring the others as if we were alone in the room.

"You."

Chapter Twenty-Two

The door hadn't fully closed behind the two FBI agents before Simon turned on me.

"What's she talking about?"

I stalled by looking over at Mack, who was smiling. Seemed everyone knew but dear Simon.

"Damn it, Donald! You're planning to offer yourself as bait was not part of our deal!" He looked over at Mack for support, but the big man averted his eyes. "Oh, so this is something you're both thinking about? Are you nuts?"

"Simon—" I started to say.

He jumped up, his face red with anger. "I was okay for going on the offensive, but that did not mean I'm ready to use you for bait."

"Would you calm down!"

"No!" he roared. "I already have Jeremy and all those poor people from the other night on my conscience. I don't need *another* corpse."

I sat waiting quietly while he paced the large room to shed the worst of his pent-up emotions. Finally, he stopped in front of us, the coffee table an ineffective defense against his anger. But he dropped into a chair as if his string had been cut.

"Are you done?" I asked.

He looked up at the ceiling as if he might explode again, but then sat back and nodded.

"First off, there should be nothing on your conscience, Simon. You didn't kill Jeremy, Russell's people did." He opened his mouth, but I cut him off. "You also didn't kill those people. I'm sickened by what happened to them, too. It was part of the reason I was ready to go home the other day. And Simon, you or I—or you, Mack—did not kill Scott or get Dillon shot. *All* of that lies on Russell."

Simon let out an enormous sigh.

"Now think about it. If I'd gone home the other day, what do you think would have happened?"

"What... what do you mean?"

"If I had gone home, like I wanted to, I would have been unprotected and therefore an irresistible target for Russell. He would have known the minute I left the tour and been waiting. I would not have had Mack and his team protecting me. So, he'd kill me anyway, but he'd have had a clean run at me. Now if we plan this right, there's a good chance we'll get shot at luring him out and making him pay for his crimes. And if he gets lucky, and he gets me, that tsunami of support that you spoke about should turn into a biblical flood—not that I'm ready to concede just yet!"

His expression told me he was at least listening, so I continued.

"Having said that, I don't think he's stupid enough to just walk out in the open. I think it would be a mistake to underestimate him. He's come out of nowhere twice and managed to elude both local cops and the FBI for months now."

"Okay, so let's say I agree with you, although I'm not in favor of this at all. What are you proposing?"

"I think we have to make it so that Russell has no choice but to come out from under his rock and confront me."

"And how do we do that?"

"By pissing him off."

I SQUINTED AT THE BRIGHT lights of the massive newscast studio as a young girl secured a lapel microphone to my uniform jacket. I had turned down an offer of makeup, which I had been told would give my skin a warmer tone since lights bleed color from unshielded flesh. At my age, what did I care about my skin?

The station, located in downtown Houston, was affiliated with one of the larger networks and had been renovated recently to give it a more open and modern feel. The studio stretched across a wide circle with the main news desk front and center. Weather, sports, and financial sections bracketed it.

The last position, used for interviews, where the young lady wheeled me, was a round table that resembled a dinner table that she said was to make guests feel at home. Bullshit! All the lights, fussing, and massive cameras that rode on sets of rails and could be positioned at any of the desks as needed made the place itself overwhelming. I squirmed with nervousness. I could watch the newscast live or I could watch it via a monitor that hung from the ceiling, behind the camera line.

Two news anchors, a salt-and-pepper-haired man in a dark blue suit and a younger woman in a stylish mock-neck, plaid, form-fitted dress stood before a tall desk, her long dark hair falling across one shoulder. Both anchors spoke into the camera as if it was a live audience, announcing the day's latest local, state, national and international news, all in condensed packages. At different intervals, one of the other sections such as weather or sports would break in, to hint at what would come up after a commercial break.

During one such break, the female anchor walked over and introduced herself, offering me her hand. She sat in the seat a couple of feet away from me, so the camera could get a good angle on both of us.

"Mr. Wilson, I'm Jessica. I'm so happy to meet you. I just wish it had been before the awful events of the other night."

"Thank you."

"We'll be on in a moment. Do need anything? More water?" she said, pointing at my half empty glass, which I had been sipping to help calm the nerves.

"No, thank you. I'll be fine."

"Fifteen seconds," announced one technician behind the camera.

"Ted will do the introduction and summary of the attack before switching over to you and me," she said, patting my hand as if she could feel my anxiousness.

When the light on the main camera lit up, the anchor at the main desk began to summarize the terrorist attack and tell how Joseph Russell was still at large. But then he dropped a bomb that I was unprepared for.

"We have an update to this story. We have learned that Clarence Walker, a ninety-four-year-old veteran who had been injured in what the Houston police now are calling a domestic terrorist attack, has succumbed to his injuries. This brings the death toll to twenty-nine." He bowed his head for a second.

I felt the hollowness in my chest dig even deeper.

The commentator continued after a staged pause, and a cynical part of me instinctively knew they had only now released this information just to get a reaction from me.

The male anchor continued, "In the studio, we have Donald Wilson, who may have been the primary target of the attack. Mr. Wilson, as most people know, has been touring America warning of the rising danger of neo-Nazism. He's with Jessica, who we'll turn to now."

The light on the camera in front of us lit up and Jessica looked directly into it. "I'm joined now by Donald Wilson, who, as Ted mentioned, has been warning of the increasing danger the neo-Nazi movement poses in recent years." She turned towards me. "Thank you for joining us."

Still shaken by the news of the latest death of yet another veteran, I just nodded and murmured, "Thank you."

"Donald, had you known about Mr. Walker, or are you hearing this for the first time tonight?"

I shook my head. "N—no," I stammered. "I talked with him and the other victims at the hospital on the day of the attack, but this is the first I've heard that he had left us. Let me express my heartfelt condolences to his family."

She stiffened and blurted, "Yes, of course. And of course, our own condolences to the Walker family from all of us at Houston News."

She clasped her hands together as she looked at me. "I have seen your entire presentation, Donald, and as moving as it was, I have to admit that, at the time, I thought it was unrealistic to think that we had much to worry about from the White-supremacist fringe. I now have to concede that I was totally wrong. The attacks the other night proved your prediction. These modern-day Nazis are a genuine threat to Americans. Maybe to the entire world."

"I understand. It's been too long. When we celebrate Memorial Day we say, 'Never forget,' but America *has* forgotten. America has forgotten the sacrifices of our veterans. And it has forgotten the horrible danger of Nazism."

I paused. "The other night was a wake-up call for America. That was just a small sample of what Nazism is like. If it's allowed to grow, it will become much, much worse."

Jessica was frozen, probably for the first time in her life. There was a shadow in her expression that I was very familiar with. Fear.

"But we have two things going for us, Jessica."

Hearing her name seemed to snap her to the present. "What things are those?"

I leaned towards her. "The enemy has revealed itself in its true form. This was a massacre, so it can't hide in a riot like it did in Charlottesville. This time it stood before the world clearly and proved how evil it truly is."

"And the other?"

"This time the enemy is different from the one I faced in Europe during the '40s. Then, Nazi forces fought with conviction. They stood their ground and fought like men without flinching. Most were not even evil. The majority were just regular Germans fighting for their homeland, either convinced or forced by the madmen running their country. Most were not even Nazis."

I turned and looked into the camera.

"The Nazis of today are a shadow of that enemy. Joseph Russell and all the other White supremacists are no better than schoolyard bullies that need a crowd to back them up or else they need to strike from the shadows. Not one of them will stand in the light of day, man to man to fight an honest fight."

"I still call on every American to push your state and federal representatives for change that will not allow this type of hatred to manifest itself. It is high time that the legislators—who are supposed to serve their constituents—develop hate laws with *teeth* to protect the innocent and punish any and all who would tear America apart.

"But I am also throwing down a challenge to those who think they can force their agenda on America through brute force, intimidation, and fear." I turned from her to look directly into the camera.

"Joseph Russell. The guy who arranged the Dallas massacre and who's on the FBI's list. Well, I challenge Joseph Russell and the other cowards who share his ideology to face *me*, man to man."

Her eyes widened in shock. "But Donald, you're..."

I smiled. "Wheelchair bound and ninety-five-years-old?" I nodded. "Yeah, but I'm still more of a man than that coward, Joseph Russell."

Chapter Twenty-Three

We stopped in three more cities so I could sit through more interviews as my dropping the gauntlet seemed to have become almost as big a news story as the attack itself. With the country as divided as it was politically, thanks in part to the president's social-media commentary, there was plenty of push-back.

The far-right attacked me non-stop, calling me irrational and senile. They even had a poster of me, in my wheelchair, with a line through it. They captioned it, 'Stop the Jew Lover!' These were popping up online and across the country as posters; but no one, not even the NMA, would step forward and assume responsibility. Of course, this was just more proof, which I promoted, of the cowardliness of both the ideology and its believers.

The political left was trying to jump on board, but Simon wasn't having it. We had one message, and no one was going to hijack it.

Our tour kept moving east, towards home. Simon was nervous that Russell might not wait for me to return home, but all that was part of our plan. If we were going to get a chance to grab him, we needed to pull him in close.

Mack left most of his team to guard us and headed back to Lancaster ahead of us to get the lay of the land. He planned to set up a base of operations and to inquire about the proposed march in July.

Meanwhile, Simon had been planning a small vacation for us. The stress of the past weeks and the pain of losing so many people in Houston had taken its toll on all of us. So, after the last interview with CNN, Simon's jet left the sprawling cityscape of Atlanta, our most recent stop, and headed southwest to parts unknown to me. Simon was trying to keep it a surprise, and he smiled gleefully at my questioning stare. He had something up his sleeve, but he was busting a gut to keep from blurting out the secret.

A couple of hours later, Emily shook my shoulder to waken me. I squinted at the bright light coming through the jet's oval side-windows. It had been dark in my little sleeping quarters when I lay down for my rest, so Emily must have slid the blind up to help me wake up.

"The pilot has announced that we are on our final approach to our destination and has asked that everyone get buckled in," she said as I fumbled my glasses out of a little cubby-hole and onto my face.

I sat on the edge of the bed, stretching neck and back muscles as she positioned my wheelchair beside me.

I ran my tongue over my surviving teeth with all their caps and the two implants. Lucky to have them. "Do I have time to brush my teeth? It feels like something crawled in and died."

"If we hurry," she said with a laugh.

A minute later, I was feeling more like my old self and she had me fully dressed and in my chair. Then she handed me a cup of water and my morning pills. While I knocked them down, she pushed me through the cabin to the common room. With practiced maneuvering, she got me into a regular seat and strapped me in, then folded my chair and secured it nearby. Then she took the seat near mine and secured herself.

Through the window, the aquamarine blue of the Caribbean rose towards us. Shimmering waves made way for sandy beaches and clusters of tropical trees. With a light bump, the jet touched down, and the engines reversed to slow us down. In minutes, we pulled up to a single-story terminal building no bigger than a bungalow.

When the forward passenger door opened, a wave of heat flooded the cabin, and I began to sweat immediately. It took only minutes before they got a scissor lift in place for disembarking.

After she got me back in my chair, Emily handed me a pair of cheap, oversized plastic sunglasses to go over my own glasses, and a straw Panama hat. "You'll need these, Donald. We'll get you into lighter clothes once you're settled."

"Where are we?"

She shrugged. "I know as much as you do."

Exiting the aircraft, we felt the true heat of the sun, and I was happy for the hat. Sun and thin hair lead to a burned scalp. Done that.

Once on the ground, we made for the terminal building. The three bodyguards that accompanied us went in first, presumably to ensure there was no threat. Simon held the door while Emily guided my chair through the entrance. After the bright sun, I was all but blind even with the sunglasses. I blinked fast and found myself the focus of a group of people gathered in the room.

"Surprise!"

I jerked in my chair, not expecting this kind of reception. As my eyes grew accustomed to the gloom, I recognized Gail and Richard at the front of the crowd, their smiles wide and overwhelming. Gathered around them were the familiar faces of my grandchildren.

My expression registered my recognition because they surged towards me. Suddenly, my family surrounded me, happy smiles mixed with tears of joy. Overwhelmed, I couldn't speak for a minute. Gail was hugging and kissing me as if I'd come back from the dead, while Richard shook my hand calmly with a warm glitter in his eye. Gail said, "Sure beats meeting you in Chicago, Dad!"

As the press of family lessened, I looked over at Simon. "Surprise," he mouthed silently. He swiped at his own eyes before turning and saying something to Emily.

All the stress and pain I'd been living with these past weeks suddenly bubbled up and I broke down in sobs right then and there. Jeremy's death, the attack, the cancer, the cracked pelvis that put me into a chair—it all tore through me in a cleansing of tears. But my family's arms around me and my joy at seeing them firmly pushed aside the horrors I had dealt with.

"Now Dad," Gail said, dabbing at her eyes, which were her mother's, with a tissue. "If we knew that seeing us would have you in tears, we'd never have come!"

That brought an abrupt laugh right from my chest, and I smiled. "You cannot know how happy I am right now!"

Simon suddenly knelt beside my chair. "There still one more surprise waiting, Donald."

"What—?"

He raised his hand and Gail and the others backed away so I could see what lay beyond them. Standing at the back of the room, looking nervous and out of place, stood my long-time friends from the Legion!

With a hand pressed to her lips, Rita almost ran to me. Her arms circled me, threatening to push the chair back through the terminal doors. Holding my face with her hands, much to my horror she showered me with kisses with my family looking on.

"Keep your knickers on, Rita," Decker said, a huge smile lighting up his face. As Rita stepped back, wiping her cheeks, the big man extended his hand and almost crushed mine. "Damn good to see you, my friend."

I patted his hand, only to have Frank push through. "Makin' us proud, buddy."

Benny and Edith had been holding back. As they shuffled forward, I realized I hadn't seen Benny since the week after his heart surgery. He looked good, and his complexion seemed normal. Edith clung to him like he was her lifeline. I lifted both hands and grasped both of theirs in welcome.

"Good to see you're doing better, Benny."

"Thank you, my friend." He took in my chair. "I see you've upgraded. Wait till Wayne sees it, he'll have it spec'd out for racing stripes—or flames!"

We laughed, and I felt a warm glow realizing how much I had missed seeing my old friends. They'd been a weekly part of my routine for so long that the past few weeks had left a hole I hadn't recognized until they stood before me.

Simon stood up and waved everyone to be quiet. "I know everyone wants time with Donald, but let's move this *mishegas* to the main house."

Everyone began to move towards the building's rear doors. As Emily pushed my chair towards the retreating group, Gail looked at her. "May I?"

Emily nodded gracefully, with a smile. "Of course." To me, she said, "Enjoy the visit, Donald. I'll be along soon."

Gail pushed us forward. "I get to be your nurse now, Dad." Her tone was questioning.

I knew she was fishing, unsure of what she'd missed.

"Simon insisted on a nurse ever since I got hurt in Portland, and he hired Emily. She makes sure I eat enough and take my pills. After the attack the other night, she even patched up one bodyguard who had a bullet hole in the arm."

Sitting in the chair, I couldn't see her face, but her silence told me she was considering what I was telling her.

"I can't say I'm too happy that you're involved with this business. I mean, don't get me wrong, Simon's invitation and the accommodations here on the island are so generous, but at ninety-five, you're no longer as spry as you used to be even ten years ago. I'm afraid for you, Dad. Hell, we're all afraid."

I reached over my shoulder to pat her hand. "I'm making a difference here, Gail. It gives me something to live for."

She was quiet after that, but I knew my daughter, and she was far from finished. She'd wait, then try to get her brother on board before making her next move. In her eyes, I should be at home, playing it safe.

But I had other plans.

Chapter Twenty-Four

"This is the Island of Caicos, and my property is on the south side of the Providenciales," Simon said, responding to my question of just where in the heck we were. We'd gathered our group in the main building for supper that was supposed to be served momentarily. "I bought the place from an estate sale and really couldn't pass it up. I spend all my free time, which is limited, here on the island."

"It's magnificent," I said, sipping on the single beer Emily allowed me. She hadn't wanted me to even have this one, but we were celebrating the reunion of my friends and family, so she conceded with a look that warned me about over-doing it.

Ceiling fans moved the warm air around but did little to cool the room. My host must have noticed the sheen of sweat on my face, because he motioned to a man in a white jacket who'd been ensuring that everyone's drink remained full. The man began to open the shutters on the windows, and soon a cool breeze from the ocean filled the room. I nodded my appreciation.

Our group moved through the large room, each taking a turn talking to me and asking a hundred-and-one different questions. They had all been following my crusade across the country, and I felt proud for what I had accomplished with Simon and Jeremy's support.

My grandson, Tyler, updated me on the grocery store I used to run and those employees I still knew. It was heartening to see how well Tyler had made the business his own.

My old crew sat together in a corner of the room, so I wheeled myself over. Using my rationed bottle of beer, I raised a toast to our reunion. Right away, Rita lit into me.

"Damn it, Donald. You refused the help of your oldest friends and then let Mr. Money-pants bankroll this whole tour." She raised her hand when I tried to answer. "Don't get me wrong, I appreciate him bringing us all down here. It's you that needs to explain. We've been sitting on our butts wanting to help you, and you shut us down."

The others nodded hesitantly.

"It was our war too, Donald," Frank said quietly.

"And my people were the main victims," Benny said, with Edith nodding at his words. "I'd like a chance to even the score."

I bowed my head because I knew they were right. But with Jeremy's death so recent and so close to my heart, I knew I could have never taken them up on their offer.

"I'd admit, when I first left, I was doing this for myself." I looked around to see if anyone was close by. Gail was talking with Emily and that caused me concern, but I put it aside as I turned back to my friends. "You all know about the cancer. It's why I was in a hurry to make my move. I only have so much time. After the success of the documentary, the rest was a blur. I wasn't thinking about you guys. Yeah, I admit it; but I wasn't thinking about myself either. Every couple of nights, it was a new town and a new group. They blended together until Portland, where Russell appeared, and this happened." I banged my hand on the arm of my wheelchair.

"After that, all I was thinking about was the danger he posed," I said. "But after Houston, I am truly glad you were not with me. What happened to those poor people—could have happened to you. It was hard enough losing Jeremy. I couldn't bear to lose any of you."

"Sugar, that's sweet. But it should have been *our* decision to make."

Decker leaned forward. "We've talked about it, Donald. From this point, we want to help." He glanced at the others, who were nodding. "We've figured out how you've been aiming to rile this Russell guy up. Insulting him. Calling him out. So, just when and where is this showdown supposed to happen?"

It was Frank's turn. "Answer me this, Donald. I can see you clench your gut every once in a while. Right? The cancer is eating away at you. Do you somehow hope that this fight might end that pain?"

His words stopped me cold. I hadn't thought about it that way—or had I? I admit, I wanted Russell behind bars—or even dead by my hand. He was the head of the snake. After all the suffering he had caused and might cause in the future, it would be a fitting legacy before I checked out.

But, if I was being honest with myself, the end of the constant burning, the ever-growing ache in my back would be welcome relief. As the cancer progressed, I wasn't under any illusion that the pain would lessen. It would get worse. Much worse. Emily and I had talked about it on more than a few occasions. Soon, I'd be unable to function, living the rest of my days sedated to the nines, oblivious to everything around me. That was no way to live. That was no way to die.

Dying for what I believed in was much more preferable.

I looked up. "Yeah, my pain might play a part, Frank. But my main reason is that it's the right thing to do and there have been enough innocents hurt because of this animal."

Their eyes lifted, and I knew someone was approaching. I felt a soft touch on my shoulder and Gail said. "This is supposed to be a party, but you guys look like you're attending a funeral. Liven up!"

The group dropped all seriousness and awarded Gail their best smiles—but I knew the discussion was not over. I had a lot to think about.

Supper was served; and, as always, Simon proved to be a magnificent host. Serving staff, all in white jackets, set the table with gold-plated china and crystal wineglasses. Simon's chef stood ready to carve a massive baron of beef to everyone's preference. Gail took it upon herself to fill my dish with all my favorites, but frowned when Emily produced one of her green smoothies and poured the concoction into a crystal goblet.

"But Daddy, roast beef is your favorite," she said as I moved the plate aside and picked up the goblet of green stuff.

I gave her a smile. "It smells divine, Gail, but my digestion hasn't been the best lately. Emily's smoothies are much easier on my system."

She smiled back, but the smile didn't reach her eyes. She knew something was out of place; and knowing her as I did, I knew she would not let it lie.

I WOKE SOMETIME DURING the night to the now-familiar burning throb in my stomach. Clutching my midriff, I rolled to my side to face the open patio door. Light from the moon showed a gentle breeze moving the white sheers in and out of the bedroom. The hiss of the sea climbing and retreating on the shore's sand was like a whisper.

As my eyes adjusted to the gloom, I made out a figure sitting motionless in a chair at the foot of the bed. I could not see their face, but my throat caught.

Was it him? How did he find me in the middle of the goddamn ocean? The figure rose, and I stiffened, my mind searching for some way I could defend myself. But between my hip and the pain in my intestines, there was no way I could fight back. I lay like a bug, waiting for the shoe to drop.

A moan escaped my lips as another bout of pain twisted my guts. The figure moved forward and sat on the bed beside me. I was helpless as a hand reached towards me.

"Shhh. Deep breaths," I heard. "I have your medicine, Dad."

Gail!

My tension deflated into the mattress, and I almost sobbed with relief. Strong arms raised me into a sitting position as she propped up my pillow before gently lowering me back. From the bedside table, she picked up a small dish of pills and a glass of water and helped me take them, one by one.

As I settled and gained back my breath, I said, "How did you know?"

She pulled my bedsheets to my chest. "Did you forget what I did for almost forty years? I've been dealing with sick and dying people all my adult life. One look at you and I could tell that you hadn't been honest with me. You've lost a lot of weight, your skin color is off, and I've seen you grabbing your stomach. But when I saw your preferred supper, I kind of guessed the rest. Emily confirmed it once I twisted her arm."

"She—"

She patted my arm. "Don't worry, I can also see that she's taking excellent care of you. What hurts is you wouldn't let me do it for you."

It was my turn to explain to her. "She came as part of the complete package. Simon insisted on it. Like you, she saw the signs and put me on a routine and pain management. As for you and Richard, I didn't want you sitting around watching me deteriorate. You especially. You had enough of that for a lifetime. I told your mother..."

Tears had been tailing down her cheeks, but she let out a laugh. "You talk with Mom?"

"Every day," I said, surprised that she found this strange. "Sometimes for hours; other times just for a minute or two—but she's always there to listen. And y'know, if I listen *real* hard, I can hear her talk back."

She reached out and caressed the side of my face. I could make out the sheen of her tears in the faint light of the night.

"What does she say?" Her voice was a whisper.

"That it won't be long now, but that I don't have to be afraid. But she understands I need to finish this before I'm with her again."

"Does she talk about me?"

I chuckled. "Oh Honey, family was the center of her universe. You know that. She's always going on about you and Richard and the kids. Never doubt that."

We sat silently in the dark, the only movement the graceful sweep of the sheers.

"I need to finish this, Gail."

She stared at me for a few moments before wiping her cheek. "I know Dad." She laid her head on my chest and I stoked her hair like I did when she was a little girl.

Chapter Twenty-Five

The morning was bright and clear, and I sat under a canopy that shielded me from the worst of the sunlight. Emily had wheeled me outside once I'd had my regimen of pills down my gullet. Then she disappeared inside, only to reappear with my morning coffee, which I'd refused to give up, regardless of the bite it would cause. She'd also found a proper pair of clip-on sunglasses for my specs to help cut down on the glare of the sun on the near-white sand that covered most of the island.

"I've had a chat with Simon's chef concerning your diet," Emily said, "and he sees no issues. He has all the ingredients needed to keep you happy and full. Who knows, you might even put on some weight this weekend."

"How hard can it be to mix up that green slop?" I grumbled.

"Now, Donald," she said in a diabolical whisper. "Do I have to speak with your daughter or are you going to behave?" She followed the threat with an innocent smile, but it left me wondering if I had any choice.

I spied one of my bodyguards sitting quietly under a potted palm at the far end of the patio. He had a cup of coffee on a little bistro table in front of him and nodded when he saw I was looking his way. Another of Mack's men was strolling through the grounds, a shoulder holster over a tight electric-blue t-shirt. Because of the private enclave, he didn't have to bother concealing the weapon. I hoped Gail wouldn't make a fuss over it.

I sat there quietly, the breeze, the sound of the waves and the heat almost putting me to sleep. For the first time in a while, my mind was empty and relaxed. Other than a mild burn in my gut, everything was peaceful. I would definitely have to remember to thank Simon for this reprieve.

As if on cue, Simon pushed his way through the glass patio doors, a cup of coffee in his hands. He looked at me and smiled.

"May I join you?"

I nodded. "Please."

"You look so relaxed, I didn't want to disturb you."

"I *am* relaxed, and I have you to thank for it."

"You have a beautiful family, Donald," he said, taking a sip. He put the cup down with the saucer on my table. "After you retired last night, I touched base with Jeremy's wife, Miriam. She's doing OK—he was surprisingly well-insured—and I let her know about an educational trust I've set up for their girls. I reminded her, too, to call on me for anything she needs."

To say I was touched by this amazing man's generosity would be to badly understate the issue.

He continued, "Then I had the opportunity to meet with your Legionnaire friends and heard some marvellous stories about you."

I snorted. "They're all lies."

He laughed. "I envy you. Not everyone has so many people in their corner. Those people hold you in high regard."

I wasn't comfortable with all this touchy-feely stuff, but hid my unease with a large swallow of coffee.

"Anyway, they asked me if there was anything they could do to help with our endeavor. Your friends really want to be part of this, Donald. Mainly, it's for the opportunity to pay you back for all the help, the *mitzvahs*, you've given them when they needed a helping hand. And although they believe in your message and what you're trying to accomplish, you've been there for them, and they need a way to return the favor."

I dropped and shook my head. This was the last thing I wanted to think about. My peace was shattered, and I could feel my old stubborn anger rise. I looked over at him.

"Do you remember what we just went through in Houston? What we lost? We have barely laid Jeremy to rest, and you're asking me to put my friends in harm's way."

"No," said Simon, a hint of scorn in his voice. "I haven't forgotten. You aren't the only one affected by Jeremy's death, Donald. You don't have a monopoly on grief or blame. Don't you think I shoulder most of the blame for that young man's death. It was my idea to start this country-wide crusade. I'm a believer in what we are doing, but don't think for a minute that I wouldn't have taken his place if given the chance."

He threw back the rest of his coffee, his cup banging onto the saucer with a clunk. Silence created a cavern between us.

"I'm sorry, Simon. Didn't mean to blame you," I said, lowering my eyes in shame. "I just don't want to lose anyone else, especially any of my friends."

His expression softened, and he reached over and took me by the arm. “I understand, Donald. Maybe we can find them safe jobs, like making phone calls to recruit sponsors or to invite attendants to the next presentation.”

I mulled over this compromise while my gaze swept down the beach, watching curling tips of the waves as the wind picked up. After a moment, I nodded. “That would keep them away from any presentations. I can’t have them at risk, Simon.”

“I understand. How about if I make sure I pass any arrangements through you. Fair enough?”

“Thank you.”

The patio doors behind us slid open and Emily came out with my breakfast tray balanced in her hands. She closed the patio door with her foot, then she slid the platter in front of me. “Sorry, Simon, I didn’t know anyone else was up. Can I get you something?”

He raised his cup. “Could you ask Ramiro to set out a carafe of coffee with the regular pastries?” He was speaking of his Jamaican chef, who he had introduced us to the previous evening at supper.

“Right away.”

“Then why don’t you come back and join us, Emily.”

She nodded and re-entered the massive home.

I skewered a piece of watermelon from the tray and shoved the still-dripping fruit into my mouth, enjoying the sweet treat. “That girl has brightened my mornings with her concoctions,” I said, patting my lips with a serviette.

“It does look healthy.” Simon peered at the bowl of fruit on the tray, his expression telling me he wasn’t sure he recognized fruit as a food group. Then he looked quizzically at the other bowl.

"Acai Muesli," I said with a snort. "Tastes a heck of a lot better than it looks. Basically, oatmeal with acai, chopped almonds, diced apple and yogurt. Emily tells me it helps my immune system and my digestion." I shrugged, looking at him. "Compared to my usual fried eggs that resembled rubber, I think I'll follow her lead."

Simon laughed. "I'll take your word on it, but I'll stick to my pastries." He patted his flat stomach. "With my metabolism, I don't have to worry about calories."

Emily returned with Simon's pastries and the extra carafe of coffee and took a chair beside me. Simon had pulled another table closer, so its umbrella shielded our nurse from the strong tropical sun. Simon began to regale us with stories of the history of the island and its slow but steady encroachment by the rich and famous.

As we spoke and enjoyed the breeze off the ocean, the others began to join us on the patio, plates filled with all kinds of breakfast fare. Then Gail and Richard and my grandkids joined us, too.

Gail had dark circles under her eyes, and I knew she had slept little after our brief talk last night. I'd fallen asleep while I held her and hadn't woken until my next bladder break. By that time, she was curled up on a sitting couch across the room. I stretched a blanket over her, but I think we were both fooling each other that she was asleep. Guilt pierced me.

Watching those I love eating and smiling at each other was another painful reminder that I had little time remaining. I tried to push aside the morbid thoughts and enjoy the moment; but all I pushed was myself, away from the table.

"I think I'll explore a little," I said to Simon and the others at the table.

I felt eyes on the back of my head as I maneuvered the wheelchair along the patio towards a raised, wooden pathway that led to the beach.

I told myself that I was too used to being alone in my apartment, and that the crowded patio was making me skittish. But you can only bullshit others, not yourself. I was getting that scared, feeling-sorry-for-myself sentiment that surely must be part of every old person's thoughts. I knew that as happy as I was seeing my family and friends, the pain of never seeing or interacting with them again was overwhelming.

I had never been afraid to die in the past. As horrifying as life was during my time in Europe and then again in Korea, dying was just something I never gave much thought to, maybe because I was too busy hunting the enemy—or just because I was young and stupid. I had seen so much death during those years that it became the norm, if that makes any sense. I don't know. I ain't no philosopher. Nohow.

Of course, it was afterward that I had problems—especially after Dachau.

So why now?

A part of me, the smart-ass part, guessed that I had to face the end because there would *be* no afterward this time around. When I took that last breath, there would be no reflection, no opportunity to wonder about my choices.

There'd be nothing.

In the back of my mind, I heard Maggie ragging me out. All the years we were married, including our marriage in 1946, I dutifully attended First Presbyterian Church on the arm of Maggie Louise Wilson. She was a staunch believer and would definitely be floating on some cloud, looking down on her cynical old husband.

But after Dachau, I would always doubt the presence of a passionate, all-loving God. What loving God would sit back and allow the atrocities of the Third Reich to ever happen? So, although I talked to her every day, deep inside I was unsure if I would ever see my Maggie in an afterlife, if one existed.

And that scared the hell out of me.

Chapter Twenty-Six

For three days, we slept, ate, talked, and told old stories and lies. It was an enjoyable break after the hell of Houston.

Gail teamed up with Emily to ensure I followed the exercise routine, which consisted of floundering in the pool like a half-drowned cat with Simon's personal trainer. My previous exercise had consisted of shuffling from my recliner to the kitchen table or the toilet, an Olympic obstacle course when pushing a walker before I finally got rid of my shag rugs.

I can only guess that because I'd graduated to four wheels, the girls had been looking for some other torture to inflict on me. The only bright spot was when my great-grandchildren joined me in the pool. Buoyed with water-wings, smiles with missing teeth, high-pitched screeches, these water nymphs lifted my spirits. Like his mother would have, Richard was busy snapping photos the entire time. I would live on in memory on a jpeg.

It concerned me that my grandson Tyler's seemed too aloof. He was always standing on the edges of the family group or walking alone on the beach while everyone else laughed and played.

Richard explained. "Her name is Anna and she's all he thinks about. The only other thing on his mind is the store, thank God."

Of course, once we all discovered this tidbit, Tyler found himself the center of some targeted teasing by both his parents, Richard and Lilly. And, of course, his Aunt Gail. Naturally, I led the charge. Tyler soon surrendered and joined the family in our get-togethers but only after filling my ears about this jewel that might well have been the inspiration of a thousand sonnets.

After my afternoon naps, I spent time with Rita and the others. Simon and I told them about the job we had thought they might help us with. They seemed satisfied. Of course, Rita had to have the last word.

"Was that so hard? We could have been helping from the beginning if you weren't so damn stubborn."

"Careful, Rita," I said with a growl. "I can always change my mind."

"Bullshit, Sugar. Simon holds the purse strings, so he's in charge. You're just hired help like the rest of us."

She looked over at Simon, who held up his hands. "I'm not getting in between you two."

"Man, he's got you two pegged," laughed Decker, elbowing Frank beside him.

THE FOLLOWING MORNING after another sunlit breakfast, a parade of taxis arrived; and in a deluge of tears, smiles, and hugs, my children and their families, along with my oldest friends, followed the road to the airport. I would see Rita and the others in a couple of days, but Gail was flying back home. Although her husband hadn't been able to come with her and the others because of his own mother's health issues, she was anxious to get home and support him. Richard, and his brood were flying home as well; but the fact we lived in the same town, meant we would hopefully get some time together when I flew home.

I hadn't wanted Gail or Richard to know about my prognosis, but now that it had come out, I felt a release of pent-up stress that came from disarming the unspoken time bomb. To anyone who did not know him, Richard seemed unmoved by the announcement; but the tightening around his eyes and the flare of his nostrils were subtle indicators that I knew well. He hurt inside, but felt it was his duty to exhibit a sense of calm and strength in times of trouble.

"Not the news I'd ever wanted to hear," he said as he hugged me before he entered the cab. "But I'm glad you told me, Dad. I'm there for anything you need."

I had nodded and squeezed him back. "You and your sister need to help each other through this."

He nodded and then was gone.

The sudden quiet was startling after the days of talk and laughter.

Simon and the others were kind enough to give me some room after the exodus. I had moved down to the boardwalk near the water's edge, allowing the wind and surf to calm my heart, and I made a mental note to look for a wind and surf app for my tablet for the next time I had trouble sleeping. My batteries charged with each minute of this calm, and I would soon be ready to jump back into the fight.

I'm not sure how long I sat by the water, but I felt the vibrations of the footsteps through the boardwalk's wooden base and turned to see Simon approaching. Emily stood on the patio, waiting patiently. Simon started when I turned to him but recovered quickly and gave me a smile.

"Emily is busting a gut to get some meds into you and Mack will be calling to give us a report in a half hour. Are you okay with doing this?"

"Definitely. Last person I want to upset is Emily. She might order me an enema if I piss her off."

Simon laughed loudly. "Let's not challenge her then."

He rolled me back to the house before going off to do something else, and I happily accepted a paper cup of pills and a glass of water from Emily. I let her hover over me without complaint and even agreed to eat some solid food for lunch. While she stalked towards the kitchen, I settled at the massive empty table so that it positioned me in front of a large television monitor mounted on the wall.

Simon returned to set up his laptop for our video conference. Simon might be one of the world's rich, but he did his own chores and I liked him for that. Heck, he hadn't even sent someone to get me from the boardwalk, but had come himself and rolled me back to the house. Good man, Simon.

With a tray of sliced tomatoes, cucumbers and a bowl of mixed nuts before me, I snacked as we waited for Mack. Right on time, the video flared to life and to show an empty desk. On screen, Mack slid into a comfortable-looking leather computer chair and gave us a smile and wave.

"How's life in the sun?"

"They call it paradise for a reason, Mack," I said. "You should have made time to join us."

"Maybe once this is all over, I'll take you up on that offer."

"What have you got, Mack?" Simon prodded.

"Well, we now have a base of operations outside of Lancaster. I was able to find a farmstead that's been on the market for some time. The owner was more than happy to rent it out for a six-month period. From my understanding, they had purchased another property hoping that this place would sell and are a little hard up trying to deal with two mortgages."

Simon laughed. "I might have to hire you for the real-estate division of my company, Mack."

"Thanks, but I'd rather take my chances with bullets rather than death by a thousand paper cuts."

We both laughed.

"I've met with local police and filled them in on what we're dealing with. I passed on contact information for the Houston detectives so they can share the findings from their investigation. The more the local police know, the better they can help us when the shit hits the fan."

It made sense, and both Simon and I nodded.

"From what we're hearing, the city is getting bogged down in the courts over this march by Russell and the other neo-Nazis. It's anyone's guess if they'll be able to stop them from marching. The city lawyer I spoke to believes the Nazis have someone with deep pockets in their camp."

"Well, I have deep pockets too," Simon said with a growl. "Hire someone who can follow the money, Mack. If we can get a name, we can make it public and see just how serious their sponsor really is."

Mack nodded. "Not sure if you'll make any headway with that, but I'll put out some feelers. The fella at the city might advise on how we could do this."

"Good."

"I hired a social-media geek who's monitoring several high-flier White-supremacist websites and forums. He's established a few avatars and is monitoring the sites for anything that might interest us."

Simon nodded and pointed a finger towards Mack's image. "That's an excellent idea, Mack. I have some really good people working for me that are into the social media stuff, and I can have them assist if you feel the need."

"I'll keep it in mind, moving forward. I don't think Russell and his people will actually discuss battle plans, at least not on social media because I'm sure the Feds are watching, too. But we may luck out and get some kind of warning about what might be in the wind."

"Is your guy going to search the dark web as well?"

Dark web? The look must have registered across my expression, because Simon raised a hand to the screen.

"Sorry, Mack. Donald, the part of the world wide web we use on our computers is only a small portion of the web. Even though there are millions of sites, you can access all of them with a search engine. But that's only the surface of the web. Below that is the 'deep' web. All the sites that web browsers like Google or Yahoo have not indexed are there, so regular browsers can't access them. Those are sites that need specific log-in usernames and passwords, like on-line banking and email clients on the regular web." He paused. "Are you still with me?"

I nodded. "Never heard about a deep web, but I guess I understand what you're saying."

He pulled his hands together; his eyes focus on the table. "But that's not all. Below the deep web is the dark web. You need special software to move through it, and it's where all communication is anonymous, and both the origin and the destination of interactions are completely hidden. Because they don't track readily, those who want to keep activities hidden use the dark web—those who traffic child pornography, weapons, drugs and any other contraband you can think of."

"So, if you wanted to plan an attack," I said, "the safest place to do it is via the dark web, right?"

"Exactly."

"So how do we access the dark web?"

Simon chuckled. "It's not that easy. You and I'd be spinning our wheels if we even tried. We need to find someone who is already familiar with the dark web environment and those who frequent it." He looked back at the monitor. "Do you have anyone that you know who can help us with that, Mack?"

He stared at us for a couple of beats, his brows clenched. "Let me make some inquires. I do have a name, but we need someone we can trust, so I need to do a thorough search on the person I'm thinking of. Do you want me to report back or can I move forward if this person checks out?"

"If this guy passes your standards, then go for it. If not, let me know and I'll put out my own feelers."

Mack nodded, but I could see he was deep in thought about how best to test this person's loyalty.

"Donald, anything else to add?" Simon asked.

I shook my head, feeling pretty useless.

"Do you have any idea when you plan on returning to Lancaster?" Mack asked.

Simon glanced over at me, and I shrugged. "I'm just here for the ride, Mack," I said, smiling somewhere in front of me, not even knowing where the bloody camera was. I could have been looking at Mack's crotch for all I knew.

Simon leaned forward and said, "Donald's family left this morning, so we might take a couple more days just to unwind and then head there."

Mack nodded. "Send me an ETA and I'll plan for the team to meet you. Sooner the better to let me know so I clear it with the airport. I have more of my people heading here to Lancaster and they should be in place before you arrive. All are topnotch and ready to go the distance."

With that, we disconnected.

Simon looked over at me. "Is there anything more you think we can do, Donald?"

I huffed. "Hell, I don't know. Don't forget, Simon, I'm a long-retired grocery-store owner. Don't know anything about dark webs or dealing with lawyers. I feel like a fifth wheel, spinning, but not moving anywhere fast. But, put that son-of-a-bitch, Russell, in front of me, and I guarantee I'll know what to do."

"Do you think it will come to that?"

"Nobody's caught him yet. He's still out there. Waiting to strike."

I turned my wheelchair towards him and added, "I don't think you following the money and exposing his backer is the right move. We want him to surface. It's the only way we'll get a chance at stopping him once and for all. Our strategy of getting him wild enough to come out of hiding to make another attempt at getting to me only needs one thing: me."

He stared at me, and I knew he had the same reservations that he'd used to try to talk me out of taunting Russell. The grief and blame he was feeling for Jeremy would be worse if Russell was successful.

"I'm going to do this with or without your help, Simon. You know that."

He nodded his head hesitantly.

"It's my decision, so there is no reason for you to feel guilt or blame. Having you help me makes it easier, and I know Mack will put Russell down like a rabid dog, if given the chance. But it takes me to stand up against him to draw him out."

"I know."

"And I'm running out of time."

Chapter Twenty-Seven

Two days later, we approached Lancaster airport from the north-east, paralleling Highway 222. We skimmed over farm fields scattered in between new subdivisions that popped up as fast as they could build them. Touchdown was uneventful. Simon's jet had made our trip comfortable and quick.

As promised, Mack and his team were waiting for us inside the airport's gate. Clearing customs was a breeze for someone with Simon's money. A signed declaration handed to a customs agent as we left the aircraft was all that was required.

The door of the Escalade closed so heavily that I knew it had to be armored. I turned to Simon. "Does anyone ever board your aircraft or check your cargo? You could have brought a shipment of drugs in, and they would never have known."

"They do spot checks dependent on the origin of the flight. Today, we lucked out. Tomorrow, we might have to wait to allow the dogs to walk through the cabin." He elbowed me in the ribs. "Don't worry, they have not subjected me to a cavity search. Yet."

The glass separating us from the driver's compartment came down to reveal Mack in the front passenger's seat. Without waiting for pleasantries, he got right to business.

"There's been a development, and we need to decide how to react."

Simon and I exchanged a look before turning back to Mack.

"What's happened?" Simon said.

"I think it'll mean more if I just show you. We'll be there in a few minutes."

Without waiting for a reply, the glass divider rose, leaving Simon and me looking at each other with trepidation.

Our convoy continued towards the center of Lancaster, the familiar mixture of old and new architecture reminding me how much time had gone by since I was last home. John Deere farm trackers and glossy, low-riding, Jaguar sports cars shared the busy streets, moving past massive brownstones and turn-of-the-century colonials, with many backing onto a sprawling modern-day mall. The town was a potpourri of time capsules that captured a progression of snapshots of American architecture.

As we turned onto the street that held my apartment, I felt a quiver in my gut that had nothing to do with my cancer. Mack's indication of a problem accented that feeling the closer we got to my home.

As we came to my street, our car smoothly turned the corner and headed south. Mack lowered the partition, as if to gauge my reaction.

The convoy stopped across the street from the building and Simon whispered, "My God!"

I was on the far side of the vehicle looking past him, and what I was seeing made little sense. Pushing my door open, I carefully stepped out, my weight on my good leg. Using the vehicle's roof to stabilize me I got my first good look at my home.

The enormity of what I saw made me go cold.

Someone had covered the entire facade of the two-story building with hundreds, maybe thousands, of swastikas. They had replicated the hated image in different sizes and colors, stretching from the base of the building to the underside of the eaves. Even the windows hadn't been spared.

The door to the passenger's compartment opened beside me, and Mack stretched his long form out. He said nothing but stood beside me to give me strength. The message centered in among the swastikas pulled my eyes. Painted in black and outlined in red, "DIE JEW LOVER!" and "Donald Wilson, ENEMY of AMERICA!"

"When?" I croaked, my voice failing me.

"Last night. We heard about it on the local news this morning."

"How... how does he know where I live? And how could he do all this with no one noticing? I mean... there... had to be a bunch of them... ladders... they'd need ladders."

Mack kept his eyes on me, letting me process it.

I snapped my head at him when one thought clarified. "The other tenants? Are they all right?"

He nodded. "Yes, they're fine. Shook up, as you might guess; but none of them saw or heard anything. One neighbor down the street took her dog out around 6:00 AM and saw it for the first time. She's the one who called it in. She told police that there was no light on in any of the units."

"You've spoken to the police then?" Simon asked.

Mack nodded. "Met with them this morning. They reached out fairly quick and have been real forthcoming. Seems Donald here is something like a local celebrity. They'll be amping up their drive-bys from now on."

"Well, that's something, at least."

My leg was aching, and I had no choice but to return to the back seat. Mack's strong arms took the bulk of my weight and eased me into the compartment. The relief was instant, although I was shocked by how quickly I had lost the strength in my muscles.

When the other two men got in as well, I asked, "Can you drive me around so I can get inside?"

Mack swiveled in his seat to look back at me with an expression that said I had lost my mind. "You can't stay here! He obviously knows you live here. You'll be like a lamb pegged out for a lion."

I looked at Simon and then back at Special-Ops Mack. "Did you forget our plan, Mack? We *want* him to come after me. That's the whole point," I said, a little more harshly than I wanted to. "I told you I wasn't running from this son-of-a-bitch, and I meant it. This is my home! And I will fight to the death to defend it. When he comes, it should be easy for you and your men to nail him. It should be like shooting fish in the proverbial barrel."

"Taking him down is not the problem, Donald," he said in his calm voice. "Doing it in a way that doesn't put you or others at risk, is. Protecting you is no different from any of my other clients, except for your mobility issue, which my team and I include in all our plans. And you just mentioned the other issue: the other tenants."

I opened my mouth to speak, but realized he was right. I hadn't taken them into consideration. I pictured Helen and David Wong and their children who called me Yéyé, Grandfather. If any harm came to these kind-hearted and happy people, I would be devastated. And Mr. and Mrs. Ziegler, who immigrated to America after the Berlin Wall came crashing down. They'd be as horrified by the markings on the building as I was. Finally, the young couple, Lisa and Charlotte, who had just moved in this past fall. My shoulders slumped; and my anger, which had been rising, deflated as fast as my hope of ending this quickly.

Mack's eyes softened as he saw that I had calmed down enough to see his point. "I'm not saying we're going to run and hide, Donald, but we need to plan this out so there's no collateral damage." He looked from me to Simon. "Let's go to the safe house so we can flesh this out so there are no mistakes."

I don't recall the trip to the safe house. My mind couldn't seem to grasp a single thought. Images of Russell and the carnage he had sowed kept flashing through my thoughts. I couldn't even feel the anger that would normally threaten to overflow the boundaries of normality. Perhaps the numbness was the shock of going from an enjoyable break with my family and friends to being plunged so quickly into this battle of hate and racism.

I only looked up as our armored Escalade turned onto a long straight driveway that ended in a weathered but well-kept farmhouse. A massive barn rose from behind the house, and I could make out several paddocks with white-painted posts and rails. There was movement in those enclosures, and

I could see a few horses moving forward to meet their new visitors.

As we neared the farmhouse, a speaker clicked on and Mark's voice, tinny because of the radio, said, "We might have an issue. There's a cargo van that's been behind us and now it's slowing down near the driveway. When we stop, wait inside the vehicle, until I give the 'all-clear'."

Both Simon and I twisted in our seat to peer out the rear window.

A white van stood parked across the entrance to the driveway, the driver staring after us. I couldn't be sure, but it looked like he was watching us through a pair of binoculars or maybe a camera.

Our convoy of SUVs circled the roundabout of the drive so my side of the vehicle faced the house. A long sloping ramp ran from the pavement to the front porch, and I grunted at Mack's forethought.

I heard one of the car doors open and turned to see Mack stepping out of the vehicle, his attention fully on the suspect van. He raised his wrist to his mouth, and I knew he was talking to his other teammates. Seconds later, he dropped to the ground as bullets struck the side of our vehicle. A cluster of white divots materialized on the window beside Simon's head, causing him to duck instinctively. The high impact shells created a 'thunk, thunk, thunk' that caused my heart to jump. But the special glass held.

Mack returned fire with his pistol as he maneuvered round the front end of the SUV, but the distance made his shots ineffective. Behind us, the other men of Mack's team were also returning fire.

Looking at the van, I could see the driver standing with a rifle to his shoulder. Puffs of white smoke burst from the weapon, but the breeze pulled the smoke across the field. The side door of the van slid open, and another figure emerged with a long, tube-like object.

At sight of the weapon, the drive threw his door open and rolled out. "RPG," he yelled. He yanked open my door and lifted me physically out of my seat and set me to lie prone on the scorching black asphalt.

On the other side of the vehicle, Mack was yanking Simon out and shoving him unceremoniously around the rear of the car.

I grunted as the driver covered me with his own body. I rescued my glasses from the pavement by me, stuck them on my face, and peered at the man at the far end of the drive. I could just see him from under the SUV as he leaned forward, weapon on his shoulder, taking aim. With a whoosh of white exhaust, the weapon fired. Almost at the same moment, a loud report from a rifle washed over the courtyard and a bullet slammed the tube-totting shooter into the van's open door, the back of his head crumpling as it hit the vehicle's frame. Dark blood covered his shirt. The RPG launcher fell with the man . . .

. . . just as a massive explosion rocked our vehicle, and it terrified me that it would roll over on us. Chunks of asphalt and gravel pelted us as strong hands lifted me and we scrambled away from the SUV, intact, but still rocking from a blast that had seemed to come from the ground beside it.

I heard Emily give a startled cry of concern and glimpsed her being herded towards the front entrance of the building as she looked back towards me as someone was lifting me off the ground to get me to safety.

Hands grabbed me again, lifting and dragging me unceremoniously towards the building. Another rifle shot echoed across the field towards the van, as screams of the terrified horses added to the chaos. As someone bodily carried me forward, I watched the van lurch forward, side door still open with the dead man's leg dangling from its maw. With no thought to his comrade, the driver accelerated, weaving through oncoming traffic, a blast of horns in his wake.

It was our driver who had carried me and deposited me safely inside the house. Simon was on his hands and knees beside me panting like a worn-out dog. Mack slapped the driver on the shoulder and they raised a high five.

"On me!" Mack called. Turning towards a table beside the door, he passed an assault rifle to the driver and a harness with extra magazines. Grabbing a rifle and harness for himself, he led the way back out to the vehicle, loading his weapon on the run.

The two men jumped into the SUV, which, remarkably, had been missed by the rocket-propelled grenade that had been fired much too low. As the car leapt forward in a sharp, tire-squealing turn, I saw the crater that the explosive had left, mere feet from where we had just parked.

Like a NASCAR racer, Mack tore down the driveway and slid onto the roadway without slowing down. The last I saw, he was heading east in the van's direction.

Chapter Twenty-Eight

Within minutes, I heard sirens in the distance, becoming louder as they approached. Now that the worst of the danger was over, two of Mack's men gently lifted me under my arms from off the floor and into an easy chair, while a third held an assault rifle to his shoulder, at the ready. I murmured my thanks, but they ignored my discomfort and shame.

Then Simon placed a hand on my shoulder. "You okay?"

"Well, other than being thrown out of a car, used as a floor mat and then dragged and dropped into a chair like a helpless child, I guess I'm just peachy."

He looked at me in shock, his mouth and eyes wide.

I laughed. "Damn it, Simon, don't mind me. I'm just pissed off at being so helpless. The mind is willing, but the body..." I shook my head.

A heavy tread of footsteps came from the stairs behind me. One of Mack's men who I had seen, but not spoken to came down the steps, a large sniper rifle cradled across his chest. A light-skinned Latino with a Mohawk cut and many tattoos, he wasn't tall, but he had the wiry look of a scrapper.

"Cops are here, Mr. Wilson. Mr. Krakow. I'm Mateo. Please stay inside and out of sight. Only come out if one of us comes to get you. No one gets to you unless the Boss gives the green light. And that includes the cops."

He laid the huge rifle gently on a long coffee table and headed towards the door. As he stepped outside, I could see four or five cruisers lined up in the driveway, police shielded behind car doors, weapons drawn, unsure of what they had responded to.

Emily rushed forward and knelt beside my chair as the guards moved to take positions at the entrances to the room. These men carried enough weaponry to start a minor war. Until this point, the Mack's men had just been carrying sidearms. Their new weapons showed a sure sign of the escalation of the threat.

There was nothing rushed in their movements, yet there was no waste of energy either. Everything had a feeling of a practiced, choreographed exercise.

Simon pulled back a section of drape so we could see the scene outside, but one guard motioned him away. Mateo slowly opened the door. He moved slowly down the front stairs towards the police, hands held away from his body. The cops were on high alert, weapons trained on the ex-soldier, their stance alert and threatening. We couldn't hear what they said, but the police officer who seemed to be in charge spoke into his radio. Seconds later, the radio emitted a burst of static, but no discernible words. But the message changed the demeanor of the peace officers. They lowered guns and finally holstered them before Mateo approached the lead officers.

The next few minutes had Mateo walking the police through the earlier attack, pointing at where everyone had been situated as the skirmish had played out. He and a couple of police officers walked the length of the drive and surveyed the ground, pointing at items that we could not discern and peering at the crater left by the explosive.

Just as yellow tape was being stretched over the entrance, Mack returned, parking the damaged Escalade on the side of the roadway. He and his partner exited the vehicle and met with Mateo and the police officers. The group shook hands and Mack pointed eastward. One officer spoke into his radio and the last car in the line along the drive backed up to the road, where he was guided around what must have been evidence on the ground. Once turned around, Mack's driver jumped into the rear of the cruiser to act as a guide and they headed east.

Mack, Mateo, and one officer walked up the drive towards the house. Another vehicle, a dark blue sedan, approached and parked along the side of the roadway, stopping just before the yellow tape. Two women stepped out, and I recognized them as Special Agents Gilpin and Pointer. Pointer carried a leather briefcase.

"Finally," I said, losing patience. "The gang is all here. This is taking forever!"

Simon game me a patient smile like he was dealing with a child. It should have made me calm down. Made me realize I was being obtuse. But it only pissed me off more. I didn't want to wait for the police and the FBI to go through the motions, taking photographs and filing more useless reports. They needed to be hunting the bastards down!

But there was no stopping bureaucratic investigative routine. They taped off, measured, and photographed the scene. They interviewed each security guard one at a time so the police could get unrehearsed statements. They kept Mack separate as well for the same reason. But in contrast to my growing impatience, Mack seemed to take it in stride, and I guessed he had dealt with similar investigations.

They tagged Mateo's rifle and confiscated it. They would return it after the police investigation as long as they identified no wrongdoing, but they warned the sniper not to leave the city without speaking with the detectives.

And I was finally reunited with my wheelchair. I never though I'd see the day where I actually missed it. But having to be man-handled to move around got old *very* quickly.

They took Simon to another room for his interview, while the detectives and the FBI Agents gathered around a large dining table near where I sat with Emily. Emily excused herself after I explained who she was to the police officers.

"I'll put on some water for tea, Donald. It's almost time for your meds." She left the room, heading deeper into the building.

"Mr. Wilson," said one of the local detectives. "My name is Cristian Torres, and my partner is Jamie Nguyen. I think you know Special Agents Gilpin and Pointer?" Torres was built like a fireplug, short but broad in the shoulders. His dark eyes matched his hair that he kept shoulder-length. His partner was Vietnamese or Laotian, a heart-shaped face making her look innocent; yet her eyes held a calculating look that spoke to seeing a lot of the worst in humanity. She sat with hands crossed, holding a notepad open and a pen at the ready.

I nodded to each of them and then walked them through my version of what had happened since I returned to my hometown.

"So, you've been by your apartment building?" Torres ask when I mentioned seeing the hateful graffiti.

I nodded. "Oh yes! We'd just left there when all this happened. It's obvious Russell, and his people had found out where I live, so Mack, the leader of my security detail, suggested that it was unsafe for me to stay there. We came here to plan our next move."

"And did you enter your apartment building?"

"No. Like I said, Mack didn't think it was safe." I sighed, suddenly tired. "Seems like nowhere is."

"Would you mind if we searched your residence?" asked Nguyen, leaning forward.

"Why?" I asked, suddenly suspicious.

"To ensure that whoever did the graffiti didn't leave you something else to find inside."

Gilpin said, "Donald, we shared our information about Russell with the detectives. If you remember, we also suspect Russell of building those firebombs that were used at the synagogues."

"So, you think he might have rigged something in *my* building?"

"Never can be too sure," said Nguyen. "Better safe than sorry."

That possibility floored me, and I once again thought of my tenants—my friends and neighbors—and the risk I might have placed them in. I nodded my head. "Please do. Do you need me to contact my tenants?"

"Not at the moment. We'll let them know what the situation is and ask them for their cooperation. I'm sure they will not want to take any chances, either."

I nodded, feeling sick that my crusade might have put those good people in jeopardy. "Should I go with you? I could tell you in a minute if anything was out of place."

The four investigators exchanged a look. Pointer, looking bored, shrugged.

Torres nodded. "Okay, but only after our people clear the building. I'm guessing you'll want your bodyguard to accompany you?"

"Definitely."

I fished out the key to my apartment and slid it across the table towards him. He nodded as he pocketed it.

Nguyen's phone chirped, and she rose and moved away from the table to answer it. She listened for a minute and wrote some information on her notepad. After hanging up, she turned to the group.

To me she said, "Your bodyguard, Mack, chased the shooter's van, but had to stop when he came across a body on the highway. The van got away, and he thinks the body turned out to be the guy that was shot after he fired the self-propelled grenade at the house. We got a sergeant on the scene right away along with a couple of cars. The man's driver's license identifies him as Hector Biggs, and he's from Lancaster. Have you ever heard his name?"

I shook my head.

Gilpin opened her briefcase and fished around the contents for a minute before pulling out a file and opening it. She thumbed through papers in it, then lifted a photograph of a man and slid it across the table to me.

I spun the photo around so that it faced me, and I saw it was a mug shot, the plaque showing that the arrest had been in the Capital, in 2012. Seeing the man's face brought me instant recognition. I slapped the photo. "Yeah, I know this guy. He was with Russell the first time I confronted him. Tried to warn me off."

"Biggs was the local leader of the NMA White-supremacist group based here in Lancaster. We always suspected he was involved with their terror activities, but this is the first confirmation we've had," Gilpin said.

"And the last," I said

Gilpin ignored my comment, but Pointer smirked, and I felt deep down inside that Pointer felt zero sympathy for the dead Nazi. I warmed to her.

"Because of his involvement," Torres said, "we should have no problem getting a warrant for both his home and the group's local headquarters. It'll take a few hours, so maybe we can clear Mr. Wilson's building in the meantime; and then," he looked at the Federal agents, "if you are interested, we can split into two teams and hit both together."

Gilpin and Pointer nodded together. They exchanged a quick glance before turning back to the local detectives. Gilpin said, "I'll take the headquarters with you, and Jennifer can accompany Detective Nguyen, if you're good with that?"

The other detectives nodded. Torres turned to me.

"Are you ready, Mr. Wilson?"

I turned my chair as Emily pushed through the doors.

"You're not going anywhere, Donald, until you've had a bite to eat and taken your medication."

The tone of her voice and the menace in her eyes were enough to make the toughest cop in the room cringe. No one argued as she took up her spot behind my chair and wheeled me towards kitchen at the back of the house.

"When you're ready, Donald," Torres called weakly.

Chapter Twenty-Nine

Mack and I watched as the police entered my building and home. They took the time to gather the tenants and had them stand across the street, just to play it safe. From the wringing hands and clasped arms, I could see it only made them more nervous after the news of the graffiti. Mack guided my chair over to the group, and eyes widened once they recognized me.

Helen and David Wong's two children were the first to reach us. Their faces reflected their fear and confusion, but it was mixed with relief and happiness at seeing me. Both reached out to hug me hesitantly, because of the chair; but I swept them into a huge hug that had them giggling. Their parents came forward.

"Mr. Wilson. So happy to see that you are safe." His eyes spotted the chair. "You are okay?"

"Yes, David. I'm fine. This," I held my hands to the wheelchair, "makes moving around a little easier."

The two young ladies stood nervously together, arms pulled into their jacket sleeves. Lisa waved shyly. Her girlfriend looked lost and afraid.

"Are you two, okay?" I asked.

Both looked furtively around before nodding. They were young, and it was the first time living away from home. The situation would have freaked out anyone. My heart lurched at their fear.

"You became famous, Donald," said William Ziegler, his accent thick. "But maybe not in the way you thought," he said, pointing at the building and the hateful symbols.

"Definitely not the way I foresaw it. I'm only worried that I have brought this down on you, my friends."

"Not to worry, Donald. These men who did this are children playing bad guy. They have nothing on the Communists. That was real evil."

I nodded, recalling some of the stories he had told me over coffee. He and his wife had grown up in the ruins of Berlin. On the wrong side of a border.

Minutes later, one of the police officers in uniform walked over to inform us that Torres had cleared the building and was ready for me. I apologized to my friends and tenants, and Mack pushed me across the street.

"Those people almost treat you like family, Donald. Strange, considering the contemptuous old-fart persona you like to portray," he muttered in my ear.

I turned back to eye his smirk. I said nothing and knew there was no way I could convince him either way. He had me pegged.

The uniformed officer held the front door open, and we glided inside. Mack only hesitated long enough for our eyes to adjust from bright light outside to the dimmer, synthetic light of the hallway. I pointed to the open door at the end of the hall.

My homecoming wasn't what I'd imagined. Uniformed and non-uniformed police officers overcrowded my small apartment. Every kitchen cupboard was open, interiors exposed to the ensemble. Across the room, Torres lifted my service pistol from its hidden compartment with a pen through the trigger guard, a surprised expression on his face.

"For Christ's sake," I yelled, and began to cough, causing every face to twist towards the doorway while I struggled with the cough. "Torres, you were supposed to ensure Russell hadn't broken in and *left* something, not gut my fucking apartment!" I tried to pull into the room, but Mack held me in place. "Get out! All of you! OUT!"

While I struggled with my cough, all the heads turned to the detective, whose eyes flicked across the room as if seeing it for the first time. He nodded. Mack pulled me back to allow the press of cops to squeeze past us.

The last of the officers left, leaving only Torres standing, my automatic still dangling from his upright pen. He'd overstepped his jurisdiction and knew it, and I wasn't letting him off the hook.

"I have a permit for the .45," I said with a growl as Mack pushed me through the door. "Do you need to see it?"

He looked at the weapon as if he couldn't remember how it got there. He gently placed it on the edge of the cabinet. "That won't be necessary."

"Did you find anything you were supposed to be looking for?"

He shook his head. "No—no evidence of a break-in. No incendiary device." He wiped his hands together. "Look—I'm sorry. We got carried away. Just the idea of a firebomb going off made us jumpy."

"No kidding. But I guess if I hadn't given you the key, you would have kicked down the door." To the ceiling I said, "Thank God for small favors."

"Once again, I'm sorry." With that, he walked past us and out the door.

I shook my head.

"Donald," Mack said. "I know it's upsetting, but you have to remember that we're all on the same side. I agree Torres and his people took it too far, but don't forget that we still need them. Be nice."

A white picture frame lay on the floor, partially under the table. Seeing my attention on it, Mack bent over and retrieved it. He wordlessly passed it to me. I turned the frame in my hand and saw that it was my wedding photo. Long cracks in the glass ran from one corner of the frame and shards had fallen out where it had made an impact on the floor. Through the ragged breaks in the glass, I saw a broken image of a happier time. The picture of my Maggie and me blurred, and I took off my glasses and swiped at the wetness with the back of my hand.

Mack left me alone as I worked out my emotions. He moved through the apartment, closing cupboard doors, and picking up fallen items and replacing them on the shelves or hooks they'd fallen from.

I rolled my chair to the table and carefully turned the frame. Easing the points from the back of the frame, I lifted the backing gingerly to avoid scraping the photo on the glass. The photo stuck to the backing, having not moved in over seventy years. I carefully peeled it from the backing and, with a light breath, blew glass dust from its surface.

I sighed with relief when I realized that the image had suffered no damage. I would have to replace the frame because the bottom corner was dented, but otherwise, the picture had survived. The same way Maggie had helped me survive all those years ago.

At that moment, I was as ready as I would ever be to let go. Being with Maggie would end my frustration at not being able to move without assistance, the anger I felt towards the bullies of the world, and the weariness I had endured for so long.

It was the loneliness that hurt the most. I missed my girl, my bride, my best friend. Until her death, there hadn't been a night that she didn't lie beside me. A day that she hadn't given me that special smile. She had been the glue that held me together.

I'd been empty for so long.

Visits with the grandkids and my friends at the legion were enjoyable, but they were just a distraction from the void that had filled me since Maggie left me.

I traced the image of her face with my fingers, the tremor in my hands more noticeable. *Won't be long, my Maggie.* I laid the photo face-up on the table.

Mack was examining the photos on the wall, pausing at the picture of me shaking hands with Eisenhower. He looked over at me, indicating the image with his thumb. "What was he like?"

I shrugged. "Firm handshake." I said with a grunt. "I remembered that his hand was dry, which told me he was comfortable with his role. I was just there long enough for the handshake and the photo op. But I did escort him around

Dachau in 1945. He actually remembered that when I got the star."

"I read how you earned that star. That took guts."

I huffed and shook my head. "Come on Mack, you know what it's like. Your training kicks in and you react without even thinking. It's afterwards that you feel like pissing yourself."

He chuckled, and I knew he understood.

Picking up my pistol from where Torres had left it, he turned to me and raised an eyebrow.

I nodded. "There are two magazines at the back of the false bottom. Grab them and then let's get out of here."

He handed me the weapon, and I slid in one magazine, engaging the safety after I chambered a round. Satisfied, I wedged the weapon between my thighs.

WE RETURNED TO THE safe house although its location had been blown. It still was a good defensible position. Mack had convinced me that to attend the raids on the Nazi headquarters or Biggs' home would be a waste of time. "We'd be left sitting outside in the car until they completed their search. It'll be more comfortable in the safe house. Besides, if I keep you from your afternoon siesta, Emily will have a fit, and I don't have enough firepower to save me from *her* wrath!"

The last had made me laugh, pulling me from the depressing funk I had allowed myself to fall into. The nap had helped more.

A couple of hours later, three quarter-horses vied for my attention and the bag of carrots that sat in my lap. After returning to the farmhouse, I found solace with these magnificent animals while waiting to hear from the police.

The largest of the horses must have grown because of his insistence on eating first. He pushed the other two mercilessly, threatening to nip exposed skin if ignored. I caught his greedy eye with a large carrot and, as he reached for it, tossed it over the animal's head. He backed away from the rail and turned to search for the sweet treat in a rush. Using his lapse of greedy insistence allowed me to pass out the remaining vegetables fairly.

As soft muzzles reached out to me, I touched the warm, velvety flesh, and felt the thrill of befriending these incredible creatures. Their warm breath enveloped me.

"When they breathe on you like that, they're signaling they trust you."

I turned my head to see Mack watching the animals interact with me.

"They're beautiful," I said. "Except that one is a greedy as they get."

"Pointer called. The group is on its way back here to fill us in on what they found," he said.

"Did she mention anything?"

"No. Pointer seems to be someone who keeps what she knows close to her chest. I'd hate to sit across from her at a poker table."

Not long after, Pointer and the rest of the investigators showed up as a group. Mack, Simon, and I sat across from them out on the deck while one of Mack's team prepared food for us. They all seemed tired. Agent Pointer and Detective Nguyen both displayed signs of dishevelment with dirt-smeared cheeks and mud-covered slacks.

Torres started the briefing. "Long day, so we'll keep it brief. Agent Gilpin and I searched the headquarters. There's nothing. Just a pile of propaganda, signs and banners. We snagged a few computers, which FBI techs will go through for any information that might help us. Our warrant covered the computers. We didn't think they would be stupid enough to leave anything important there, though, in the first place."

Pointer looked over at Nguyen, who nodded. She leaned forward, grasping her hands together. "Biggs' home address is a farm. Not as elaborate as this one, but it has a lot of acreage. We, too, found a laptop that will be turned inside out. But we also found a large cache of weapons."

She allowed her eyes to sweep the table. "A *very* large cache."

Nguyen took over. "There was everything from automatic weapons to claymore mines. There were even several self-propelled grenade launchers like the one they used this morning. From the markings in the dirt, we figure this is where the weapon came from that Biggs used."

"But why would they jeopardize their stash like that?" Torres asked. "They must have known we'd find it."

Pointer shrugged her shoulders. "I'm guessing the attack today was not planned. It was just a quick opportunity, and they took it without thinking it through. Of course, with that kind of firepower, maybe he didn't reckon on the fact that he might be a casualty."

Mack nodded. "It goes back to the paper-target thinking. They think they're superior until the target shoots back."

"So," Simon asked. "I'm guessing there was no sign of Russell?"

"None," Nguyen said. The house was big enough to house a small army, but there was no evidence that anyone other than Biggs ever stayed there. We did dust for prints and the forensic people vacuumed for DNA, but that will take a while."

"What about my tenants? Are they safe?"

Torres shook his head. "He knows where you're staying, but it's anyone's bet whether or not he would strike at you by burning down your home. If he thought for a minute that you cared for the people you rent to, he'd have already targeted them."

"I could have my people make arrangements to relocate them until after the march," Simon offered.

"That's going to cost a lot."

He smiled. "It won't be a trip to a private Caribbean Island, but they'd at least be out of harm's way."

I nodded my thanks. I turned to the two groups of cops.

"So, we're back to waiting for Russel to make another move." I said, frustrated. "One of these days, he's going to get lucky. I'd rather not wait that long."

"There's no evidence that he was in on today's attack. None of Mack's people recognized him as the driver," Pointer said. "We don't even know if he's in town."

"Oh, he's nearby." I said, looking over the faces around the room. "He might be hidden, but I can *feel* him."

Chapter Thirty

I really hate being proved right.

I hadn't heard the phone, but the minute Simon cracked open the door to the bedroom I was using, I was fully awake.

"What's wrong?"

"Russell," he said in a hoarse voice, exhaustion clear. "He's surfaced."

"What? Where?"

"He fire-bombed the Legion, right here in Lancaster!"

"That son-of-a-bitch," I growled, throwing the sheets aside and reaching for my pants.

Forty minutes later, we sat in an armored Escalade, a twin to the one with the shot-up windows, down the street from the building. Dark smoke drifted across the roadway, red and blue emergency lights creating a kaleidoscope as it cut through the gloom. The street was a tangle of hoses as fire fighters moved back and forth across the scene.

A large white fifth-wheel trailer sat along the curb downwind of the building. COMMAND CENTER was stenciled in large red lettering. A uniform at the perimeter directed Mack to the trailer, and we sat waiting to hear any news.

"We can only be thankful that this happened so late at night," Simon said, trying to lift my spirits. "At least the building was closed and there would have been no one at risk."

I didn't bother to answer, and he fell quiet again. I was beyond being pissed off. Now, the urge to kill was strong within me. I knew I was being unreasonable, but I was at a point that I didn't give a rat's ass. This all had to end before Russell hurt anyone else.

I wanted to lash out at the cops and the FBI, but knew they were doing everything they could. Even from our distant vantage point, I could sense the frustrated expressions and body language of the detectives as they met at the entrance of the Command Center trailer. Even Pointer and Gilpin seemed worn-out and tattered. No one was getting much sleep. For all the technology and manpower, Russell was a ghost that seemed to move freely without concern of being exposed.

At long last, the trailer's door opened, and Mack dropped to the street. He made his way to where we waited, his eyes roaming the neighborhood. He stopped beside our vehicle and spoke through the driver's side window.

"It was definitely our friend," he said without preamble. "Fire and police have identified and confirmed the device as the same type used a few months ago to firebomb the synagogues and mosque. The place was alarmed, but even the fire department arrived well before the inept security company that monitors the building. The place is a total write-off."

I thought about all the history now gone forever. Many of the photos that covered the Legion's walls were one-of-a-kind, with most of the service personnel displayed in them already passed on. There might be some digital record, but unless someone had safeguarded that record on a cloud service, the important memories of my generation would be gone forever at the strike of Russell's match.

"No one got hurt, Mack?" Simon asked, and I knew it was for my benefit.

"No, a working smoke-alarm gave the tenant in the upper apartment plenty of time to get out. He'll be looking for a place to live, but he'll live to talk about it."

Listening with half an ear, I watched the scene down the street with creeping defeat as exhaustion pressed me down. I knew I was allowing myself to descend into self-pity and despair. The continuous attacks were taking their toll. All this wouldn't have bothered me thirty, or even ten or fifteen, years ago, but now it was becoming overwhelming. Between the mix of anger and frustration and the constant pain that gnawed at my innards, I wasn't sure how much longer I could last.

What was worse was the guilt I had for those who were there for me. For Simon and Mack and his team. And for poor Jeremy, who paid the ultimate price for my pride.

A vehicle's movement shook me from my dark thoughts. A light blue Dodge Caravan crept past our position to park three car lengths ahead of us. I cursed under my breath as I recognized the van.

"What is it, Donald?" Simon asked.

I lifted my head towards the Caravan. "That's Decker's van."

Sure enough, the driver's door swung opened, and my friend extracted his long frame from the vehicle. He turned towards us, but only to pull open the side sliding-door. Benny and Edith exited from the open door, while Rita and Frank walked around the van from the passenger's side to cluster together, all eyes on the smoking ruins down the street. With them was the Legion Commander who immediately headed toward the command trailer.

"Damn it!" I muttered.

"Donald, what does it matter. It's only natural that they come out to see this. From all that you and they have told me, this place has meant a lot to all of you."

"That's not the point. If Russell is anywhere near here and sees them with me, he'll target them just to hurt me."

Mack leaned lower towards the window. "Donald's right. Windows are tinted, so stay inside and out of sight, Donald." He reached in and tapped the driver on the shoulder. "Give it ten minutes and then head back to base. I'll have Drake shadow you home to make sure you haven't picked up a tail."

Our driver nodded, but said nothing, his eyes on the scene ahead.

Mack looked back at me. "Your friends never met me, so it shouldn't be a problem if you stay out of sight and if they stay away from the car."

I nodded and stared ahead at the cluster of my friends who stared at the devastation of the building we all considered our own. So many memories, both good and bad, had played out inside those walls over the years. Celebrations, last farewells, and remembrance for all those who came before us—and those still serving in a country that no longer appreciated the sacrifices they often asked us to make.

Mack stood up and made his way back to the command center, passing my friends on the opposite side of the street so they never even noticed him, their attention on the dense smoke and flames and flashing lights just down the block.

I watched with mixed emotions as my friends dealt with this latest blow, and I wanted to be with them, to share their grief. Even from here, I could see wetness on Rita's cheeks and the slack expressions on Frank and Benny's face, as if someone had kicked them in the collective gut, which, in a way, the assholes had with the loss of our sanctuary. Our home. I wanted call out to them, to exchange stories and memories, anything, to keep alive what that building had held, not in the torched building, but at least within our hearts. And I wanted to lend my shoulder to help carry the awful expression of pain I could see in my friends.

But the cynical side of me knew that piece-of-shit, Russell would pray I would do just that. It would give him another reason to hurt someone else I cared about.

And I would *not* give him that opening, even though it broke my heart to stay hidden in the dark. It wasn't out of fear of him, but of what he might do to my friends.

As the driver pulled away from the curb, I caught a flash of lighter material against the night. When I recognized what I saw, I yelled out for the driver to stop. The car rocked on its suspension as he did, and as I pulled my phone from my jacket. Hitting speed dial to Mack's phone, I ignored Simon's look.

"Knight," Mack answered.

"Russell is here," I said in a rush. "He's heading towards Rita and the others." I twisted in my seat and could see the flash of a cell-phone camera tearing apart the night. He stood only feet away from my friends, casually taking photos of their surprised faces. Dropping my phone to the car seat, I groped for my pistol.

As the pistol cleared my jacket pocket, Simon's eyes went wide, and he placed a hand on my arm.

"Don—"

"Stow it, Simon!"

I hit the window button, but nothing happened. Turning to the driver, I snarled an order. "Open my window."

"The rear windows don't open," he said. "Mack's on his way."

"Then unlock the damn door."

"Sorry, Mr. Wilson. Mack would fire me on the spot if he didn't shoot me first. Let him deal with this."

I was so upset that I saw spots in my vision, my gun visibly shaking.

But then Mack was there, his weapon trained on Russell's head. Around him, the two FBI agents, Pointer and Gilpin, spread out to one side, while Lancaster's top cops, Nguyen and Torres, flanked the special ops man, each with their weapons leveled.

"Russell!" Torres barked. "Get down on your knees."

Even with the rush of the police towards the group, Russell was unperturbed, continuing to center his cell-phone camera on my friends. With a last flash aimed at Decker, he calmly turned to face the gauntlet of weapons. His face held a sick expression of amusement, like a child who was watching the activity of an anthill just moments before he stamped on it.

Torres leaned into his firing stance. "Don't make me repeat myself, Russell."

Russell's eyes slid to Torres briefly before centering on Mack's. Those dark eyes resembled a snake's, not giving away a thing.

He slowly raised his hand, like a child ready with an answer to the teacher's question. He grinned as two red dots floated across Mack's face, causing him to squint at the brilliance. The soldier stiffened and his weapon dropped off its mark.

I swiveled in my seat but could not make out any threat in the street's darkness.

"What is it?" Simon asked, confusion sweeping his face.

The driver was whispering into his radio. "Car One to Shadow."

"Shadow here."

"We got at least two tangos with IR, marking Maestro." He was telling the others of the team that the enemy was using infrared scopes and that Mack was the target of at least two of them.

"Stand by, Car One."

Outside, one of the red dots danced across Mack's chest while the other seemed to play tag on the other officers, first skating across Agent Pointer's torso and then climbing Torres' chest, clearing his Kevlar vest and centering on his forehead. At that, Russell laughed out loud.

"I'm guessing that vest won't help you with a head shot," he said with more of a snarl than a smile. "Of course, with metal-jacket rounds, the vests won't help you much, regardless."

"Shadow to Car One. I have one shooter. He's at your six, three stories up. Can't find the other shooter. Lights from the fire and responding vehicles are interfering."

"Roger. Standby. I have eyes on Maestro."

Outside, the stalemate stood, with both sides eying the other.

Behind Russell, Decker and the others stood frozen in either fear or indecision, or both. Edith clung to Benny with no recognition on her face that she understood what was happening around her. But I could see fear in Benny's eyes as he tried to keep himself in front of her frail body. Rita was holding Decker back as if the man was ready to take on Russell barehanded, and I knew that was exactly what he was thinking.

"If any of you heroes are thinking about getting brave," Russell said, "Remember, there are others you're responsible for." He half turned towards Rita and the others, and one of the red dots flickered across the profiles of my friends. "Just kidding!"

"What are you hoping to gain with this?" Agent Gilpin, her voice tight with tension.

"I just wanted to meet the people who call Donald Wilson, a friend," he said, waving his hand towards Rita and the others. "I figured if I burnt down their watering hole, they'd come out and introduce themselves. And rats always show themselves once you torch the ship."

He slowly backed towards my friends and the others followed until he raised his hand. "The way this ends is entirely up to you. Try to stop me and these five are the first to die. My men have their orders."

Mack had taken his eyes off Russell and was staring intently at our vehicle. The driver gave an abrupt nod and Mack returned his attention to the Nazi.

"Car One to Shadow. Any luck on second shooter?"

"Negative."

"Waiting on Maestro. When we get the light, take the shot. Watch for muzzle flash and engage."

"What are you planning?" I demanded.

"If Mack gets an opening, we're going to back this car up to cover your friends. It's armored, so should give us and them some protection until we can get rid of the other shooter," he said, looking at me in the review mirror. "Mr. Wilson, when we stop, throw open your door to let your friends take cover."

I licked my dry lips and nodded.

Russell had reached my friends and gave Benny a vicious shove. The tank man tumbled backwards, glancing off Edith, who went down as well, like a pair of bowling pins. A weak shriek came from Edith as she hit the ground beside the Caravan's front wheel. Russell was reaching for her when Rita stepped in between them.

"Leave her be, you animal," she screamed.

From behind his back, Russell drew a pistol that his sweater had hidden. He shoved it roughly into her neck. "Then you'll take her place, hag!" Without waiting, he twirled around to face the law enforcement officers who had moved forward.

"I don't think so, people. Did you forget my two friends? You try to follow, they'll start shooting. I got what I came for." He pointed his gun at our car. "Too bad, Donald didn't want to come out and play, but at least I have one playmate."

With a savage tug, he pulled Rita into a tighter embrace his pistol tucked under her chin. He pulled her after him as he plunged towards the same park I had first glimpsed him at.

"Rita!" I screamed.

From the corner of my eye, Mack gave a sharp nod and the driver put our car into reverse and tramped the gas pedal while crying into the radio, "Weapons hot."

If I expected the crack of a rifle, I was disappointed and it unnerved me as I thought that Mack's man, Shadow, hadn't heard the command.

The car plowed backwards, throwing Simon and me forward against our restraints. I managed to put up my hand to avoid hitting the back of the front seats before the car impacted with Decker's Caravan. I bounced off the rear cushion, glasses flying off, scrambling for the passenger rear door. Above us, there was a loud crack of a rifle and Simon's window ballooned like a white blossom, but the thick poly-carbon glass held against the titanic force of the high-powered slug. The impact caused the car to shudder, and Simon let out a cry of surprise.

I screamed to my friends, "Decker, Frank, get in!"

The two hobbled forward, bent over towards the sanctuary of the limousine, herding both Edith and Benny, who crawled on hands and knees.

The radio crackled. "Sniper one down. Sniper two, down."

I glimpsed Pointer and Mack running all out after Russell and Rita but lost them once they entered the foliage of the park. Other officers crouched behind the two vehicles, weapons at the ready, scanning surrounding buildings for threats. Torres had a portable radio at his lips and was shouting orders. From a distance, multiple sirens pierced the night.

I helped Edith into the car, her terrified sobs wracking her frame. Benny crawled in beside her, blood oozing from his hands and one cheek that had met the pavement. Seeing the messy scrapes caused Edith to wail, even louder, in the enclosed space.

"It's all right, Edie," Benny said, trying to comfort her. "At least nothing's broken. I think."

Decker and Frank crouched low against the car outside the open door since we'd run out of room in the rear compartment. With luck, there would be no third sniper.

"Damn it, Donald," Decker said in a growl. "Just in case you need it said out loud, I think you got that asshole's attention."

I looked over Edith's shuddering shoulder at my old buddy with an expression I hoped showed how pissed off I was.

It was then that we heard two distant shots, fired one right on top of the other.

There are times when you feel with all certainty that you know something, even though you have no proof of what's transpired. I remember that during the Korean War, a New Yorker named Tony Benzo had ducked into a cluster of trees to take a shit in relative privacy. Then we heard the crack of the rifle. To a man, we knew without even seeing the corpse that he would not return home and marry Maria, his childhood sweetheart.

It was that same feeling when I heard that double tap in the night.

Rita was dead.

I wasn't alone. With looks of open-mouthed, mute horror on their faces, Frank, Benny, Decker, and I exchanged knowing glances. Only Edith, now quiet, seemed blissfully unaware. At that moment, I was jealous of her affliction.

Around us, the chaos of more law enforcement officers arriving on the scene seemed like the calvary that always arrives too late. I caught glimpses of Torres directing his men in the direction of the park while Agent Gilpin held a cell phone pressed to her head, the other hand blocking her other ear. A curtain of blue uniforms surrounded our vehicle, but the shield of police officers was a waste of time and energy.

Russell was long gone, and he'd left my friend, dear Rita, dead behind him.

Chapter Thirty-One

Hours later, which felt like days, my friends and I sat numbly in the living room of the farmhouse. Or rather, what might have passed for a working ranch to someone driving by.

Now it was a fortress.

Mack and Simon had pulled out all the stops. Men and a few women had been arriving continuously since the fire, with more coming in the next day or two. Except for a cluster of Escalades and a couple of other high-end black SUVs in the circular drive at the front of the house, they stashed all other vehicles in the barn.

Through the closed blinds, I could make out the beginning of false dawn and knew I couldn't last much longer. I was beyond tired, but I seemed to see Rita's face every time my eyes closed for more than a moment or two. My other friends must have been feeling the same because as I squinted at them without my lost glasses, they all had the same vacant, lost expressions—except for, God bless her, Edith. She was curled up on the couch, head on Benny's lap as he stroked her thin white hair. He didn't seem to notice the thin line of drool that soaked his pants.

In a windowless basement room, I knew that a bank of computer screens displayed multiple views of the property from cameras equipped with lenses that could penetrate the darkness and distance in all directions. It was like being at a launch site for NASA or SpaceX.

We were safe for the moment.

Most of the others in the room were strangers who moved with purpose. Security consultants, armed to the teeth, with shoulder- or hip-holsters and a few knife scabbards in the mix, stalked the property.

Last night, Mack had returned to the vehicle long after the gunshots with the news we expected. If our lack of reaction had surprised him, he gave no sign.

"He killed her," Mack said, his jaw clenching. "It might have been to slow us down, but it might have been because Rita was fighting him. We found evidence beneath her fingernails that shows she took a piece of him before he shot her. He had a car waiting a couple of blocks away. I heard it tearing off in the distance, but I was too late."

Total silence in the car.

"When can we see her?" I finally asked.

"Probably not until tomorrow, Donald. I'll have more answers once I talk with Torres and Nguyen. It definitely will not be before the medical examiner has shown up."

I nodded my understanding. "I'm guessing the others will want a few minutes with her as well."

"Can that wait until the funeral service?"

I raised my eyes to him before glancing at the cascading emergency lights that created a false dawn. "Will there even be a service?"

He started to say something, but his mouth closed firmly, knowing nothing of Rita's family or faith.

"We're about the only family she has left," I said. "Her husband passed years ago, and they had no children. I know she had no family living. Nigel, her husband, was born in England and any family he might have never visited in all the time I knew them."

He nodded. "Let me make some inquires."

He spoke with some of his men and then left again to deal with the fallout of the night's activities.

As that awful memory faded and my head returned to the farm, my nurse, Emily, entered the room and put her hands together as she addressed us all, now a whole group of geriatric cases instead of just me. "I've had beds made up for all of you. Are there any specific meds you require before bed or can they wait until tomorrow?" Seeing no one raising a concern, she continued. "Simon will have someone collect your medications and a couple of changes of clothes for the next few days. Anything else you need, let me know."

She looked at Edith's sleeping form and smiled softly. "Let's start with Edith. She'll sleep much better in a double bed upstairs, Benny. I'll help you." Gently coaxing Edith to get to her feet, she guided the older women and her husband up the stairs to their new room. I don't think Edith even woke up.

Minutes later, Emily returned to lead away the others until I was the last one left standing—or rather, sitting. "Come on, Donald. I haven't forgotten about you." She wheeled me to my main-floor room. She'd turned my bed down, and my nighttime pills and a glass of water waited for me on the night table along with the glasses that had flown off my face in the car. "Try to sleep as long as you can tomorrow—er—this morning. I'll leave a bedpan here, so you don't even have to leave your room. The more rest you get, the better off you'll be."

I nodded tiredly, unable to gather the will to argue. "My daughter—"

"I have your phone and will make the call," she said as she pulled the covers over my chest. "Besides, I promised her on the island that I would keep her apprised of any issues. It's way early, Donald, so I'm just waiting a bit so I don't wake her needlessly."

"You're a lot like her, Emily. You have a good heart."

"Now you got me worried, "she said with a laugh. "It's not like you to throw around compliments. You're either exhausted or off your meds. Better get some sleep, so I can tell the difference."

She patted my chest and turned off the light on the table before slipping out of the room, leaving me in almost total darkness.

With my guilt.

I WOKE TO MY INNARDS on fire and lay curled on a bed of pain. The late night and messing with the regularity of my medication would take their toll until the pills that Emily had waiting took effect. By the time the opiates had worn down the sharpness of excruciating agony, I was stuck to the sheets, my body clammy and cold.

Knowing what to expect, Emily helped me into a bath already drawn and ready for me. Twenty minutes later, I was feeling like my old self. While she helped, she told me of her conversation first with Gail and then with Richard. I think she kept the worst of the details from me, but I could imagine the anxiety and hurt Gail and Richard would be feeling. She'd be bouncing off the walls to find a way to get to me so she could help nurse me and, of course, convince me to quit this insanity. Richard would brood and hold everything inside, but would never challenge me even when he thought I was in the wrong. There was no way I could avoid that now. Even if I gave up this crusade, it would not stop Russell. It had gone too far.

I had pushed it too far, said a little voice inside me.

The house was quiet as Mack's little army slept in shifts. After breaking my fast with a fruit, yogurt and granola mixture, Emily wheeled me out to the back patio that was partially fenced more to cut the wind than for privacy. The sun was warm, and I welcomed it; but it wasn't long before I had to hunt for shade. One of Mack's people sat with his back against the fence facing the back fields and paddocks, occasionally raising field glasses to his eyes. He'd nodded when I came out, but kept his attention on his post.

One by one, the others joined me; but we spoke little as each of us grieved for Rita, quietly, and in our own way.

Silence was becoming heavy when Simon and Mack come out of the house. Both men grabbed a folding lawnchair and my friends moved aside for them, set themselves around the table. Without any orders, Mack's man pushed away from the fence and repositioned himself further into the yard, so he was out of earshot.

Mack leaned forward, rubbing his hands together nervously as he looked around the table at us. "First off, I'm sorry I could not protect Rita." He looked straight at me. "I'll fully understand if you feel the need to find another contractor."

I hadn't for a minute blamed Mack, and was taken aback by the suggestion. I leaned towards him and started to speak, but he cut me off.

"My job is to protect people and so far, I haven't been too successful doing that."

"Your job has been to protect Donald," Simon said.

"And Jeremy," Mack reminded him.

"Maybe so, but Donald was your priority," Simon said. "He's been Russell's primary target from the get-go. You can't be responsible for all the collateral damage that *paskudnyak* and his people have inflicted."

"Mack," I said. "No one is blaming you for Rita. That's all Russell. Don't cloud that with ego or guilt. Rita stepped in to save Edith, her friend. If you knew her like we all do, you'd know she did it without thought. It was who she was. She always gave more than she took."

Benny, Frank, and Decker nodded in agreement.

Benny reached over, took Edith's hand, and gave it a squeeze. She smiled absently. A tear rolled down Benny's cheek. "That was Rita."

"You know," I said, looking at my hands. "Rita had an idea how to handle Russell and his cult of losers. She wanted me to let others help me with that plan. Kept telling me I didn't need to go it alone."

I looked at Mack and then at my friends.

"Maybe... she was right."

"What was the plan?"

I looked over the faces and saw desperation that must have mirrored my own. We all hurt and we all needed a win. If anything, we needed to make sense of Rita's sacrifice, to ensure her death wasn't for nothing.

"We know the date of the march here in Lancaster. It's three weeks away."

A couple of heads nodded.

"Rita wanted to use the Legion to reach out to every living veteran of World War II and invite them to march with us. It would give us a united statement to send to the politicians and to the Nazis or any other hate group out there."

Decker's head tilted with a look of incredible. "You can't think that everyone that fought in the war wasn't a racist. Hell, they segregated my people, Black people, right up to until the incident with Company C of the 24th Infantry back in '50."

I knew about the incident. Everybody who served in Korea knew it took the Chinese Army to begin to rid the US Army of segregation. With the surrender of a Black-only company on grounds that the Chinese promised to treat the men better than their own countrymen, the US changed its policies not because it was the right thing to do, but because they feared more capitulation of Black-only forces.

I shook my head. "No, Decker. I don't think that doing this will end systemic racism, but times have changed since then. Not everyone thinks or acts the same way as we did back then." I opened my hands towards him. "Look at you and me."

The warmth of his eyes touched mine, and for a minute I knew he was back in Korea, in that foxhole where we met in a life and death struggle, neither caring what color of skin the other wore.

"Times have changed, and I hope people have too. The Black movements have made major strides, and fewer people think the way they did in the '50s and '60s. I'm not saying it's perfect, but the road gets shorter every time we take a forward step."

He nodded, content with that perception.

"What kind of numbers are we talking about?" Simon asked, and I could see interest in his expression.

"No idea." I looked at Frank and Benny. "You guys been working with Rita on her idea? What can you tell us?"

"We can send out the invites, but most of the vets from World War II are either in nursing homes or not mobile anymore, and the same is true with Korean vets. The numbers are fluid. There were still over three-hundred-thousand vets still alive as of 2020, but we're losing many as time goes by. Vietnam, Afghanistan and Iraq vets may well join us, too; but it would be from solidarity, not because of their direct investment in our cause. Sadly, some of them are major players in White-supremacist movements."

"No surprise there," Benny snorted, causing Edith to jump in surprise. He patted her hand softly to assure her everything was okay.

"There just no way of knowing just how many can travel or have the inclination. As Dexter said, many of those guys came from states that—"

"Not to make light of it, but right now, we have to concentrate on the bloody Nazis." I looked over at Dexter. "We all know that the two groups are sometimes interchangeable, but Russell is our immediate threat."

"After Houston, I would think a lot of veterans might want a crack at these idiots," Mack said, his face a mask. "I know, I do."

"We can hope for the best, but plan for the worst case," Simon said. "But I can work with this." He looked over at Frank and Benny. "What do you need to push this message out to the vets? Put your heads together and make me a list. At the same time, I'll get my marketing people to build a nation-wide campaign to spread the news."

I felt a trickle of excitement and knew it stemmed from having a plan and an end-goal. It was better than sitting still.

THE FOLLOWING DAY, we were able to say our goodbyes to Rita. Simon had arranged a proper burial through a local funeral home. Because we were under guard, we held a small service among our group in the barn. Rita would have loved to see her old friends working side-by-side with these muscle-bound security specialists as we swept out the central floor of the barn. I could just hear her laughter and less-than-lady-like encouragement at our efforts. With Emily looking on with a concerned expression and my pain pills, as well as a ready supply of oxygen and nitroglycerin pills for the other oldies helping, we got the job done.

I'll be the first to admit it, but although it wiped me out, the work was also therapeutic. Working together for a fallen comrade brought us together and helped salve the wound her death had caused.

"I swear," Decker said with a smile. "I can hear her cackling right now watching me wheezing in this dust."

Rabbi Lehrer agreed to say a few words. We'd asked him as none of us knew what faith Rita had followed, if any. I shook my head when Simon questioned me about arrangements. "I've known her almost my whole life, and that was one thing that we never talked about." The kind words that Rabbi Lehrer expressed were, although generic, him having never met Rita. He did speak of her sacrifice to protect her friends and that it showed the power of her friendship and commitment to those friends. Most are never given such an opportunity to prove that commitment.

One by one, each of my friends said their own goodbyes. I waited until only Rita and I remained, everyone else having stepped out to give me some privacy.

I rolled myself up to the open casket; and, after ensuring the locks on my chair were secure, struggled to stand so I could look at my friend one last time. I took her hand, trying not to think about how cold and lifeless it was in mine.

"I tried to keep you out of this. And look what happened." Pain and loss bubbled out of me. "It was supposed to be *me*. This was *my* crusade, not yours! It should be *me* lying there, not you, my dear friend." I wiped my face with the sleeve of my jacket, knocking my glasses askew. I fixed them, then I took a ragged breath to pull myself together. "You'd be laughing yourself silly about now, wouldn't ya? Got old, cantankerous Donald to shed a tear. But did you have to get yourself killed just to get me to listen to your plan to get the others involved? I can hear you now, good woman. You and my Maggie are probably laughing like two loons."

I smiled at the thought of those two old friends together after all these years. "Don't get too comfortable, 'cause I'll be there soon enough. Save me a dance."

I gazed at her calm face, hoping that we would be together soon. She had been a good friend. She, we, could have been much more if I hadn't been so stubborn and set in my ways; but the loss was mine. Now that she was gone, I saw how much she had meant to me. It was like the old saying about not knowing what you have until it's gone. Everyone around us is a part of us, and we ought to appreciate every minute we have together.

Before it's gone.

The rabbi brought a small group with him, and I was pleasantly surprised to see Jacob and Uri, burdened under trays of sandwiches and fresh-cut vegetables, being harassed by Sarah, one of the Jewish survivors who had helped me begin this journey of mine. Her short stature took nothing from her demand for perfection and her contagious energy. The two men did exactly as told; and before long, she had everyone munching on the food put together by a thankful group from the synagogue.

There was no escaping Sarah's hug when I tried to thank her for her kindness.

"What? After all you have done for my people. This nothing." She looked towards mounds of flowers and an open polished-walnut coffin that sat on a wheeled trolley at one end of the space that we had cleared. "We owe you and your friends so much more." The tear that slid down her dough-like cheeks broke my heart; but just as suddenly, her mood became happy again. "Eat. Eat. You're such skin and bones! You should stuff your pockets with change, or the wind will take you."

Chapter Thirty-Two

Steam rose off the pavement as the morning sun flexed its muscles, drying the dampness from the night's rain. It boded for a hot and humid day. Ground fog hung gently over the fields, broken only by the plodding movement of horses as they eased their way towards me and the early sounds coming from the rear of the farmhouse. We had our routine worked out, the horses and I, and I felt that we'd miss our morning greeting: me with my morning coffee, and a few sweet carrots for my equestrian friends.

As always, the enormous male pushed its neck past the bay for the first treat. I flicked the first carrot over his shoulder that caused him to turn and move away from the fence. He still hadn't caught on to my little trick that allowed the quieter and more docile mare to move forward. She daintily accepted my offered tribute and stepped back to chew, giving way to the big, solid quarter horse. As was his habit, he swung back to the fence looking for a second treat, not even finished with the first, the chomp and grinding of his teeth loud in the morning air.

His large neck extended greedily over the wooden barricade, a shiver running across glossy hair. Fog from his warm breath covered me, and I felt content with these magnificent creatures as friends. I filled my hand with his velvet-soft muzzle before the lip rose, exploring for a second carrot. I smiled at his hunger and gentle greed. The female showed so much more patience, knowing full well that she would not do without.

The slow twang of the door's spring expanding told me that my solitude was over. I pushed my chair forward under the big horse's chest and tossed a second carrot to the female. She gently accepted it and turned away while I waved the last one at the big male with a smile. He accepted it with another blast of breathy horse-fog.

Turning towards the house, I saw Mack waiting patiently. I appreciated the courtesy with a nod.

"Were you able to sleep?" he asked, squinting at steam rising from his own coffee mug.

I nodded as I pulled my chair towards the table and out of reach of the male, who was looking for another handout. The female had already begun to amble across the yard, satisfied with the treat.

"Emily's cocktail did the trick."

He studied me for a minute. "Are you ready for this?" He was referring, of course, to the march.

I grunted, tapping my gut. "Wasn't sure I'd make it, so yeah, I'm ready." I thought about all the phone calls, the strategy meetings, media releases, and the interviews. The countless letters of encouragement and the massive amounts of money raised by improv Go-Fund-Me pages for Legions and vets, or against racism from all across the country. All of it was coming to a head.

I looked at the ex-soldier. "We just need Russell to show."

"He'll be there. He couldn't stay away if he wanted to."

"That's what we've been playing towards. Do you think he'll have something planned for us? Another ambush?"

"My old daddy used to say, 'Hope for the best; plan for the worst,' and we have definitely planned for the worst. I've stationed men around the route and the park all night, keeping watch. The cops have been moving around as well. And so far, there's been no sign of either Russell or his people."

"He's here. I can feel him." I said, my guts churning.

Mack nodded but said nothing.

I wheeled around the patio table. "Let's see if Emily has any extra concoctions for me before this show begins."

With a grim smile, he turned to hold the door.

WE HAD ARRANGED TO meet before leaving for the march. In fact, the police insisted on it. As Mack and I entered the rear of our farmhouse, I could see the common living room packed with officials, my friends, and multitude of different-colored uniforms from seemingly every law-enforcement organization in the country.

Before I entered the room, I veered to my small bedroom and, after swinging my chair around, closed the door. Emily had my uniform laid out; and even from the wheelchair, with all the practice I'd had, it took only minutes to dress myself. I allowed my hand to fall across the Golden 'Thunderbird' that was the insignia of the 45th Infantry, with all the horrible memories close to the surface and threatening to overwhelm me. After pulling on my blazer and adjusting my tie, I ensured the door was locked.

From the night-table drawer, I pulled out my service pistol and checked that the magazine was loaded. I placed the weapon in its holster and wedged it between my legs, before covering my thighs with a light blanket that I had used earlier in the tour to ward off cool spring air. It would be far too warm with today's temperature apparently headed into the 90s, but it kept the weapon out of sight. I slipped the spare magazine into the front pocket of my pants.

Now, if Russell attacked, he'd find this old dog still had teeth.

Now armed and in my uniform, I pushed into the living room, nodding at those I knew. I recognized our town's mayor and wondered what that blow-hard could offer. Was he here for a photo-op? There were several unfamiliar faces, and I could only hope someone was keeping track of these people as potential security risks, but Mack caught my eye and rolled his own eyes in exaggeration. Neither of us had patience for meet-and-greet bullshit, though both of us knew its value in our campaign.

So, there was no helping it, and I settled back in my chair to wait it out. But one politico in a grey suit and a red tie began the meeting like he had called it. He thanked everyone for coming; and as he began what might have been a drawn-out speech, I could take no more of it and rolled into the center of the room.

"Mister, sorry to rain on your parade, but who the hell are you and why are you here?" I said, not attempting to hide my irritation.

"Ah... I'm from the Governor's office."

"Really... ." I let the word hang. "And where was the useless son-of-a-bitch when I first tried to talk to him? He had no time for me then, but now that this is making front page—"

"Donald—" Simon started, but I raised my hand and turned my head away, closing any argument.

"No, my friend. Unless he's planning on marching beside those of us who'll risk harm from these modern-day Neanderthals to prove that America is about freedom, or unless he plans on tabling anti-hatred legislation with teeth, then he—and you—" I said looking right at the governor's flunky "—can take a hike." I let my gaze fall across the wall of fresh faces. "Get out," I snarled. "*All* of you!"

I looked over at the mayor and pointed a finger towards the door. He didn't need to be told a second time and pulled his ponderous frame from the leather chair and slunk after the others without a word.

Torres was grinning from ear to ear, nudging his partner, Nguyen, in the arm. She kept her face neutral and did not rise to his nudge. Torres might catch hell later from his superiors over his attitude concerning the mayor, but for now, he was enjoying himself.

I turned my attention to Agent Gilpin. "What's the latest?"

She took a deep breath, giving herself a moment to look over her notes. "We're working with the local police force," nodding at Torres and Nguyen, "and have all the *major* routes to and from town covered. I stress the word 'major' because there are a lot of other avenues into town. On another note, you cannot find a hotel or motel within here and

D.C. Everything is booked. We have reports of both civilian and Legion members descending on the town—by the busloads!" She looked at Simon and me. "You and your team sounded the alarm, and the response looks to be astronomical. Within the next few hours, the entire town will be gridlocked."

"Any word out of Washington?" Simon asked.

She shook her head. "Everyone is waiting to see what happens. Even Twitter is quiet."

"Maybe someone took his phone away," Decker said, his tone disgusted.

The remark allowed a lot of the tension in the room to ease. Leave it to Decker to voice what we all were thinking but were too political to say out loud.

"We are also aware of a huge Antifa gathering at a farm thirty miles out," Torres said. "If someone started singing Janis Joplin tunes, it'd look like the re-birth of the Free Love movement. Our sources at State said they had huge bonfires and a ton of speeches through a bullhorn, but mostly, they behaved themselves. We should see them arrive soon. They'll gather around chokeholds like intersections where they can block the Nazis, but have room to escape if things get too crazy."

"As you might have heard, had you not thrown out the Governor's people," said Gilpin with a smirk. "The National Guard has set up in secluded areas on the outskirts of town. Once the parade begins, they'll move in closer and shut down all traffic in and out of Lancaster. Their orders are to stop and apprehend any disorderly Nazi sympathizers, with Russell being their main focus. Laws about free speech won't permit us to arrest all of them, but we've handed out photos of all neo-Nazi heavyweights within the organization and some of the off-shoot White-supremacist groups to all the agencies."

Agent Gilpin raised a folder over her head, looking in my direction. "I have a set of photos for you and your friends, just in case you get pressed by any of these people."

I nodded my thanks.

Agent Gilpin wasn't finished. "We have approximately forty agents who will be in plain clothes mixing with the crowd. We've assigned them Channel 6 on the Lancaster Police frequencies. They'll communicate and work directly with local forces to locate and identify Joseph Russell, and if able, to apprehend."

Nguyen stepped forward. "I know it's a waste of breath, Mr. Wilson, but the Chief wanted me to ask just the same for you to consider not taking part in this event. She feels strongly that without you, the chances of violence are extremely low, or if anything, manageable."

"Thank the Chief," I said with a smile, "for her interest in my safety, but I am within my rights. Those that have planned this march are not."

She raised her hands in surrender. I knew she was only doing what had they had ordered. Now that it was out of the way, we could continue.

"All vehicle traffic has been re-routed around the entire area. There is a drop-off area at the north of the sports field, and this is where most of the veterans will enter the area, but they will still have a fair walk. I'm afraid we do not have the resources to set up shuttles."

"We let everyone know that transportation was their responsibility," Frank pointed out.

"How many veterans are you expecting?" Torres asked.

"We had around thirty-five hundred at last count. Those were confirmed. How many will just show up is anyone's guess."

"Damn," Torres swore, his eyes wide. "That'll fill the park."

"It might be their last outing," Benny said. "Remember, most of these people are in their nineties. We are losing over three hundred every day to old age, so many are looking for a hero's send off. One last kick at the can."

Torres bowed his head in his hand. "This is going to be a fucking nightmare! Even if there is no violence, we could lose a bunch of people to heart attacks. I better give the hospital the head's up." He turned and stepped from the room, his phone tight to his ear.

Nguyen continued. "We will set our SWAT up around the central area of the park with an urban assault team out of sight. The last thing we want to do is challenge these people. The team'll be called in only if there seems to be no alternative."

Mack stood next. "My people will protect Donald. Because the police will deploy their urban assault teams, all my teams will be in the park. For identification, I will deck all my people out in green wind breakers." He raised a light jacket so all could see the dark emerald green. "Let your people know. I don't want any confusion if things get hairy."

"So, all we need is for Joseph Russell to show," I said.

"I think from a law-enforcement point of view, we would much prefer picking him up, say, trying to cross the border into Canada," said Agent Gilpin.

I gave her a tight, humorless grin. "Why would you wish *that* on our neighbors? I certainly wouldn't wish that on such a good friend and ally."

As the meeting broke up, my friends moved towards me. Like me, they were decked out in dress uniforms that represented the service they had served in. Frank's navy-blue air force blazer made the gold wings pop off his chest, while Benny's army-green uniform of the Second Armored Division, 'Hell on Wheels' made Decker's and my uniforms look drab in comparison. But it was the goddamn fly-boys who always had it best.

Frank and Benny, being officers, both wore their service pistols on their hips, as part of their uniform. I was considered a non-commissioned officer and technically not entitled to carry the weapon as part of my uniform.

Decker had noticed as well, because he leaned over to reveal his own pistol, stuffed in his pants behind his tunic. "Better safe than sorry, I always say," he murmured. He threw me a wink and stood with hands folded in front of him, hiding any telltale bulge the weapon might produce.

This might be my fight, but it gave me confidence that my friends were armed and ready for any stunt Russell might pull. He might have a harder time than when he killed Rita. He was lucky the old girl hadn't been armed, because he might be sporting a couple of holes himself.

Chapter Thirty-Three

The farmhouse emptied, the operatives checking their weapons one last time. Benny hunched over Edith, whispering words of assurance. Emily hovered just out of earshot to give them privacy for what might be their last conversation.

Last night I had tried to talk Benny out of marching with us, mainly for the sake of his wife, but the man had made his decision.

"Donald, I appreciate what you're saying, but neither of us have much longer. Even before what just happened to us, my poor girl doesn't remember me most days; but I know that deep down, she would march right beside me if she could." He looked across at Edith's face and his features seemed to soften. "She had been all set to hunt down escaped Nazis after war, except I had seen enough blood and guts for a lifetime."

He paused, lower lip trembling, before he turned back to me. "My God, you should have seen how ferocious she used to be. Twenty-two, and ready to take on the entire Third Reich herself. Even tried to get me to go back to Israel and live a life on a kibbutz." Those sad eyes looked back at his wife of almost seventy years. "I never understood why she stayed with me. I'd been worn out by the war, not a dime to my name, yet ..."

"Then, maybe that's why you have to stay back today," I said, my voice hoarse with emotion. "For her."

He patted my hand. "It's *for* her that I have to go through with this. The adventure I denied her all those years ago. If there was a shred of the old Edith left, I'd let her come along—hell!—there'd be no holding her back." A single tear rolled down Benny's pale, wrinkled cheek. "But now, she'd just be scared and confused. Better she stay back. Emily will watch her for me."

"But Benny, what would happen to her if something were to happen to you?"

"She'd forget within minutes ... and at least I wouldn't have to watch her waste away. And there are . . . people . . . who would care for her. I've set that up." His lip quivered as he turned away.

Benny spilled fresh tears as he said goodbye to Edith, and I had to turn away for his sake as much as for my own. "Damnit, Rita," I muttered to myself. "This is why I wanted to do this myself!"

Of course, both Frank and Decker stood near enough to see both the tender moment between Benny and Edith, but also my reaction to it. There was no way they hadn't heard my comment either, but both stared at their hands and said nothing. I felt my face heat up and pushed my chair towards the front entrance. Before I could reach it, the now-familiar dark Mohawk of Mack's sniper, Mateo, poked through the entrance.

"Mr. Wilson?" he began to call in a loud voice until he saw me approaching the door. "Do you know a Wayne Saxon? Drives for the VA?"

"Wayne? Yes, why?"

"He's outside and says he's got to talk to you before the march." He threw up his hands in frustration. "Right now, he's a real pain 'cause Mack wants us moving."

"He's a friend, Mateo," I said. "I'll make it fast."

I pushed through the door and heard the stocky Latino following me as backup.

Wayne was standing beside his familiar passenger van, bouncing from foot to foot, nervously. His face brightened when he saw me come between the parked cars. He stepped forward, but Mack stepped out to intercept him. Mack didn't stop Wayne physically, but just stood there, posture and silence speaking volumes. Wayne's excited expression morphed to one of wariness and caution.

"Donald, do you vouch for this person?"

"Oh yes! Wayne has been driving for me for a couple of years now."

To Wayne, Mack said, "If you know Donald, you know the trouble that's been following him. Do you mind?" he asked, miming a pat-down.

"No. No. Not at all," Wayne said. "Glad someone is watching his back. Do what you have to do."

"Thank you."

Mack did a quick, but professional, pat-down of the large man. He pointed towards the van and Wayne nodded.

"There's something in the back for Donald. Figured, it might come in handy today of all days."

Leaving Mateo to keep watch over Wayne, Mack walked around to the rear of the van and opened the door. I couldn't see what he was studying, but after a minute, he reappeared and nodded to Wayne. "Nice! Go ahead."

Again, almost bouncing like a child, Wayne scooted to the van's rear compartment. "Saw you had traded your walker for a set of wheels, so it got me figuring." He disappeared behind the door and his voice was muted but clear. "You doing what you're doing has showed us all that the real enemy is right here in our backyard. I wanted to do something that showed my appreciation for all of that, Donald."

He emerged from the vehicle with another wheelchair, but this one decorated with the insignia of the U.S. 45th Infantry Division. The back panel held the red diamond with the gold Thunderbird emblem. He'd painted the entire chair the same brown/green as my uniform and put my company number on one arm and my name and rank on the other.

"My God, Wayne," I said in surprise. "It's a lot more impressive than racing stripes!"

He beamed from ear to ear. "I added a little surprise for you, just in case that psycho shows up." He said this while looking at Mack. Tilting the chair backwards, he exposed a built-in holster under the chair. "Just in case."

"Saves hiding it under that blanket," Mack said in a droll voice. "It's warm enough today that with a blanket, people will think you pissed yourself after an hour."

Sheepishly, I pulled back the blanket and hefted the pistol. "Would you do the honors?"

With a smirk, Mack took the pistol and inserted and secured it into the compartment under the chair. He examined the setup and smiled at Wayne. "Nice job." He eyed Wayne for a minute before asking, "Where?"

Wayne looked down at the tattoo that Mack had been eying, "256th Brigade out of Louisiana. Served '04 and '05. Attached to the 10th Mountain."

"Armor?"

Wayne shook his head. "HMMWV, out of Tigerland."

"You saw your share."

Wayne nodded but did not elaborate. Mack didn't press. He pulled out a business card and handed it to the tall ex-soldier. Lifting his head towards the handi-van, he said, "Always on the lookout for a skilled driver. Pays good, but there's a lot of traveling."

Wayne stepped back, surprised, and I had to contain a grin. He looked at me before returning his gaze to Mack. "Donald and his buddies are the only family I have 'round these parts. Traveling is good for the soul, I hear."

"Look me up," Mack said. To me, he said. "If we're going to beat the crowds, we'd better leave now."

"Aren't we really early?"

He nodded. "I'd rather be early with room to wiggle if things get hairy."

I nodded and shook Wayne's hand. Nodding my head towards Mack, I gave Wayne a wink and said, "Luck."

"You be careful today, Donald."

Without another look, he ran around the van, hopped in, and pulled away from the farmhouse, clearing the drive for the procession of vehicles filled with old and young warriors ready to make a statement.

Turning towards our vehicle, I caught sight of Decker and Frank, both hobbling, each with two large canvas bags. I had to look away since the two idiots looked like something out of a Martin and Lewis comedy, trying so hard to be inconspicuous that they stood out like a pair of clowns at a Sunday School. I heard rather than saw the tailgate of Decker's truck slam closed and I didn't think anyone had made them.

We hadn't been sure if Mack or Simon might put a kibosh on our carrying weapons, but figured it was better to be safe and ask for forgiveness later, then risk being shut down. The two would follow the convoy for the time being and would slip off at the right moment and make their own way to the parade.

Chapter Thirty-Four

A few non-armored vehicles preceded our especially shielded SUVs, while the remaining ones fell in behind us. The Lancaster police gave us an escort and were made aware that nothing was going to stop us from attending. Because of the number of vehicles in our group, and because of our interaction with Torres and Nguyen, we flew through the city that Maggie and I had called home since our return from Europe in early 1946—without worrying about traffic lights.

The high golden dome of Beit Israel Synagogue came into view sooner than I thought, and then I realized that it was because we were approaching from a different direction than the last time I had visited it. The massive building and grounds had undergone a transformation in anticipation to the march today. Not trusting the law to keep the neo-Nazi march from happening, Rabbi Lehrer and the congregation had a security company erect a six-foot, temporary fence around the perimeter of the property. Hired security personnel mingled with a group of younger men and women standing vigil. Off to one side, two State and County Sheriff cruisers sat nose to nose across the synagogue's parking entrance, in front of the metal fence. They were leaving nothing to chance.

In their original petition, the Nazis had planned their parade route to run defiantly past the Court House, two synagogues—including Beit Israel—and one mosque. Then they planned to march to a local sports field at Buchanan Park where they could continue to shout hate speeches to whoever showed up to listen.

But we would be meeting them there and it would not be to listen. These idiots had no idea just how cantankerous, we old farts could be.

We pulled over by the parked cruisers at the synagogue, and Mack hopped out and moved towards the gate. Before he could reach the enclosure, Rabbi Lehrer squeezed through it and, with Mack watching the surrounding area for threats, approached our vehicle. Our driver opened the passenger door for him, and he dropped into the front passenger seat then turned to greet Simon and me.

"*Boker tov*, my friends," he said with an expansive smile. He threw his head back towards the synagogue. "Do you like what we've done with the place?"

I laughed, feeling stress bleed from me. "Very fetching, Rabbi."

"It doesn't hurt to be prepared." He nodded to both of us, becoming serious. "Are you both ready for this? Is there no way I can convince you to join us behind the barrier?"

Simon smiled nervously, and I answered for both of us. "It's time to end this, my friend. One way or another. Together, we've made some noise and brought attention to the dangers of their cause. People seem to be waking up and demanding change. No matter how this all ends up, I think we might see actual change. Maybe not with the present administration in Washington, of course, but there's always the next one."

"And it is all because of the two of you. Donald, you've shared your memories and your courage to remind the world of the menace. And you, Simon, have given your never-ending support in so many ways. From the depths of my heart, and I am confident to say, and also from those I represent, thank you—and go with God."

He reached over the seat and shook both our hands. There wasn't much more to say. He pulled himself from the car and leaned in one last time. "So, go with God, my friends."

Seconds later, Mack took the rabbi's place in the Escalade, and we were on our way. It was quiet for a while as we talked with our personal visions of a creator, each in our own way.

Every once in a while, we passed a group of police vehicles pulled together in a parking lot, with officers milling around as if passing the time. I noticed that there were a variety of crests on the vehicles and realized that other police services had sent extra personnel to back up our own department and the state police. This march would not catch them short, as had happened during past events. The support and organization really impressed me.

"Seems the powers that be are taking this seriously."

Mack nodded. "They've brought in massive amounts of resources. They don't want another Charlottesville."

I kept my mouth shut. Mack knew some of my plans, but not everything. Would he try to stop me, if he knew it all? I'm not sure. He was and is a warrior and knew the difference between right and wrong. Like so many generations of soldiers, he'd been asked to fight a war that had no endgame, and therefore no way of completing what others had started. It was only loss or stalemate. I liked to think he would appreciate bringing our fight to a legitimate end with a clear winner and loser.

The closer we got to town center, the thicker the traffic and crowds became. Multitudes of people packed sidewalks. The stream of participants and spectators was fast becoming a torrent on both sides of the street. There actually seemed to be some sense of order as crowds moved forward without pushing and shoving.

But, of course, even a river runs smoothly until it comes up against an obstacle in its way.

It surprised me to see such a variety of ethnic groups merging towards what was about to become the worst racist event on the planet, until I realized it was the perfect place for these people to be. They were here to stand witness to the event, but also to show a unified statement for equality. Together, they were standing up to a group of bullies.

Simon nudged me.

"You notice how well-behaved the crowd is?"

"I was just thinking about that," I said, nodding.

"Look at the signs they're carrying."

Studying the mass of pedestrians moving on either sidewalk, I pulled my glasses up my nose and focused on the banners and placards they carried. One group carried messages of equality and living together in peace, while the others, many in khaki uniforms, carried familiar swastikas and the lesser known *Schwarze Sonne* or Black Sun. Based on the ancient sun wheel of a Norse faith, Himmler himself had adopted the symbol. They had inlaid the symbol in the floor of the Wewelsburg castle, home of the SS during the war.

Antifa members marched alongside neo-Nazis, but you could see an increasing tension in each group.

"It's hard to believe they're not at each other's throats," I said in wonder.

"Almost like they're saving their energy for the main event," Simon suggested.

"More likely the whole bunch of them are cowards and need a bunch of like-minded people to give them backbone," Mack said from the front seat. "No different from a schoolyard bully that gets separated from his posse."

But two intersections further, we came to a full stop. Ahead, the two groups had moved to opposite sidewalks. Now, amongst their own, they gained the bravado Mack had mentioned mere minutes ago. Both groups, Antifa and neo-Nazis, were screaming obscenities and threats at each other. Perched on either side of the intersection, some from both sides leaned over the curb, waving fists and signs at their opposites, each certain that they held moral right.

I noticed right away that the spectators and those calling for peace stood back, open-mouthed, observing both groups with a nervous eye. They were there because of what they believed in, but from their posture and lack of fervency, it was obvious they wanted to present their own messages peacefully and might bolt if things became violent.

Police were beginning to move in quickly with mounted officers. Using their well-trained horses with practiced efficiency, they pressed twelve hundred pounds of horseflesh in between combatants who had begun to move beyond the curbs. Rather than risk a crushed foot or be knocked down under prancing hooves, most broke off their protest and backed away, eyes on the equestrian barriers as much as on their opponents.

"That was anti-climactic," Simon said with a smile.

"That's the point," Mack said. "It's best to shut down trouble before it has a chance to even develop."

As both vehicular and pedestrian traffic resumed, I started wondering about our own plans. Would fast mobilization by police stop any confrontation with Russell before we could finally end this feud? Looking at the peaceful demonstrators pressed up tightly against the brick facade of the businesses, I knew we had to end it, somehow, without putting any of the public or police at risk.

This was between Russell and me. He might have his followers of hate, but I had some very pissed-off friends who had just lost a dear comrade to this animal. We also had, I gathered from the briefing this morning, a flood of WWII vets who were not happy that their sacrifices of over a half century ago had been ignored and forgotten. Vets from Korea, Vietnam, Bosnia, Afghanistan, Syria, and every dirty war the US fought were still being tossed aside and forgotten by an ungrateful country.

Mack seemed to sense my apprehension because he turned in his seat to look back at me.

"The crowds at the park will hinder any rapid response, Donald. By the time they arrive, your plan will be complete, or it won't be happening." There was a pause, then, "Donald," he said, looking me in the eye, "there's a chance that the asshole won't even show. His MO has always been to strike from the shadows. Coming out into the light might not be something he's even capable of."

I stared back, but in my heart I knew differently. I had looked into those dead, dark eyes and knew nothing would keep Russell from confronting me. He had to do that or forever doubt himself. And he knew what I knew: I didn't have much time left.

He had to act. And so, did I.

Chapter Thirty-Five

Any movement of the crowds and traffic we were in had slowed to an almost complete standstill. With the clock ticking and in our current position, there was no way in hell we'd make it to our destination before the parade began. Mack was getting updates from those of his group either further up the convoy or sprinkled over various locations on the parade route. Unfortunately, from both Simon's and my perspective, because Mack was wearing an earpiece, the communications were all one-sided and both of us were getting a little restless.

"Mack, we're in the dark here. Can you fill us in?"

"Sorry. I'm trying to find us an alternate route. Traffic has come to a complete standstill. Seems someone used a Molotov cocktail on two cars about a block and a half farther up. Even the fire department can't get in with their equipment. They're going in on foot with hand extinguishers. You ought to be able to see the smoke just above that bus in front of us."

"Russell?"

"My gut is saying yes. My people are on high alert. We're sitting ducks, here in the streets." His hand went to his earbud, and he leaned forward, checking the street. He had a tablet in his hands and was sliding between a couple of screens. I could just make out highly detailed maps of the town. Into the microphone, he said, "Delta team, can you leave the convoy and run parallel to us on Shepard Street?" He listened to the reply and then ordered. "Roger. Tell me when you're in place. Echo team, reposition to back them up."

He turned in his seat and looked back at us. "I'm concerned that Russell and his crew are planning on hitting us while we're stuck here in traffic. So. We're going to cut through that department store on our right and meet up with a spare car on the next street."

"But we'll be in the open," Simon said.

"If they are using Molotovs, then we're sitting ducks in here. It's bulletproof, but not fireproof." He motioned to his driver, who I'd recognized earlier on as Mateo, the sniper, who was guarding us. "Mateo will grab your wheelchair, and when he has it ready, you'll slip out with Simon on the curbside, and we'll enter the store together. There's a loading entrance on the next street. We'll get picked up there and use an alternate route to the grounds. Donald, once you're in the chair, you might want to arm yourself."

Simon's head came up in surprise. "You have a weapon?"

I just looked at him for a minute. He seemed to deflate and looked away, muttering under his breath.

"Simon," Mack said. "Do you want a gun?"

"No!" he said with indignation; but then he sighed, "I'd only end up shooting myself in the foot."

Mack nodded and said nothing more. He looked down at his tablet and I could see a red dot flashing parallel to our position on the map. He nodded to Mateo and, after checking the street once more, both left the relative safety of the vehicle. One of Mack's team that I only knew by sight emerged from the crowd and without being told, slid behind the wheel in Mateo's place.

Mateo ran around to the back of the Escalade and retrieved my chair. He unfolded it as he circled up to the door nearest the sidewalk, Mack scoping out the surrounding crowd. "Two tangos, ten o'clock on the sidewalk," he said matter-factually, no panic in his voice.

As Simon turned to help me out of the rear compartment, I swung my head in the intersection's direction as two men wearing paramilitary camo outfits with AR-15s at the ready, trotted towards us. The crowd was staggering back in fear, some crying out, giving them an open route. Seeing us exiting the car, they put on a burst of speed and crossed between two vehicles to our side of the street.

My butt slammed into the chair as Mateo pushed it forward leaving me gritting my teeth with pain. He wheeled me towards the entrance of the department store just behind Mack and Simon while I wrestled with the clasp of the holster beneath my seat. Clearing the weapon, I jacked the slide, loading a heavy shell into the chamber of the .45. I kept the weapon low as Mateo pushed my chair forward, following Mack and Simon.

The crowd on the sidewalk parted at the sight of Mack's pistol. He held open the large glass door, and we swept inside. As we pushed deeper into the store, Mack skipped behind us, keeping his large frame between us and the entrance, his gun held in two hands, pointed at the ground.

Mateo wheeled me around a set of stairs that led downward, washing machines and driers spreading out of sight on display below. A man, I'm guessing a salesman by his dark suit and clipboard, stood with his faced raised in anticipation of a sale. Until he noticed Mack's gun. He disappeared behind a railing as we slipped deeper into a furniture showroom. Around us, living-room displays with easy chairs, coffee table and couches stretched wall to wall. Further back, bright colors of massive televisions flashed on a hundred screens. It took seconds for me to pick up the red and white emergency exit sign and I pointed towards it although I doubted that Mateo had missed it.

"Gotcha," he confirmed, pushing me at a quicker pace. I could hear Simon panting behind us.

"Get to cover!" Mack yelled, causing Mateo to veer to the right into an aisle of bedroom suites. I looked back, past Mateo's flapping jacket, to see the front of the store cut off from sight.

Ahead, I could hear startled voices being raised.

The floor turned to tight-woven carpet and sounds of our running feet were silenced. Simon was behind us, his face beet red as he labored to keep up.

There was no sign of Mack.

At the end of the long series of simulated bedrooms, another walkway followed a wall that turned both to the front of the building and to the rear. A glassed-in office room with a service window held a number of employees, wide-eyes and open mouths expressing their surprise. Without slowing, Mateo pushed us towards the rear, still headed towards the exit. The slap of his and Simon's feet returned as carpet turned into lino tile.

From behind us, there was a yell followed by a pair of gunshots, loud in the low-ceilinged room. The panicked voices of a man and woman rose near the back of the store. I heard Mack's voice yell, "Clear," and felt a wave of relief knowing he had not been on the receiving end of the weapon's report.

Mateo slowed down a fraction so that we were no longer at risk of crashing into anything. As we neared the end of the hallway, it opened up to an order desk where two wide-eyed salespeople stood. Upon seeing us, both dove out of sight behind the counter, the man whimpering loudly.

Mateo parked us behind a large wooden hutch and pulled out his pistol. He kept it at the ready while watching the way we came. In seconds, Mack arrived and with a nod, the two moved us towards the exit with a red-faced Simon pushing my chair.

Waiting to one side while holding the door, Mack spoke into his wrist microphone. We pushed through the door into a large warehouse.

We crossed the open area to the surprise of two men in fall-arrest harnesses on a massive forklift. They stopped loading crates of furniture to watch us, with open mouths, as we made for the far exit. Nobody said a word.

Once again, we waited while Mack spoke to his people on the street where we were headed. Once he got the all-clear, we pushed through the exit where a copy of the vehicle we had just vacated sat idling at the curb, rear doors open, with two agents watching the street, each with an automatic rifle at the ready, aimed at the ground.

Simon slipped in through the opened door and Mateo helped me in before collapsing the chair and putting it into the Escalade through the open rear hatch. Once Mack and Mateo settled inside, the team that we'd exchanged with entered the department store warehouse to retrace our path to join our former armored limo.

Mack talked non-stop on the radio. Getting updates and issuing orders, he spoke in the calm voice I had gotten used to. Nothing seemed to excite this man. If it did, he contained it so that he could make rational decisions despite the heat of the moment. His voice was like those of pilots recorded talking calmly as their planes fell from the skies to certain death, never losing control of their emotions.

Over the downtown district, we could see a dark plume of oily smoke and I guessed it was the cars that had been set on fire to close the roadway and that trapped us in the closed-off street.

Beside me, Simon was catching his breath after the run. His tomato-red face was covered in sweat. He stared at me, and it took a minute to realize that he was staring at the pistol in my hand. I had forgotten I still held it. I switched it to my other hand before reaching out for his.

"It's okay, Simon. We're safe."

His eyes fluttered away from the weapon to settle on mine. He took a shuddering breath and nodded. He glanced back down at the gun. "Where did you get that?"

I held the pistol in the palm of my hand, so it did not look threatening. "Carried this through both wars. Took it off an officer who had been killed in early '44 when we were holding Anzio."

"You took his gun?"

"He wasn't going to need it."

I nodded, remembering. "They only gave sidearms to officers as part of their uniform. I was an enlisted man, but a handgun, in close quarters could mean the difference. All the enlisted guys grabbed one when they had the opportunity."

He nodded slowly. I wasn't sure if it calmed him, but he moved his attention to the route we were taking.

I was glad I didn't have to explain to him that anyone's courage or fortitude could be enhanced carrying the firepower of a Colt M1911-A1.

Chapter Thirty-Six

Mateo stomped on the gas, and the armored vehicle lurched from the curb. Ahead of us, three figures raced around the corner of the building from the other street. Two carried black, mean-looking pistols, while the third heaved a pump-action shotgun.

"Down," Mack commanded, his hand reaching for his sidearm.

Simon didn't need to be told twice. He dove for the floorboards, hands covering his head. I bent over with morbid curiosity, my face pressed up between the Mateo's headrest and the post separating the front and rear doors. I couldn't seem to take my eyes off these relentless bastards.

Of the three approaching, the two pistol-toting neo-Nazis were both garbed in the familiar brown Khaki that gained them the nickname 'Brownshirts' in the 1930s. Both stopped when they saw us and dropped into classic pistol-shooting stances. Smoke erupted from their weapons, but the armor and the roar of our large V-8 turbo engine swallowed most of the noise of their gunfire. Mateo, Mack, and I all flinched as the rounds walked across the windshield of the car, heavy thuds accenting their trail. Simon remained on the floor, which is where I was supposed to be, too.

As we approached the trio, the third man, a broad-chested, muscle-bound stereotype of a redneck, dressed in only a pair of coveralls, displaying sleeves of tattoos on his arms, lifted his shotgun. He shot from the hip, but the pellets bounced harmlessly from the reinforced glass of the side window, leaving only scratch marks in their wake.

Mateo tapped brakes while holding firm on the accelerator. With a quick flick of the steering wheel, the rear of the car slid sideways, slamming all three like dominoes. I felt a sudden weightlessness in the pit of my stomach as the car slid, then multiple thuds shuddered through the car. The heavy vehicle straightened and rocketed up the street before Mateo put it into a screaming skid, heading away from city center.

"Scenic route?" he asked with a toothless grin.

"I'm game," Mack said, leaning into the turn.

Into the microphone he reported, "All units! We're taking a road-trip south. Link up on the far side of town at the conservation center. Acknowledge."

As the other units replied to confirm the new rendezvous target, Mack reminded me about the large public area where I hadn't been since my wife passed. Set aside as green-space buffer between agricultural and residential, a whole collection of parks stretched between the Conestoga River and Mill Creek. The huge park area boasted a swim center, family picnic areas, a trail system and, as I recall, a skate park. You could hide an army in any of the picturesque trails that covered its whole expanse. From there, it would be an almost straight run to Buchanan Park, the area that these born-again Nazis were aiming for. If all worked as planned, they would find my group there as a welcome party.

Mack switched frequencies and repeated the information on a channel that had been designated for the law agencies. He added the fact that there might be three injured assailants at the intersection where the department store was situated.

I heard Special Agent Pointer's low growl, followed by Torres's gruff voice, acknowledge the change in plans and could imagine the chaos that would ensue as their vehicles forced their way with sirens and lights through crowded streets to the altered rendezvous.

Seeing no pursuit, Mateo eased off the gas and our heavy vehicle settled into a more leisurely ride.

I reached out a hand to help Simon back up onto his seat. The poor man was pale and wide-eyed.

"Breathe, Simon. C'mon, deep breaths."

He did as I suggested, but his eyes rolled back and forth like a cornered animal. I placed a hand on his arm, and it seemed to center him.

"Make a wide loop, Mateo," Mack said. "If we take the road up the east side of the green space, it will give the others time to get out of that parking lot of a town."

Simon twisted violently towards me. He grabbed my hand desperately and clung as if I was a life preserver, keeping him afloat in a sea of fear.

"Where in the hell are the *police*?" he said, voice shaking with shock. "How can those people just attack us in broad daylight without *any* fear of a response? This is not some third-world country!"

"Simon," Mack said, his tone patient, understanding that my friend's shaking voice came from stress and fear. "You're safe in here. Look at the windows. Bullets had little effect. They just bounced off. As for those guys shooting at us, you can relax. Mateo took care of them. Those three won't be hurting anyone soon."

Mack's calm, smooth voice touched that part of Simon that was ready to bolt, and I watched as his breathing slowed. Finally.

Simon looked at me, and I nodded.

I knew, but did not say, that the saving grace was that the rounds had been from small-caliber weapons. Things might have been dicier if any of those thugs had carried any weapon with higher velocity and weight. Of if they had loaded that shotgun with deer slugs, it might have done more damage than scratching the paint. Or, I could have reminded him what happened to the Escalade that had been hit with heavy armament at the safe-house farm we'd been at. But I said none of this.

As Simon calmed down, I cleaned my glasses and then watched as we drove toward the edges of Lancaster. The landscape flashed by, a mixture of farm fields and lush forest that hugged meandering creeks and rivers in the area. I think the scenery had a calming effect my friend, because he finally released my arm and sat back in nervous exhaustion.

I'd followed Mateo's twists and turns across the outskirts of Lancaster and knew exactly where we were. At one point, we had to slow to pass a long line of military vehicles lined up facing the town. I knew this was the National Guard waiting to block off main entrances to the town, hoping to capture any lawbreakers among the gathered White-supremacists as they tried to escape after the march. Part of me felt secure knowing they were there. There were a lot of resources and firepower on our side. But after the past few months of playing this insane game of hide and seek with Russell, I wouldn't let my guard down any time soon. The slippery bastard had been one step ahead of us the whole time.

Twenty minutes later, we entered the south end of the park from Hwy 222. Pushing north on Eshelman Mill Road, I felt the vehicle slow while both Mateo and Mack craned their necks to read the road sign on our right.

"Long Rifle Road?" Mateo read out loud. "There has to be a story there," he said, glancing at his partner. His eyes flicked to the rear-view mirror. "You know anything about it?"

I was grinning from ear to ear as I realized this warrior, who was no stranger to long-distance shooting, did not know where he was.

"The Martin Meylin Gunshop was supposed to be the birthplace of the long rifle, also known as the Pennsylvania rifle or the Kentucky rifle. It sits just down the road in Willow Street."

"Damn." Mateo whispered in reverence. "Boss, after this..."

Mack laughed. "Relax. I'm way ahead of you. Some of the other boys might want to visit it too."

The car surged ahead and the grin behind those dark glasses Mateo sported was blinding. He looked like a kid seeing the presents under the tree for the first time. His eyes flashed towards the mirror. "You've been holding out on me, Donald. Any other sites I should visit around here?"

"What? Do I look like a tour guide from the Lancaster Tourist Information Center?" I said in mock anger. "Google it yourself."

The men up front chuckled, but the mirth cut off as two camo-painted pickup trucks appeared in the distance ahead of us. By the way the rear end of the trucks pulled sideways as they came out of the turn, it was obvious they were traveling too fast for the winding road. The road straightened and as they bore down on us, I saw two or three figures in the boxes of the vehicles. They were standing, hanging off a light bar that was fitted over the cab.

With little warning, they began to fire at us. The windshield puckered, causing divots to appear on the ballistic glass, but the polycarbonate layer dispelled the force of the bullets. Although visibility was hindered by webbing of the exterior glass, Mateo easily guided our car forward and toward the trucks in a wild game of chicken.

The second truck swerved out to allow their gunners to fire as well, so that both trucks filled the roadway but with one truck thirty feet in front of the other. Firing from a speeding truck ensured that most rounds missed our vehicle entirely, but that didn't deter the shooters in the least. They kept up the barrage.

"Hold on!" Mateo yelled over the near constant thumping of bullets. As we barreled towards the oncoming attackers, he maneuvered our SUV close to the center line. Neither group slowed down or turned 'chicken', but as we flashed by the first truck, Mateo jerked the wheel, so we slid alongside the first vehicle, tearing off our side mirror, but glancing off the truck's rear bumper, causing it to swing uncontrollably towards the spot where we had just been. The suddenness of the movement launched the shooters from the rear of the truck as if a catapult had fired them.

Mateo jerked the wheel in the opposite direction to clip the second vehicle the same way, and I wrenched my head in time to see the truck, which had twisted violently, begin to tumble. It spun itself towards the first truck that was desperately trying to stop without rolling, but I watched the second vehicle overtake its partner. The two became one as crashing metal came together in a rush. A flash of something falling passed so fast that it took a minute to realize that it must have been a person, one of the shooters, tossed skyward like a dry leaf.

Our heavy SUV swerved a couple times before Mateo had it running straight and true.

"Anyone hurt?" Mack called out.

Simon and I looked at each other and I guessed his shocked expression mirrored my own as we both assured Mack we were fine. I'd have bruises from the seatbelt, but without it . . .

"Find somewhere we can pull over," Mack said. "Out of sight."

I leaned forward. "Why? What's wrong?"

"Only my team and the cops knew we were coming through the conservation area," he said, his eyes searching for new threats, "yet these yahoos got here first. Unless they have their own encrypted police scanner, we might have a rat."

Chapter Thirty-Seven

We sat in the car with doors open to allow a natural breeze to flow through the compartment. The windows did not lower, as it would weaken the integrity of the ballistic glass and armored panels. Mateo leaned against the front fender waiting for orders, while Mack tried to get a clear picture of the tactical map.

Mateo had moved a barrier and tucked us deep into one of the hiking trails so that we were not visible from the road. Mack was outside on his mobile phone, no longer trusting radio frequencies. He was sure that his team hadn't been compromised, but the police were another matter altogether. Most police departments used standard radio frequencies, so that anyone with a scanner bought off the internet could listen to everyday police business; but they also incorporated encrypted channels for security or privacy issues. What had disturbed our security contractor was that the police had assigned us one of those secure channels for today's activities. Somehow, the neo-Nazi group was getting strategy information that should have been secure.

Which added up to a leak in the police department. Any officer who held extreme-right beliefs could easily pass on information to third parties without drawing attention to themselves, unless they were stupid enough to use text or email. We could even trace phone numbers back; although doing so would be well after the fact, if at all.

Mack broke the connection and walked over to my side of the car. He crouched on his haunches and looked towards Simon and me. "According to Torres, when I announced the meetup at the conservation area, there were several reports of vehicles leaving the downtown area heading south. Torres immediately shut down all the entrances to the park—he says that because of the river, there are only a few ways in or out."

I nodded my agreement.

"In any case, it seems we're fairly safe at the moment, but our adversaries must know roughly where we are and where we intend to go. Their combativeness tells me they don't want you, Donald, making a stand during their march and they seem desperate to stop you before the event. I think Russell fears the outcome." He held up his hand to stop my retort. "I don't think he's scared of dying, but rather of the public condemnation his group would fall under if he attacked you. There is absolutely no upside if he shows any aggression towards you despite the hatred he must surely feel."

"So, what are you considering?"

He glanced over at his partner before answering. "Although our ride is drivable, it's also a huge target. Any of those guys see us coming, we can expect a gunfight."

"Any more hits to the windshield and we'll be blind," Mateo said.

Mack nodded. "So, we need something that will not attract attention, and I think I might have just the right thing on the way here."

IF I TOLD YOU I HAD an idea what Mack was planning, I'd be lying. My mouth dropped as a large, open, produce truck rumbled into view and parked directly behind our armored car. Someone had decorated the sides of the truck with Nazi and White-supremacy flags, the hateful symbols mocking everything we were fighting against. From the cab of the truck, Dillon emerged with a huge grin. His right arm supported in a sling, he seemed to have recuperated. He waved and walked over to us.

Mack and Mateo smirked at my expression, exchanging glances, while Simon let out a tired sigh.

"You actually expect Simon and me to travel in this hunk of junk?" I growled.

"Can you think of a better disguise?" Mack smiled. "Hell, Russell and his group will give you an escort right to the playing field, if we let them."

Simon was shaking his head. "But those flags..."

Mateo gave an evil grin. "Simon. I'll supply the gasoline so you can fire them up while Nazi bozos march towards our group. That ought to *really* piss them off!"

Simon chuckled and shook his head before nodding. "I hope I'm not paying for this?"

Dillon beamed like a kid in a candy store. "When Mack called for a new set of wheels, I figured what would be better than to borrow some from the idiots who are giving us so much grief."

"But won't they know you've snatched the truck?" I asked.

Dillon shrugged. "Considering the driver is hog-tied in the back of the truck, there's no one to spill the beans. I won't be squealing."

Mack grabbed his man by the back of his neck. "Great job. Give it an hour before you take the SUV back to the farm. By that time, we'll be at the field and the goons won't be hunting for us anymore. Until that shoulder heals, I don't want you in harm's way."

"Boss, I'm ready to toss the sling. It's not an issue."

"Regardless. You have your orders."

His head bobbed acceptance and he moved towards Mateo. I watched as Mateo pulled off his suit coat and Kevlar vest as Mack pulled my wheelchair out of the trunk. I slid from the rear seat into the chair, my gut clenching as pain reared up. I gasped and would have fallen but for Mack's powerful arms.

"I gotcha," he said in a whisper as he eased me into the chair. Pulling back, he searched my face, which felt hot. "You're white as a sheet, Donald."

"Just need a painkiller. Been a busy morning."

"Maybe we should get you to a hospital."

"I'm dying Mack. We all know it. Nothing is going to change it. If I wimp out and let you take me to a hospital, we'll miss our window to stop Russell. We—I—need to stop him. For Jeremy, for Scott, and for Rita. It's got to end today! Mack and I can't do it from a goddamn hospital."

I was panting as I forced the pain down. I reached out and grabbed his coat. "Help me stop him, Mack."

His eyes bored into me. I could feel Simon and the others watching, but I refused to take my eyes away from the former soldier.

He took a deep breath and nodded.

I washed down a combination of pills with bottled water, but it took the pills a full ten minutes to ease the worst of the pain. My hand shook with the effort to wipe cold sweat from my face. I didn't trust my voice, but just nodded that I was ready to proceed. Mack pushed my chair to the rear of the produce truck. Mateo had the gate down and hopped up into the bed.

While I'd waited for Emily's concoction to take full effect, Mateo had undergone a transformation. He and Dillon had cut the arms off his shirt, so he looked like a muscle-bound criminal, especially with the sleeve of tattoos that marked both his arms. Dillon passed him the former driver's hat, a dark green beret with a bright gold-trimmed, red swastika as a badge—and he covered his familiar mohawk. Instantly, he looked like he'd fit into a White-supremacist parade.

Mack slapped him on the back. "Just remember to pull off the stupid cap when we get to the field so none of our own people mistake you as one of the bad guys."

"Right."

Mateo slid the tied neo-Nazi across the truck bed and let him drop to the ground. He threw me a vicious smile when the man grunted in pain. Mack dragged the man by his bindings so that he lay beside the battered SUV.

"The others can deal with our friend when they pick up the Escalade," Mateo said.

Mack bent over my chair, picked me up like a child and passed me up to Mateo, who carried me effortlessly to the front of the stall.

"Not the most comfortable accommodations, but it should suit our purposes," he said as he put me down.

He walked back to help Simon up and then the wheelchair, which he folded and left on its side so it wouldn't roll around. Simon dropped on the truck bed, not masking his disgust for his surroundings.

"Cheer up, my friend. You can wipe your ass with that swastika flag when we get to the playing field."

He grunted but remained upset.

The truck's huge diesel engine growled to life. After some grinding of the clutch and a few attempts to turn around on the tight walking trail, we lumbered back towards the road. At the entrance, the truck slowed to ensure we had no one sitting in wait for us. With no more excuses, Mateo ran through the gears and brought us to a decent speed. We retraced our original route, but then turned north on Highway 222. I had advised Mateo to hang a left on Conestoga Street to avoid getting turned around with all the one-way streets. It would also skirt the business area that might still be congested by the marchers and their opponents.

By the time we turned off 222, I was determined to have our fair town's mayor and his councillors travel these roads the way we were travelling. By the way my ass felt, I knew they'd agree that there was a dire need of resurfacing the area roads. At least thinking about that partially blocked the continuous burning in my stomach.

As we approached the southern side of Buchanan Park, we could see only glimpses of the chaos through the slats on the rear bed. The massive field was completely surrounded by people of all stripes. Nazi and White supremacist flags and banners competed with signs and banners of Antifas protesters. From my vantage point, I couldn't even see how any group of marchers could enter the park because of the multitude of onlookers, supporters and protesters.

Mateo eased the truck through crowds on the road that paralleled the field, stopping and starting as traffic allowed. Demonstrators, seeing our truck, gathered around, yelling and booing. A few grabbed hold of the truck and began rocking the bed back and forth. Simon mumbled his annoyance, but neither of us got up, as it would announce our presence to those who were attempting to keep us from attending the rally. As protesters tore the Nazi symbols violently from the truck's sides, we could see more of the surrounding area.

It did not take long before police muscled the crowd away from the vehicle and we could pull up to the drop-off area that the police also were keeping open and clear. In seconds, the rear gate dropped, and Mack and Mateo were there to help us down. Four of Mack's team materialized from God knows where and made a shield around us as they settled me into my chair.

As a group, we moved towards the barricades, but when the crowd recognized me, it surged forward, some screaming defiance while others, support. Mack yelled an order, and the team pushed hard for the entrance to the field and the wall of blue uniforms.

Simon steered my chair, using Mack's back as a sort of compass heading. He was bent over, and I could hear his breath rasp against my right ear. He sounded like he was on the tail end of a marathon. I worried about his heart giving out. Simon is younger than I am, but that isn't saying much.

As we escaped being the center of the crowds, those on both sides of the argument set to pushing and shoving each other. The noise was tremendous, and I cringed.

The wheels on my chair dipped as we crossed a cattle gate that stretched over a ditch, and I feared I'd go down in a heap, but Simon righted me while one of the security team pulled an armrest forward and we rattled over the obstacle. Like a cork from a bottle of champagne, we broke out of the human wall, with a suddenness that was startling. The police closed their ranks to the crowd, and Mack wasted no time making for the playing field.

The access to the field that we were to use brought us right by the baseball diamond where Frank, Decker, and Benny were waiting for us. They had come using a shorter route than the one Mateo had taken us on and had been busy helping to mark different areas for those attending to position themselves. As I looked over the field, they'd driven a line of stakes down the foul lines that ran from home plate to first and third bases. Yellow nylon rope rose and fell from each of the stakes to mark off areas for the veterans had joined us. My friends had done well. And they knew it.

The boys had also grabbed four players' benches from the dugouts and had placed them right at home plate. This, I knew, was going to be where my trusted friends and I would wait for Russell and his cronies.

One either side of the field, collapsible bleachers had been erected over the past couple days. Now, they were filled to capacity with veterans in a multitude of colored uniforms. In front of the stands, wheelchairs and walkers stretched the length of the field, following the foul-ball line on either side. There were even people behind the bleachers, pressed up to the chain-linked fences.

On the outside of the fence, the media was lined up with raised platforms so they could film the event. Others stood on the roof of their vehicles, waiting for something to happen, camera bags at their feet. More than a few had armpit-sweated shirts from standing in the sun.

"We had to turn them away," Decker said with a smile that cut across his ebony face; his eyes lost in wrinkles. "There's absolutely no more room. We sent the rest of them to wait at Hartman Green, across the way." He pointed to the north of the field.

My eyes took in the size of the group. I couldn't believe so many had responded. Rita had been right. Whether it was the cause or the injustice of what happened in Houston, not only the veterans of my war, but other American soldiers had decided to make a stand against the vermin slighting the reputation of America. There were both men and women in the crowd with much younger faces then their neighbors. Their posture was more erect and contrasted with the bent and broken soldiers from past wars.

Even from the distance, I could see old warriors in faded and worn uniforms. Some with bodies like my own that caused the fabric to hang as if on scarecrows

My hands were shaking as I took it all in. Real tears blurred my eyes, but tears of joy at this show of support. I was overwhelmed.

Almost like Simon could read my mind, he put a hand on my shoulder and said, "You did this, Donald. All these people have heard your message and have left everything to be here today to add their voices to yours."

I nodded. "I have you to thank for that, Simon. I'd still be a pissed-off old fart, cursing into my beer at Legion Hall, if not for you."

I looked up at the man who'd become so much more than just a financial backer to me. "But I have to remember what I am asking of them."

Frank, who had been standing off to one side, stepped forward, handing me a megaphone with an attached microphone. "Donald. It's *their* choice to be here. Most feel exactly the same way about Nazi vermin as you do. Some are looking for a last kick at the can, while others want their lives to have renewed meaning. You've given them that."

He shook my hand and then Simon's before moving to stand a couple of feet away from me, but in the front row.

One tall and thin, almost emaciated, individual walked towards the field. Something about the man's gait sparked a distant memory, but for the life of me, I couldn't nail it down. He carried a long, hard case in his right hand. He stopped directly in front of me and studied my face intently.

Mack moved closer protectively, his hand under his jacket.

"Donald Wilson," the man said just as the moment became uncomfortable. His voice was dry and gruff, as if he hadn't used it for a long time.

I nodded. "Do I know you, friend?"

"Long, long time ago, we called each other friends. And after watching all your recent adventures over the past few months, I still would."

The surrounding crowd evaporated as his mesmerizing eyes held mine as tight as a vice. It was as if we were the only two left in the world.

"Only difference," he continued, "is I would never have recognized you after all that time, had your puss not been plastered on every newspaper in the land."

"Well, you have me at a disadvantage, sir."

"Fox. Dillon Fox."

My mind instantly snapped to the quiet yet friendly boy whose first trip off the San Carlos Reservation was to death fields in France and Germany. His MC1 sniper rifle had saved many of his own men while dispatching countless German soldiers.

His eyes crinkled as he saw recognition cut across my face. His grin deepened, and he held out a hand.

"You've done us all proud, Donald."

I clasped his hand and struggled to stand against the sudden pain. I have to admit; It overwhelmed me seeing my old friend. He helped me up, and we stood together, two worn-out warriors from a lifetime ago.

"Seems like yesterday, don't it?"

I nodded, not trusting my voice.

He lifted the case and smiled. "I brought old Alice with me. I've already found me a place where I might do some good. I'll have your six."

I squeezed his hand. I chuckled at the mention of Alice, knowing it was his nickname for his MC1. "It'll be like old times, my friend."

With a sad nod, he eased away and moved against the continuous flow of veterans towards a fitness store that sat next to the field.

I sat back in my chair, my emotions in turmoil as I stared after him. That bond—that brotherhood from a lifetime ago was as strong now as it was all those years ago. Hell, I hadn't even recognized him, yet I was floored by the love and camaraderie.

Dillon might have been a member of my old company, but looking around at all the support from these strangers who I had never met was so encouraging that I was speechless.

I was feeling the old familiar nervousness that every soldier from WWII and Korea back to Roman foot-soldiers and Greek spearmen experienced before facing a battle. For me, a lifetime had not changed that. Even knowing that my days were ending and that my cancer was destroying me from the inside out, it made little difference.

I didn't want to die.

THE OTHER ENTRANCE to the park was on the far side and I knew police were keeping it locked until the parade of intolerant bigots reached the field.

This sports field had been my concession to public safety. There was no way the police could stop my friends and me from confronting Russell and his group, so I had suggested that the meet take place in an area that the authorities could easily control so that it would not turn out to be a riot. When I mentioned the sports field with its fence and secure entrances, they jumped at the suggestion. They were all for keeping the public away from anything that might become violent.

Now, the normal empty space, except on warm summer nights under bright lights felt cozy and warm with all the soldiers waiting patiently. Banners that identified 'Veterans of America,' 'Vietnam Vets' and unit names and numbers. Division flags peppered the crowd; some large, but most small enough to wave in your hand. It created a kaleidoscope of colors.

I planned to keep Russell's people trapped in one place.

This would be my OK Corral.

Chapter Thirty-Eight

As it was, just to the right of the bus drop-off, there was a small contingent of Brownshirts waiting across the field from us. At a glance, I counted fifteen to twenty individuals. All seemed armed; those in uniform had at least a sidearm in a black leather holster on their hips, while others carried rounded shields with the "othala rune" of the National Socialist Movement painted on the face of each, looking like crude vertical fish. The shields looked like someone had cut them out of garbage cans and I wondered how much good they would do against a baseball bat, let alone rounds from firearms. Each man carried a homemade truncheon, a thin wooden baton cut from a pool cue or a hoe handle.

A smaller group of rednecks stood loosely to one side, part of, but separate from the other group. At least three wore army-fatigue pants in a green camouflage pattern and matching t-shirts. Covering these, new flak-jackets that had obviously been bought from Amazon and had never seen action, but buffed up their chests while enhancing their beer bellies.

It was almost laughable. These lard-arses would never have been able to march across Europe—but I wasn't sure about this field. Probably why they were not marching in the parade.

The group of losers milled in front of the barricades that kept the general public out of the park for their own protection. These guys were waiting for backup. Mack was right, no coward stood alone.

Torres and his partner appeared at my side. His eyes scanned the various uniforms within the collective group from the buses that had eventually settled into the areas that held our supporters. They filled over half of the massive park.

"There's a good number of younger vets, but most here are closer to ninety years," he said in wonder.

I chuckled. "I'm considered a young 'un at ninety-five and I lied about my age to enlist. Quite a few centenarians out there." Looking over my shoulder at him, sobering. "Most of these people will be gone in the next couple of years. And with them, the stories and the sacrifices they lived through."

Torres had no glib remark, but I saw him studying the faces with more scrutiny.

"Just to let you know," he said after a minute. "The parade is being delayed by Antifa. They've confronted the fascists at every intersection." He raised his arm to the east.

I could see pale, white smoke beyond the barricades and the gathering crowds. I looked back at the police officer for further explanation.

"Tear gas. It's been the only thing that has been effective in separating either group."

I twisted in alarm. "You can't start throwing that stuff around this group, you're going to end up hurting more than you help."

"Donald's right," Simon added. "Half of these people are on oxygen as it is."

Torres cursed under his breath. "This is turning out to be a royal cluster-fuck!" He tugged out his portable radio. "Torres to Command Post Alpha..." We missed the rest as he strode towards the far end of the field, his partner, Nguyen, almost running to keep up.

Looking across the ranks of veterans and their companions, I saw, as I'd reminded Torres, the small cylinders either strapped to the backs of wheelchairs or sitting on their little rolling trollies by the feet of individuals. More than a few had compact portable oxygen-concentrators beside them, freeing them from cumbersome bottles.

The frailty of the group struck me, and I shook my head, realizing that, after all, I'm part of that same group. Even ignoring that I'm sitting in this damn chair, I constantly have to remind myself that I'm not capable of a tenth of what I could do, even twenty years ago, let alone in my younger days. Throughout my life, I get these wake-up calls that remind me I'm no longer looking out through the eyes of a younger man, even with my glasses on. It feels like I'm that same person inside, but this old shell has almost completely dried out. Yet it comes as a surprise every time I get a wake-up like seeing this sea of wrinkles in a mirror.

I think that we all see ourselves from the point in our lives when we are at our peak. When we are in our mid-twenties and don't have a health issues and don't require help to move around, or even in our forties when, so the ivory-tower set tell us, we are at the 'peak of our powers.' No matter how old we get or how broken we become, internally we see ourselves from that magical point and sometimes need the continual reminders of the aches and pains of age.

Any of those romantic fools that talk about the 'grace' of growing old hasn't gotten up five or six times a night to plead for a release of a temperamental bladder. Nor for the burning in your gut to subside so you can at least function. "Age is just a number," they say, but sometimes it is a *big* number.

THE FIRST INCLINATION that the show was finally about to start was a strange hush that had all of us sitting up straighter, more alert—ready for any surprise Russell might spring.

Obviously, I couldn't trust the bastard. It would be like him to hit from concealment or from another direction while all our attention was somewhere else.

He had almost perfected a strategy of guerrilla warfare: striking where least expected, only to fade away before we could assemble any actual reaction to counter his attack. Like a feral dog, he darted in to snap at his prey, only to dash back before the desperate foe could bite back. Once his prey's back is turned towards another threat, Russell, the mongrel, would attack again. Little by little, he wore his adversary down.

Death by a thousand cuts.

Like I said, I didn't trust the bastard. My eyes kept roaming the field edges, looking for that gray hoodie.

However, part of me wondered if he'd even show up today. It was not his style to put himself at risk. In Houston, he had let others lead and risk, while he hung back waiting to see what kind of response might wait for him. He had allowed his men to die so he could escape.

Seeing as how there was so much law enforcement here and around the town, I could see him just not showing up, especially with every cop in the country after his ass.

In the distance, the barricade was being dragged back. A gauntlet of police officers stood on either side as the first of the fascists marched onto the field. Even from that distance, I could make out that some were decked out in the formal, black uniforms of the notorious Schutzstaffel, the SS. They used to be Hitler's private army and were in charge of surveillance, security, espionage—and terror—in the Europe I'd risked my life for.

I shook my head, wondering who in the hell would ever want to identify with a group as vile as those vermin, especially with all the documented crimes they'd performed.

Feeling the warmth of the sun beating on my own neck, I hoped that those black uniforms were sucking a ton of heat and that they were suffering from it. I'd accept any advantage.

As a collective "Boo!" rose from the crowd, they goose-stepped towards us with an arrogance that was almost palpable. It was intimidating, there was no denying it. But knowing what they stood for and having seen the horrors their kind were capable of gave me a stiff resolve. Many in the crowd had stood up, raising their fists in anger.

Behind them marched a looser group of Brownshirts. Their uniforms were sweat-stained both from the heat of the day and from clashes with Antifa. Many boasted dried blood and torn shirts. A few hobbled with their comrades supporting them.

Finally, those wearing tattered t-shirts with nasty messages that shouted hatred of Jews and non-Whites or proclaimed "taking back America." Many wore familiar red MAGA ball caps. Scattered through this last group were wannabe commandos sporting a mixture of military garb and standard automatic rifles slung menacingly across chests or beer bellies, showing everyone how tough they were, or trying to be. I could see these idiots standing before a mirror, brandishing weapons to ensure they looked tough. Or posting straggly bearded selfies to social media.

But I had seen grown men, as well as young boys, loaded with weaponry, soil themselves and cry for their mothers at the first barrage of enemy gunfire. Weapons don't make you brave. What you *do* with the weapon when the world around you goes to shit determines your bravery. Even then, action is usually over before you can make a conscious thought. Either your training or instinct kicks in, or you fold.

My eyes flicked back and forth, searching for the one hateful face that had brought us here.

I looked over at Mack, but he shook his head, not taking his eyes off the approaching fascists.

Where the hell was Russell?

Chapter Thirty-Nine

At a harsh command, the first squad of racists thumped to a stop just fifteen feet before my line of veterans closest to their entrance but across the playing field from me. Even from here, I saw that their shiny, tall black boots were dulled by a fine film of dust from the march.

Through the files of men, I could see that the police had formed a wall of blue across the entrance to the playing field. Although local police had not known what we had planned, they were smart enough not to rush in to assert authority. It could have been a slaughterhouse. They stood on full alert, waiting to see how this played out.

The leader of the group stood just over six feet and was as broad-shouldered as any prison lifer. His face was red with exertion and rivulets of sweat streaked down to darken his stiff collar. His discomfort gratified me, and I smiled unconsciously.

In a deep voice that would have been the envy of any parade ground drill-sergeant, he bellowed at the crowd in front of him, "Stand aside, Jew-lovers. Enemies of America and the free White world will not force *us* from our path!"

Without my meaning to, a burst of laughter tore out of my throat. Even now, I cannot tell who was more surprised by it, him or me. But as my laugh moved outward, it gained in volume and substance as the ranks of all the other 'Jew-lovers' began to join in to laugh at the black-booted band at the gate and their cosplay outfits.

The faces in the Nazi ranks became scarlet with indignation and rage.

Once the field quieted, I pulled myself up from my chair, shaking off Simon's helping hand. "The America we fought for," I called out with a strength I'd almost forgotten (but helped with a little battery-powered bullhorn that someone handed to me) and gesturing toward the veterans that sat in their various-colored uniforms, looking regal on both sides of the field, "stood for freedom and equality. We fought against people like you and we're ready to do it again. Right here and right *now*!"

To emphasize my words, I sat back down and traded the little bullhorn for my service pistol from the compartment in my chair and held it with my elbow on the top of my thigh. I made sure I aimed the barrel at the man.

Seeing a threat, the man's nostrils flared, he shouted a harsher command and flicked his arm in a downward chop. A collapsible steel police baton appeared in his hand like a magician's prop.

Others of his group pulled out knock-off 9mm Luger pistols from imitation-leather holsters making up part of their cosplay outfits. Farther back in their group, I watched AR-15s being cocked and pointed menacingly towards the sea of ancient servicemen and women.

"Big man!" I yelled into the bullhorn. "Threatening a bunch of old soldiers during their last days. Where is your cowardly leader, Joseph Russell? He started this and like the rest of you bullies, he's scared to stand and face us, man to man."

"Joseph stands with us," said the leader with a snarl. "And old man, I'm here to fight for what I believe in. America was founded by and for the White race. There's no room for the rest. We won't stand down until the others leave."

"You seem to forget your history, boy. It was Whites just like you who brought your 'non-Whites' and they've already paid for their freedom many times over. It's *you* who are the last of your kind since the world doesn't need haters and complainers. Like all of us, *you* can leave if you don't like it here, but the rest of us are here to stay. Face it."

"And you and these walking corpses are going to do something about it?"

I stared hard at him.

"Yes."

I raised my hand over my head.

Across both flanks and directly behind me, there was a wave of movement as blankets that covered legs that no longer supported their weight were tossed aside. Carrying bags were opened and contents drawn out. There came a riot of clicking and snapping as hundreds of weapons, many vintage World War II, were armed and presented at the ready.

A brief bark of laughter rose from my right and my gaze shifted to see the tarps on the side of a parked garden wagon dropping. Somehow, one old soldier had managed to bring in a M1919A6 machine gun! A standard tripod bolted to the wagon supported it. He caught the flash of sun on links of brass cartridges as he slammed its cover plate into place and charged the deadly gun. Anything in front of this weapon would be rendered raw meat.

Alarm and sudden fear flashed across the line of movie-costumed Nazis. Confronted with a threat that carried more weight than just a busted head, the bullies froze, impotent with no backup plan . . . or even words.

The group before me seemed to shrink as they realized for the first time what they had walked into. The ropes that we had set up across the field for our veterans had, in fact, positioned our people so that there was no chance of over-lapping fields of fire. With the primary group at the center, our lines were at ninety degrees to each other.

A baseball field is a perfect killing field.

As a unit, I could see the line of police at the end of the field move forward in alarm, but someone restrained them. So far, the confrontation had gone without gunfire or blood-shed, so they were content to give me my moment. I'm sure I would hear a more stringent protest later. Might even have Torres throwing my old butt into the clink.

A number of reporters to our right moved closer to stand along the chain-lined fence that ran parallel to the first-base line.

With armed men on either side, two lines of weapons confronted the enemy. There were enough M1 carbines to make it look like a wall of spears, both threatening and dead-ly.

The young Nazi leader's face had taken on a sickly pallor, slick with perspiration. His eyes darted from side to side, and I wondered if he would lose his nerve altogether. He looked ready to bolt.

"What? You don't seem so sure of yourself as you were a minute ago," I taunted, glaring at the man.

His fist flexed on the handgrip of his extended baton with a kind of nervous energy. He clearly wasn't expecting this kind of reception, and he had no clue as to how to extract himself or his group without losing face.

"The thing you really have to remind yourself is that these 'walking corpses', as you referred to my friends, have little time left."

He turned from me as he surveyed the faces behind me and beside me.

"And with little time, they also have little to lose."

His gaze snapped back in my direction at the implied threat, but this time I knew they were full of fear.

"You and your bunch need to ask yourselves if your ideology is something worth dying for." More of his people were leaning forward in an attempt to hear exactly what I was saying and I remembered the little bullhorn still on my lap.

"What...?"

"Do you think we're here just to trade *insults*, boy?" I spat, this time speaking with the megaphone and causing him to take a step back before he caught himself. "You bunch of racist assholes have been following me since I started speaking out against you. You made a point of coming to my hometown with your evil shit, even when the city denied your request for your parade of fools."

I waved my arms towards the many armed soldiers who waited for my lead.

"And you knew that my friends and I would be here to oppose you, but you thought you'd be able to push us aside.

But all of us have fought your kind before and we aren't backing down. So, I hope you came to fight."

He looked back through his own ranks for some sign of what his group wanted to do, but he saw only a sea of scared faces on the edge of panic. Boys with bad weapons dressed in Halloween party costumes facing rows of old soldiers, trained and armed.

"You're talking crazy, Mister." His eyes were wide, and his baton shook with his tension.

"Crazy? I'm not the one talking about killing or deporting people who might be different from me. Or worshiping one of the most evil groups in history." I put down the megaphone and took a deep breath to force myself from really losing it. I had to stay in control. "We're here to stop you idiots here and now. You decide, right now. Is this the hill you want to die on?"

Except for some nervous shuffling amongst the fascists, nothing moved on the field. I could feel the light breeze that blew across the grass sluggishly shifting the honor colors of one of the representative regiments.

The leader's head was on a swivel as he kept moving his gaze from the veterans and their threatening arsenal to his own people, who looked as indecisive as he did.

"What... what do you want?"

I eyed the man, not believing that he was caving so quickly. Deep down, I didn't want to kill these people, fucked up as they were. But being American, I figured they might still have some kind of backbone. I had hoped they would stand down, but was surprised at how easily they folded. I figured we might have to scare them with actual gunfire to get them to comply, but they were ready to sell the farm.

I began to speak, then remembered the megaphone. "After all the damage you and Russell did to me and my friends, there is only one way this will play out. It's not up for negotiation. You and every one of your toy soldiers do exactly as I demand, or there's no deal."

He swallowed hard but his head bobbed in a rush as he nodded.

I looked at Simon, who nodded quickly, as if to get this over with before they changed their minds.

"First," I began, leaning back in my chair and stifling a groan as a flash of burning pain erupted through my abdomen. I spoke slowly and plainly into the little megaphone to emphasize the point and hide my discomfort as I said, "Your weapons. Drop them on the ground and leave them."

His arms dropped, fists curled tight. For the first time, I realized he no longer held the baton. I did not know what he had done with it. Was it tucked in the back of his trousers or in his jacket pocket? I prayed Mack or the others had seen where he had secreted it. Not knowing if he was still armed bothered me.

"You're asking too much. You know the Constitution. We have a right to bear arms."

I nodded, know this might be the tipping point. "You're right, but there's nothing saying that you have the right to use those arms on defenseless people who don't agree with you."

His arm went up, pointing at the weapons aimed at his men. "And what the fuck to do you call that?"

I leaned forward. "I said 'defenseless.' You and your men are *not* defenseless. You're armed, most of you, to the teeth, and that's not acceptable. I have no problem with you using those weapons to protect your home, but threatening American citizens is not constitutional."

He glared at me, his nostrils flaring in suppressed rage.

"We're not thieves. I'm sure the police will return your weapons afterwards, but that is our first demand. I warned you from the beginning, it was all or nothing. Non-negotiable."

He stepped back, running a hand across his face. Pacing in front of his group to help bleed off the worst of his rage, I thought he might lose it right there and then. His fists, almost as large as a child's face, clenched and unclenched as every scenario he could imagine swept through his brain, but were discarded just as fast. Even with my weak eyes, I could actually see in his body language the intellectual battle he was having, but I was completely unsure of the outcome.

I became more certain as I felt Mack's hand grip the back of my wheelchair, as if ready to draw me out of the line of fire. The grip on my own pistol, which lay flat on my thigh, was saturated with sweat; but I stopped myself from wiping it dry, as I feared any distraction that might set off this powder keg.

I swear, those few moments felt like hours. The black-uniformed leader finally stopped his pacing and stood directly across from me. "All right, old man. We'll leave our weapons, but you are personally responsible for each one of them. If even one goes missing, you'll be facing an army of lawyers that will strip you of everything you hold dear, any *inheritance* you planned for your family."

I nodded, but kept my mouth shut. I knew better than to sprinkle salt over this very raw wound. To let them leave without a single confrontation was more than any victory I had ever dreamed of. I let my gaze flicker towards the groups of ancient servicemen, whose threat and vigilance were making this possible. Frank, who sat just down from me caught my eye and gave me an encouraging wink. This might really work.

The Nazi leader made an exaggerated show of laying his pistol on the ground, fully aware of the number of weapons that were aimed directly at him. He and his Untersturmfürer or lieutenant slowly made their way through the ranks to ensure that each man followed my directive. Carefully but defiantly, their weapons were laid on the ground beside their feet. As I'd expected, there was some very loud disagreement and I thought that all hell was about to break loose, but the leader managed to get every one of his members to lay down their weapons, even the red-necks at the back of the line.

Here, I thought I would be dead by now. The man trudged to the front of the column and glared at me, waiting for the next command.

"Second," I said, not wanting to give him time to reconsider. "I want every stitch of clothing or flags that represent your vile group stripped off and dropped on the ground."

To his credit, he began unbuttoning the jacket in rough but precise movements. Those closest to their commander, having heard the ultimatum, also pulled off their fear-inspiring garb. Those at the back of the formation were leaning forward, wondering what was happening.

"Best send someone to let your guys at the back know the terms." Seeing one fellow in the front-rank tugging at his belt, I said, "You can keep your pants on. No sense offending the lady folk." The man nodded his thanks and refastened his pants.

"I'll pass on the orders," the young man said to the leader.

Before he could move, I reminded him, "Move slowly." I motioned my head to the rank of soldiers to his right sitting with fingers on many triggers. He nodded and, with hands halfway up, he moved through the loose line of Nazis.

"And finally," I said into the megaphone, "every one of your people must denounce Nazism and everything it stands for, and do it on live television." I pointed towards the line of media vehicles parked tight against the playing field's metal fence.

I paused, so it sank in. As his eyes pulled from the battery of cameras back to me, and he nodded, eyes hooded in ill-contained anger.

I looked back at Mack who had stood patiently behind me through all of this drama. "Can we get one cameraman over here to witness these men making their pledge to denounce this shit?"

Mack simply lifted his hand and murmured into his wrist microphone. The leader of the group seemed to notice Mack for the first time and seeing the white curled cord that dangled from the security specialist's ear must have assumed he was government, because he blanched, mouth open with wide eyes.

Standing in his black trousers and a white wife-beater shirt, the leader stood with arms crossed, waiting for the next demand. Without a uniform jacket, his physique showed that he was truly an enormous man. His two bulging arms sleeved with tattoos framed a well-muscled chest. I wondered if he'd had to fight for the position of leader. A monster his size would tear apart an average guy.

Behind him, uniforms were being tossed to the dirt and the messenger had to coerce only a few of his members who tried to refuse. He only had to focus the aggrieved protester's attention on the battery of weapons facing them and the wagon-mounted machine-gun before the uniform was pulled off and angrily thrown to the ground.

Following the progress of his people, their leader finally looked back at me. "What else?"

"Nothing else. Once you've made your declaration, you and your people are free to leave the field."

But then, the first rounds of automatic gunfire began to thunder over the field.

Chapter Forty

The first round did not strike me as I would have expected. Rather, as Mack pulled my chair backwards to the relative safety of the security detail, I watched the young neo-Nazi leader—who had one second before begun yelling for his people to drop their weapons—get hit. That first round took him in square in the back and exited out his stomach, while a second round clipped the back of his shoulder as he fell over in a heap.

The report of the rifle seemed to come from a commercial building near the entrance to the field. Now most of the police officers who'd been strung across the trail leading from the street were running, bent over, guns unlimbered, searching for a target. The gunman, meanwhile, began to pick off both Nazis and veterans indiscriminately.

I strained to watch the horror unfold even as my chair with me in it was toppled sideways to the ground to give me some cover as Mack lay over me, supported by the side of the chair. Simon had also materialized on the ground beside me.

A couple of shots slammed into the left flank of the old soldiers with a sound like a wet towel striking a tiled wall. Walkers fell like dominoes as bullets slammed into old limbs, knocking the owners off-kilter. A small group of seniors fell in disarray, pulled down by their younger neighbors. Rifle fire swallowed low mournful wails. Loud shrieks of pain came from the former Brownshirts standing in ranks before us as bullets cut them down, too.

The shots set off a chain reaction since as old as these warriors were, there was no slowing down their trigger fingers. Seeing their comrades being cut down like brittle wheat stalks before a stiff wind, they unleashed their vengeance on the remaining Nazis, who were busy trying to retrieve their own weapons. In an attempt to protect themselves, shirtless bodies dove for weapons that had just been surrendered, but it was too little, too late. Both sides fired on each other, not caring in the heat of battle that the shooter at the far end of the field was the true enemy.

From my cramped but meager shelter under Mack's leaning form, I shuddered at a sudden bone-shaking thumping from the heavy .50 caliber M1919A6 machine gun mounted on the garden wagon. While I struggled to roll over to get a better view of what was transpiring around me, I saw that poor Simon had curled himself into a tight ball in the dirt, whimpering.

Nazis at the front of the column took brunt of the machine gun's barrage, point blank. It slaughtered even those who had laid down the weapons. The heavy 416 grain bullets shredded flesh, creating a red mist over the green sod. Yesterday, children had played here vigorously with screams of joy and excitement. Today the screams were of pain and terror as the sod became saturated with lifeblood of modern-day monsters, most who had no time to cry out.

I kept trying to rise, but Mack held a gentle but firm hand on my shoulder. The steady firing of the distant rifle continued to create chaos in the ranks of both groups. For a split second, I thought Dillon Fox might be the shooter, but to my relief, the rounds were coming from the wrong direction.

"Where is the shooter?" I gasped, realizing I wasn't getting up any time soon.

"Somewhere near the entrance," Mack said, voice calm as ice. "Whoever it is, he's taking his time. Making each shot count."

"It has to be Russell."

"That'd be my guess."

"Someone needs to take that son-of-a-bitch out," I grunted.

"Looks like the cops agree. They're finally moving that way."

I couldn't see a thing from on the ground even though, mercifully, my glasses somehow were still on my nose. Being on the ground might have been a good thing for me, but it left Mack defenseless as he lay over my chair. The pile of corpses that lay in front of us blocked my vantage. All I could see was that there were no Nazis still standing anywhere near us. A phantom-like haze hovered over the dead and I realized with a sniff that it was the familiar smell of cordite from the vet's ammunition.

Over the deluge of gunfire, one new report fractured the air over us.

"Damn," Mack growls, flinching and pulling himself tighter onto my prostrated form. "That's sniper fire."

"That's Alice," I said, my nervous snicker sounding like a raspy cough.

Mack pulled back his head to eye me in confusion.

"Remember that tall gent that stopped by earlier? He was our overwatch, back in the day."

A second shot rang out.

Mack risked a look and then hunkered back down. "The cops are storming that building. Looks like your friend Alice is acting as overwatch for the police, too."

I chuckled at the idea of calling Dillon Fox, Alice. He'd find that hilarious as well, and I reminded myself to seek out my old friend to share the story. Lying there in the dirt with Mack while bullets criss-crossed over our heads, and I'm laughing at something so ridiculous, was incredible.

From down range, towards the shooter's building, there were two muffled thumps that crunched over the closer gunfire. Even pressed into the dirt, I recognized the sound of explosions.

"Flashbangs?" I asked.

Mack's shoulders shrugged, but his mouth tightened in a hard line.

The roar of firing around us faltered and then stopped as quickly as it had begun. Of course, by now there were no more targets left standing in the middle of the field. Among the veterans, there were clusters of survivors, lying on the ground where minutes earlier they'd been sitting, weapons on guard. Now there were gaps in their ranks on either flank, like missing teeth.

It took a minute for my ears, deafened by gunfire, to return to my usual numb hearing, but I immediately wished it had not. Cries and wails of the injured competed with those who'd found their friends, neighbors, and loved ones dead or cut down. Around me, people began pulling themselves off the ground, moving in a daze of shock as they took in the carnage.

Mack rose cautiously, pistol held ready but tight against his leg. With his free hand, he up-ended my wheelchair. Seeing that I still clasped my own service pistol, he shoved his into his holster and used both his hands to lift me onto my chair. Simon used the arm of my chair to pull himself up to stand beside me. His hand rose to his mouth, and he sobbed as his mind took in the surrounding death.

"Mack, forget about me and help the wounded."

"But..."

"Damn it, Mack. There's no one left to protect me from. These people need help. I'll be fine."

His lips tightened across his face, and he nodded. He spoke into his wrist microphone as he knelt beside Frank, feeling for a pulse. I could see the blood spreading and darkening his uniform jacket and knew my old friend was gone. He had been sitting not more than five feet from me, and yet he caught a round while I hadn't even been scraped. I didn't need Mack's eyes to tell me. With the utmost care, the security specialist draped Frank's hand over the wound, so that he looked like he was taking a nap.

My hands were shaking as the scene blurred out of focus. It was exactly what I had feared. I had gotten Frank killed for my crusade. This was my fault. I took in the other veterans who were lying still on the grass and others who rocked back and forth in agony from their injuries. Biting my lip, I slammed my fist against my leg in anger and self-pity. Why did I let my friends—Rita!—talk me into asking for their help? I wanted to do it alone. I'm the one who was dying.

Not these others. Frank's death was on my head and so were all these other brave souls. They had already done their duty, sacrificed so much, and I asked them to do it again. And now they're dead because of my stubborn need to confront Russell—and I didn't even get to do that. If Dillon hadn't tagged that bastard, then all this was for nothing. All these people died for nothing but my own pride and pigheadedness.

"Donald," a voice pulled me back. It was Benny. He was walking carefully around the dead and injured. He grasped my hand and hugged me. "Thank God, you are safe."

I turned towards Frank's body so he could see. He looked and nodded slowly, then reached out and patted my shoulder.

"He died standing up for something he believed in, Donald. It was what he wanted."

"What?" I said in horror.

"You're not the only person who felt the need to stand up against these evil people, Donald. Don't you dare try to take his sacrifice onto yourself. Frank would have been the first to tell you to take a long walk off a short pier." He squeezed my shoulder. "We were all here because we believed those people needed to be stopped. As your friends, we expected you to understand that. God knows, Rita tried to hammer that into your thick skull."

He leaned over and said hoarsely in my ear, "You have one more friend to say goodbye to."

"Decker?"

He nodded before taking a hold of the handles of my chair. My eyes searched for my other friend, but there were so many people milling about in shock that I could not spot him. I grabbed the wheels of my chair to help Benny push it across the soft ground, and even so, I could hear his breathing laboring. And then I saw Decker.

One of Mack's people sat on the ground, holding Decker in a semi-sitting position, so that he saw us coming and waved a tired welcome. He had been shot through the chest and the security professional had his hand over the wound trying to stem the flow, but from the amount of blood, I knew it had to be fatal. He didn't have long.

I slide out of the chair to sit beside him, grasping his hand in mine. I looked at the security guard and he shook his head, confirming the worst.

"Can't I leave you for a minute without you getting shot up."

He smiled and tried to laugh, but it comes out as a whimper. He contorted his lips and spat out some reddish spittle. "Want to say—thanks, Donald."

"For what, buddy? Getting you into this mess?"

He shook his head, and I could see he's having trouble keeping his eyes focused, so I shut up so he could finish what he was trying to say.

"For being my friend. For Korea and everything after. Especially today."

"Today..."

He nodded heavily and struggled to lift his eyes to mine. "For giving me one hell of a send-off and... the best reason I can think of... to make a difference."

I reached up to my tunic and unpinned the Bronze Star. I leaned over my friend. "You earned this today, buddy."

He smiled, blood showing between his teeth, and patted my hand.

His eyes glazed over as his breath slipped out of him, and he deflated against the guard's chest, his hand limp in mine.

I looked up to find a reporter, with a large video camera pressed to his face, recording Decker's last moments for the world's twenty-four-hour entertainment. Normally, I would have been enraged at the callous sensationalism, but just then, I couldn't give a damn.

I was numb.

Chapter Forty-One

As the ball-park's survivors were assessed and triaged, Simon, Benny and I sat in numb silence. Mack was busy helping the wounded, but he had assigned Mateo to stand guard over us.

About an hour ago, a company of National Guard had pulled through the far end of the field. Like a horde of disciplined ants, they dispersed across the field. Some were dealing with the wounded, while others were finishing up erecting a massive military tent with the familiar red cross. The injured were being taken there, while another group of soldiers under the direction of the local coroner and his staff waited with black body bags to collect the dead and transport them to local morgues for processing. Except for the odd yelled command or order, they worked silently, recognizing that these ancient warriors had once again stood for American freedom.

I saw how gently they lifted both living and dead; and although I was sickened by the surrounding carnage, I was heartened by the reverence the National Guard was showing. Hopefully, this young generation would now see the worth of these fallen men, and remember.

The cameras at the edge of the field recorded it all. I was certain that the media's talking heads would get their fill today with enough material to keep them occupied for weeks to come.

I had to take another painkiller to blunt the worst of the pain, but painkillers were only sugar-coating now. The ache was constant, which was consistent with what Emily had warned. The added stress of the past few weeks, capped by today's drama, was not helping. Stress was something she no longer nags me about. She knew it wouldn't have mattered.

Mateo stood as four suits made their way towards us. He radioed Mack a message, then waited with arms crossed. Special Agents Pointer and Gilpin moved across the massive crime scene, taking care not to step in pools of sticky blood that saturated the ground while Detective Nguyen had to practically skip to keep up with her partner, Torres, who strode towards us, features dark and unforgiving.

"Now we're in for it!" Mateo said out the side of mouth. He moved between the approaching police officers and me.

Torres stops in front of the barrel-chested security consultant. "Get out of my way."

"No sir," Mateo growled back.

Torres almost vibrated with anger.

"I'm about ready to arrest the bunch of you assholes. I'm sick of you," he said, pointing at me, "And your group of rent-a-cops, who think they can shoot up my town..." His hand curled into a fist, but Mateo didn't even flinch. "We have four dead cops. Four!" He twirled away and stalked a few feet away, peering over the carnage. I saw his shoulders rise and fall as he took deep breaths to calm himself. But I also saw the shudder that racked his body as he broke down as his protective anger drained, and the horror finally hit.

I averted my gaze.

I felt for the man. I had felt something similar, except I also knew that I was the cause of all this tragedy. Regardless of Benny's words, and even Decker's, I knew it was my obsession with Russell—and if I'm going to be truly honest, my mission seemed to have become more about Russell and less about American-Nazi ideology. He may have personified the evil that group stood for, but after Houston and even more after Rita, I wanted to kill the bastard myself.

The death of all these veterans and now, four police officers *were* on me. Regardless of the imagined need to die for what they believed in or going out in a blaze of glory, I had stolen their right to die in their beds, in their homes with family at their side.

I looked over at the FBI agents. "Russell?"

Pointer shook her head, frustration clear in her expression. It was Gilpin who explained what had happened.

"He was the shooter. He was the catalyst of all this," she said. "One of your people, nodding at Mateo, hit him with sniper fire, but only got a little piece him, didn't kill him."

"Not one of us," Mateo said.

The two stared at each other until Pointer looked directly at me.

I nodded without waiting for his question. "My guy has been protecting me since 1943. The fact that Russell isn't dead we'll have to chalk up to old age or poor eyesight, 'cause I've never known him to miss."

"Oh, he didn't miss. There was a lot of blood, but no Russell. He had a rabbit hole and a car waiting. He also had a couple of IEDs waiting for the local police that stormed the building. It gave him the time to get away, but from the amount of blood he was trailing, I'm guessing he's gone to ground to bleed out."

This was natural. Even in the wild, once a deer puts distance from the hunter, it lies down, usually in a thicket. Hidden, it will lie on the wound to try to staunch the bleeding. If the aim was true, though, it would bleed out in a matter of minutes.

Mack had made his way back to our group, and Gilpin filled him in.

"My people have been helping with the wounded," he said, "but until Russell turns up dead or alive, my primary concern is still Donald and Simon."

Torres turned, and although he regained control of himself, he still wasn't happy. "That's fine and good, but make sure none of you leave the area. The District Attorney may want to move forward with charges."

"For what?" scoffed Mack. "And who the hell are you going to charge? None of our group fired a shot. Donald was on the ground with Simon, while I covered them."

"How about inciting a riot? This is all on Wilson. He put the call out to all these World War two soldiers, and as far as I know," he said pointing at the still-smoking .50 caliber, "he told them to come armed. Probably advised by you."

Mack stepped towards the police officer so quickly that the startled officer took a pace back, his hand going to his holster.

"Don't even think about it, Torres," Mack said in a low, but warning tone. "I don't care if you're a cop or not, I'll put you down."

To her credit, Jamie Nguyen had her hand on the butt of her service pistol, ready to draw.

"Would you two rein in the testosterone," said Special Agent Gilpin, shaking her head impatiently at her partner. "Donald is not going to be arrested."

Torres' mouth opened to argue, but Pointer stopped him with a look.

"How is going to look, Torres, when you arrest America's sweetheart? Especially since both FBI and local police knew about—and were involved with—his peaceful confrontation with an *illegal* march. Unless his gun is empty, I'm guessing he might not even got off a shot. Not to mention that Russell shot first."

Gilpin picked up the thread. "You saw the Nazis were dropping their weapons. It was almost over and would have gone as peacefully as promised, except for Russell. Besides, there's another reason you can't arrest Donald."

Torres glared at her.

"He's dying. He'll never make it to court, let alone jail."

This time it was my turn to gap at her. "How did...?"

"We've known from day one. Because the American Nazi movement is a threat to national security, we do in-depth background checks on anyone who comes into contact with them. We know about the cancer."

I looked over at Simon. "So much for doctor/patient confidentiality."

"Doesn't hold a candle to the safety of the country."

I looked from Simon, who just shook his head And than back at her.

"Now," she continued. "That is not to say that those that did fire into the crowd won't be investigated, especially with guy with the .50 cal., but I'm guessing they'll be dead before any of this gets through the courts. Look how old they are.

Torres tilted his head to the sky, and I watched as his broad shoulders rose and fell and I knew he was trying to stay in control. He threw his hands up suddenly, and without another word, stalked off. Detective Nguyen gave the rest of us an embarrassed smile and followed her partner.

"So now what?" I ask, looking at the two federal agents.

"Now we wait until we get a sighting at one of the blockades around the town, or we find a corpse," Gilpin said. "Until he's accounted for, we have to believe that Russell is still a threat."

Mack only nodded. "The National Guard seems to have everything in hand, so I'm guessing we ought to go back to the farmhouse until we hear from you."

She looked over at her partner and then nodded. "Yeah. If we learn anything new, we'll let you know."

"Thank you," he said and then began to call over the radio for his men to regroup with us.

The two women left us and walked towards entrance of the field. Their day would be a long one.

While we waited, Mack looked over at me.

"Did your guardian angel stop by?" he asked, meaning Dillon Fox.

I grinned. "I would have been surprised if he hadn't. He was always one of the boys, but never had much to say.

He patted my shoulder and pushed my chair towards the road that ran parallel to the park. Police had set up a checkpoint there, collecting personal information for future witness statements before those on the buses left the field. Behind the last bus, I saw our familiar SUV. As we plodded over the sod, which had been trampled by so many feet, weariness settled over me and I could not wait to return to the sanctuary of the farmhouse. Excitement, anxiety and grief—to say nothing of guilt—had sucked out all my energy and I was running on fumes.

Having Emily scold me was something I was actually looking forward to.

Chapter Forty-Two

Even though we got back to the farmhouse by late afternoon, because I knew what the media would make of the day, I took the time to call both my kids to let them know I was safe. It was a hard call, especially with Gail and her tears, and I could hear emotion in Richard's words, both spoken and unsaid. I told them we were just waiting to hear about Russell. Once the police found him, I agreed to have them visit, but I made both realize that they would not talk me into any extended hospital stay. I wanted to die on my own terms, in my own home, surrounded by memories of their mother and the life we had. I assured them that my crusading days were done.

Emily demanded that after a quick bite to eat, I head to bed, and I didn't argue. I couldn't remember the ride back to the farm and only ate because there was no arguing with the damn woman.

Neither my bladder nor the pain in my stomach had been enough to wake me, so I got up to find that it was the next day. Emily must have slipped me some pain medication before I slept, but I couldn't remember a thing. Without a window for fresh air, the heat of the room made me groggy. Finally, fully dressed, I rolled my chair into the kitchen, where a breeze pushed at the bright, white-lace curtains.

Emily rounded the kitchen table with a smile and a handful of pills. "There he is. I was getting worried. I looked in on you a few times, Donald, but you were out like a light, so I figured that was a good thing."

"Lucky for you, I didn't wet the bed, otherwise you'd have had more work on your hands."

I accepted a glass of water and swallowed the pills, two or three at a time.

"Why don't you go outside. Your horse-children are waiting for their carrots," she said with a laugh. "I'll bring your coffee out."

I nodded, but stopped at the door. "Any word?"

She pursed her lips and shook her head.

I went outside, and I was welcomed by the clomp of hooves making for the fence at the edge of the patio. The big male greeted me with a neigh as he rushed the fence. His mate took her time, refusing to lose her dignity and knowing who was to be first to breakfast. The male's head bobbed with anticipation, and I couldn't help grinning. I dug into my pocket and pulled out an apple that I had snagged from the table while Emily had her back to me. Although she never scolded me, her one raised eyebrow at my antics scared the heck out of me.

After relieving my pockets of the sweet treats I'd brought them and rewarding me with a palm rub, both horses meandered around the paddock. I wheeled over to the steaming coffee that Emily had brought out for me. She had retreated into the house, leaving me with my thoughts, such as they were.

I think I was just on autopilot. My mind was numb, and I sat there oblivious to everything around me, my only companions the flashes of yesterday's violence. Even though I knew Frank and Decker were gone, it felt unreal—like a bad dream. If they walked onto the patio, Frank with his cool demeanor and Decker with his ready-to-please attitude, I wouldn't have been surprised.

Instead, Mack joined me.

He had two cups of coffee with him, and it was only then that I realized mine had gone ice cold and that I hadn't touched it. He placed the fresh cup in front of me.

"You okay, Donald? You've been staring off into nothing for a while now."

Swallowing hard, I wrapped my hands around the new mug, absorbing the heat. I hesitated, but then said, "I don't know what to feel. I lost two of my closet friends and it feels like it never happened."

"That's just how your brain protects you from the shock of it all. You just need time to process it."

"Maybe." I took a sip of my coffee and enjoyed the sensation of warmth. I could at least feel that.

"You told me yourself that you can't keep things inside or they'll eat away at you."

I grunted. "You can throw my own words at me, but have you ever talked about your own ghosts?"

He looked away and stared towards the horses before returning his gaze to me. With both of his big hands enveloping his coffee mug, he said, "It was in Afghanistan. We were returning from a mission in the northwest, having taken out a couple of key Taliban leaders who were forcing the opium farmers to sell their crops for weapons. Everyone was in a good mood, as the job had gone well."

Although his eyes had centered on the mug of coffee, I knew he was there living the experience as he told me the details.

"We got a call to make a detour as there had been a report of an attack on a school in a small farming community east of our position. The Canadians had built and equipped a bunch of these schools across the country in an effort to bring education to rural Afghans, especially the girls. The Afghanis would travel for miles for the opportunity, and there were even a couple of buildings to lodge the children, one for boys and one for girls. Before us westerners had arrived, women and girls were not allowed to be educated. That was strictly a male privilege under the Taliban.

"Our trip overland to the community was unremarkable, and we had no encounters with any of the fighters. As we crested the last hill, we saw right off that something was wrong. This town acted as a gathering spot for all the farms in the district and served as a market of sort. Yet, as far as we could see, there was no movement in the valley.

"We went in slowly, expecting to be hit the whole time, but there was no opposition. They'd burnt the school to the ground with all its books and supplies. Charred pieces of paper were scattered all around the structure, the wind tossing black-and-white segments every which way. All the outbuildings were empty. We found ovens still smoking, with husks of burnt bread inside. Kitchens still had uneaten food on the tables. We searched the entire village building by building, but could not find a single person.

"There was blood sign, though. Dried pools of blood showed where someone had bled out, but we also saw blood trails and drags, that told us that some were wounded and tried to escape while they dragged away others.

"It made no sense. We fanned out in ever-increasing circuits around the community until a couple of our men stumbled across an open, communal grave. They also found what was left of the teacher; and, tied to a tree, still barely alive, the village's headsman. It was from him we learned what had happened.

"The Taliban, wanting to make an example, had killed every schoolgirl, but not before chopping off both of their hands for touching blasphemous teachings. They gave the young boys the choice of joining the females or becoming a fighter for the Islamic extremists. Not surprising, all agreed to join. The Taliban then forced the remaining villagers to make the journey to the next community, thirty miles away, as this village was no long safe for them. They poisoned the well and planned to raze the homes. For the villagers to return, was to die.

"That had been six hours before we got there.

"They had done a good job setting up the ambush. We were caught off guard when the first RPG exploded. They killed two guys instantly. I had been standing over the grave and Dillon and I got tossed into the hole. It might have saved us, but..."

Unseeing eyes flooded with silent tears.

"... those little hands... I'm lying in the pile... they're covering me... and I have to climb through them... to get out."

Blood oozes from his mouth and I realize the poor man had bitten his lip to hold himself together. And then this massive warrior breaks down completely as sobs wrack his frame. I sit silently, knowing from long ago that although this is incredibly painful, it's like lancing a blister. Once all the stored grief, pain, and horror is drained, he can begin to heal.

I was pretty certain that the horrible slaughter we survived yesterday had brought all the baggage he had been carrying around to the forefront: and, like an unwatched pot of oil, it finally boiled over and ignited. Knowing the pain he was experiencing, but also the relief he would feel once done, I was so glad I was able to play my part, if only as a sounding board.

When Mack's shoulders sagged in exhaustion, I knew the worst was over. I remembered how tired I was the first time I opened up to Maggie. It had been like I had been carrying the weight of a thousand-pound sack over the Alps. I never had noticed just how worn out the stress and memories had made me.

And it hadn't been a one-time cure. The healing would still take years and another war to get all the hate and anger out of my system. It would take time for Mack as well.

I handed him my handkerchief, and he wiped his eyes, then his face. Surprise crossed his features as he saw blood on it, and he had to explore the lacerated skin of his mouth to realize what he had not even felt at the time.

He cleared his throat. "Sorry," he grunted, and began to hand me the handkerchief.

"Keep it," I said, and gave him a gentle smile of understanding. "So, how did you get out of that ambush?"

The question clearly startled him. After a moment, he lifted his cup and drained the now cold coffee. "Mateo," he said with the hint of a smile. "Even from inside that hole, I could hear rounds from that big rifle of his zinging off the rocks. Like any good sniper, he had never come into the town, but found himself a nest overlooking the area. He took out thirteen before the others gave up and disappeared into the mountains. We had lost our original two, but would have lost more if he hadn't had our back."

"You had Mateo, I had Dillon Fox."

He just nodded.

Chapter Forty-Three

The call came in some time after dark. It wasn't the police this time, but Lisa and Charlotte, the young couple from my apartment building, on the phone. Emily hadn't wanted to wake me, but the girls had been insistent.

"Mr. Wilson. It's Lisa. We heard about the shooting at the park, so we figured it was safe to return home. Charlotte's boss was ragging on her to get back to work. So, anyways, we're hearing noises from your apartment, like whimpering—but the cops still have it taped up."

I sat up straight and fumbled my glasses on as her words broke through my fog of sleep. Emily could see alarm on my face and her eyes grew wide as she mouthed the word, "What?"

"Listen, Lisa. Get out of there. Don't wait. Don't pack. Just get out! I'll call the police. This is not over."

"Okay, Mr. Wilson," she said, her voice shaking with fear.

"Call me back when you're safe."

"Where should we go?"

"The police station on Chestnut."

"Okay."

"Call me." I broke the connection. To Emily, I said, "Get Mack." I immediately called 911 and explained who I was and that there might be someone in my building. Told them to contact Torres or Nguyen.

A couple of quick phone calls assured me that my other tenants, the Ziegler's and the Wong's were still safe at the hotel that Simon had put them up at. They would stay put until they heard back from me.

A rushed trip to the building, and then Mack, Mateo, and I waited in tense silence in the shadows cast by the trees that lined the park. Mack had a second car join us with four teammates parked further away but in radio communication. Across the street, a line of heavily armed police officers were stacked on either side of the main entrance to my building.

I fidgeted in my seat as pain in my pelvis competed with agony in my back. Pain was becoming worse, and I would soon have no choice but to reach for stronger pain killers than oxycodone. My biggest fear was these heavy drugs might make me oblivious not only to the pain, but to everything else around me. With my clock ticking down, at least I wouldn't have to worry about addiction. Emily had assured me that wouldn't happen anyhow, but with the news constantly talking about the opioid crisis in this country, it scared the hell out of me.

It had surprised me at how fast the police had organized themselves. They weren't taking any chances after the shootout in the ballpark. Russell had injured or killed several of his own people, and now they too were looking for some payback.

Lisa and Charlotte called me back while Mateo was driving us towards the apartment building. Both were at the police station, giving statements of what they'd heard. I breathed a sigh of thankfulness once I knew they were out of harm's way.

Although I had my pistol secure in its compartment in my wheelchair, I felt an urge to feel its weight. I felt resentment at the thought of anyone other than me finding and putting an end to this evil son-of-a-bitch. Maggie would have scolded me, and our old priest would have thrown his arms up at my focus on retribution, but I couldn't help the way I felt and all the do-gooders in the world could pound sand. It was time for Russell to die. And I had to do it.

But as long as I had all these cops around and Mack and his crew, there was no way.

At some unheard command, the assault group moved into the entrance of my building. Before the exterior door closed behind them, a pair of blinding flashes like welding arcs emanated from the apartment windows. Hollow thumps of flash grenades accompanied them.

And then silence.

My heart thumped in my throat as we waited in the dark. For what felt like an eternity, nothing on the street moved; but then a group of detectives and forensic personnel began moving from around the corner, where they had lain in wait. They must have been given an all-clear from the interior group.

The front door opened, and a line of SWAT members emerged to make room for the investigators. The shaking of heads told me right away that they had not found Russell. I could see Torres and Nguyen had their heads together with one of the assault group, and figured they were getting the lowdown on what the team had encountered. I watched Torres enter the building as Jamie Nguyen began walking towards our vehicle.

Mateo opened the door at her approach, and she spoke in a voice loud enough that we could all hear. "Russell was definitely here. There was a ton of blood and you're not going to believe it, but he lost an arm."

"What...?" Mateo said for all of us.

She was nodding; her motions exaggerated, as if she didn't believe the news herself. "The team found a severed arm. Either Russell amputated his own arm, or someone helped him do it. We knew he'd suffered a significant wound during the attack at the field and this only proves it. Forensics will collect DNA and prints from the hand to ensure it belonged to the suspect, but he's badly hurt and it's only a matter of time before he bleeds out or someone reports seeing him."

"Until I see his corpse," I said, leaning forward in the seat to look at her, "Russell is still a threat."

"You won't hear me disagree, Mr. Wilson. But I gotta say, the blood loss is supposed to be significant."

I leaned back into the leather seat and Mack caught my eye and nodded his agreement. He knew something else, too: a wounded animal is the most dangerous.

I had to believe that. I moved again to relieve the pain from my hip, this time I tasted blood as I bit down on my lip with a breathless grunt.

Simon's hand touched my arm, but I just nodded.

"We have to get Donald back to bed," I heard him say, and I was in no condition to argue.

Mack and Nguyen exchanged a few more words, but I was beyond that as I surrendered to my growing agony. With my eyes closed, I felt the vehicle pull away from the curb and, like a kid past his bedtime, allowed the motion to lull me to a restless sleep.

I AWOKE TO FIND EMILY reading a paperback in the chair beside my bed. Seeing me awake, she slid a piece of paper to mark her place.

"Morning," I muttered.

"Good afternoon," she said with a smile. "You have to start keeping better hours, Donald. You're only hurting yourself needlessly."

I closed my eyes and nodded obediently.

"Simon says you were in a lot of pain last night."

"Yes, it's becoming more intense and fairly steady now. There's no real let-up, except when I'm asleep."

"Diarrhea?"

"Some," I said not feeling comfortable with the topic.

"Do you recall anything about the stool. Was it loose? Color?"

I thought back. "Yeah, it was strange. Nothing sunk. It all floated and I had to flush a few times. It was the color of pale cream."

She sighed.

"That can't be good."

"It sounds like your bile duct might be blocked. The pancreas breaks down the fat in our food. If it's not working the fat passes through the digestive system unprocessed, causing diarrhea. And being made of fat, floats. The color confirms it.

"So, it's getting worse?"

She nodded, her face a mask of compassion. "It's time for you to accept that you're at the next stage. Home remedies and diet can only help so long. Although they are still going to be important, you're going to need stronger pain killers than I can offer. That means a doctor."

I nodded but said nothing.

"I'll speak to Simon to see if he has any friends who make house calls." She laid a hand on my shoulder.

Lying there, now afraid to move in case the pain reasserted itself, I could hear murmurs of voices in the house, but nothing concrete. I could faintly hear traffic on the road and the odd neigh from the horses.

I had almost fallen back to sleep when I heard a loud bang as if something heavy had struck the building. A scream followed it. I lay there, ears straining against the silence to ensure I'd actually heard it and not dreamed it, when a crash of glass and the far-off report of a rifle echoed through the house.

Ignoring the pain that coursed through my lower body, I sat upright and swung my legs off the bed. One hand reached for my pistol that sat in its holster on the night table, while the other pulled my wheelchair closer to the bed. In a lurch, I heaved my old, near-naked carcass onto the chair, landing with a painful thump that made my eyes water with pain. I fumbled my glasses from nightstand to my nose, and then I pulled my pistol from its sheath and chambered a round.

Glancing down at my body, all skin and bones with crepey skin hanging limply, I'm sure I wouldn't scare off a flock of pigeons, let alone Russell and what was left of his friends.

Awkwardly, using my left hand to twist the doorknob, I swung the door, holding the .45 in my right, ready to fire at any threat. Not seeing anyone, I pulled my chair forward slowly.

More shots came from the front of the house, and it sounded like someone was taking out all the windows from a distance. There was return fire, and I knew that Mack's team were still in the fight.

Turning left towards the kitchen, I found Emily's limp form on the ground. Her kind face was relaxed, but a stream of blood dripped down the side of her face from a cut at her temple. A small puddle was growing. It relieved me to see the swell of her chest and knew that for now, she was alive.

There were multiple shots from around the corner, but I wouldn't venture that way in case I was mistaken for an assailant.

Above me, on the second floor, I heard a heavy tread of boots, followed by the thunder of a rifle, and assumed Mateo was using his Remington R11 RSASS to good effect. The firing at the front of the house died down after he threw a couple of .308 shells that way. I could hear him moving from room to room as he searched for other threats from their windows, and I thanked God he was on my side.

I wheeled out of the kitchen towards the dining room and ran into a stranger, a wide-eyed man holding a bayonet in his right hand. He was around thirty-years of age with a red MAGA ball cap pulled down over a head of long hair that challenged the dark full beard. He wore a white shirt with the Norse Valtnot over his right chest, three interlocking triangles that identified Nazi followers willing to die for their cause.

Two other men stood behind him, one carrying a pump-action shotgun, while the other held a nickel-plated Walther P-38 that might have been the sidearm of an actual Nazi officer.

Without hesitation, the young idiot in front of me stepped forward and drove the mean-looking blade into my stomach. “Die, Jew lover!”

The blade went deep, but I hardly felt anything. Maybe it was because of the pain I was already dealing with or because the edge was so sharp. Either way, I lifted my pistol, flicking off the safety as I did.

“You first,” I told him and squeezed the trigger. The bullet caught him high in the chest as he was leaning over me. The heavy slug lifted him off me, tearing the blade from my gut, and threw him backwards towards his friends and the kickback nearly took my hand off.

My left hand went instinctively to the hole in my stomach as I tried to lift the .45 towards the shotgun-toting inbred now swinging the business end of his weapon towards me. I extended my pistol to take aim—my damaged hand doing its best—and fired off a shot that went wide.

The man smirked as he saw the Colt I was holding fall to the floor as this time its weight and the pain in my hand making it unbearable to hold. I figured that this would be it, when the big guy’s head suddenly evaporated in a cloud of red mist. Before I could even register it, his body tumbled away to land in a heap beside the wannabe Nazi with the

P-38. That man's head snapped in time to catch two rounds to the chest as Mack fired from a classic shooting stance. The man joined his comrades in death.

Not wasting time, our ex-soldier-turned-bodyguard re-holstered his Berretta. Then he pulled the tablecloth from the table with a snap, rolled it into a ball around his one arm, and placed the ball into the hollow of my stomach. He told me, "Press down on the wound."

I gasped at the burning sensation that quickly overwhelmed my long-standing pain from the cancer. I had seen many abdominal wounds during my war years and knew that most were not fatal if treated. The biggest threat was infection.

Mack was calling his people through his wrist mic, trying to get a handle on the enemy, and how they'd got in. It was a one-sided conversation. Before long, members of his crew began closing in on the dining room. Mateo guided Simon down from his bedroom on the second floor. Upon seeing me, Simon rushed over, staying low like he was dodging a barrage of gunfire.

"Donald," he said, his eyes wide. "You're bleeding."

I motioned to the dead Nazi in front of me. "He thought his knife could outmatch my Colt. Grab my gun for me, will you?"

With disgust, he picked up the weapon as if it were evil and handed it to me wordlessly. I could barely hold its weight with my damaged right hand, and let it settle on top of the cloth bandage. Just having it made me feel more secure.

"Mateo, could I get you to check on Emily? She's out cold in the kitchen. Make sure she's okay, please."

He nodded and left to check on her. Minutes later, he returned with her leaning heavily onto him, a dish towel held to her forehead. Seeing me hunched over, holding the cloth to my stomach, she tried to stagger to my side, and would have fallen if not for Mateo.

"It's okay, Emily," I said, to ease her mind. "With luck, the knife might have stabbed that fucking tumor." She rewarded me with a weak smile and took the seat the wide-shouldered sniper had guided her to.

"Keep your eyes peeled," Mack was saying into his mic. "Cops should be here and then we'll do a recon to flush out any stragglers."

"Where the hell did those guys come from?" I asked aloud.

"They had a couple of shooters on the road while they charged down the driveway with a pickup truck," Mateo explained. "They rammed the front entrance to keep us pinned and came through the side door." He pointed at the three corpses in front of me.

"Two more out back," Mack said. "Fortunately, they only clubbed Emily, before they found me."

"Any one-armed shooters among the dead?" I asked.

Mack shook his head.

Chapter Forty-Four

The ride to the hospital was uneventful, with Torres and Nguyen giving us a police escort and Mack and his crew following to serve as tail gunners. Emily lay on a stretcher next to me and, for a change, I was the one assuring her that everything would be fine rather than the other way around. I was appreciating this lady in a brand-new light.

Of course, as she was pretty groggy, we weren't having long philosophical discussions. I was thinking maybe a concussion. And I was working hard to hold back my own pain that had separated into three distinct throbs: one in my gut, and the other all over, and a new one in my right wrist. My joints seemed to compete with the stab wound. I'm sure I felt every crack in the city's streets and I vowed again that after I finished with Nazis, I was going to take issue with Lancaster's city council.

While I might bitch about the local roads, there was no doubting the expertise at the hospital. They whisked Emily and me into the building where a platoon of nurses, orderlies, and doctors took charge.

Before the curtain on my cubicle closed, I saw Simon speaking with a nurse as Mack stood guard, eyes glaring as he scanned the people in the room. Knowing I was safe from Russell and his people, I relaxed and answered the nurse's questions. When I explained I was a stage-four cancer patient, that stopped them for a minute while the doctor called upstairs to the oncologist for his input.

Seems like I was causing a fuss.

Finally, a doctor pushed through the curtain. He wasted no time examining the knife wound. Making a notation to chart, he nodded at the nurse.

"Doc, any chance you can tell me how Emily is?" I asked through gritted teeth. "She came in with me with a blow to the head."

For the first time, he looked at my face. He was in his sixties with a head of silver over a pair of thick glasses that made his eyes look like an owl. I saw recognition cross his features.

"You're the fellow who's been raising cain with the extremists?"

"Guilty as charged," I said.

"Was it one of those who did this?" he said, pointing his chin at my gut to indicate the wound he had just covered.

I nodded.

"I hope you got a piece of him, because he almost made you forget the cancer you've been dealing with. Even so, this wound might make things a lot more complicated. Your oncologist should be here momentarily to determine what she can do for you."

"At least you don't have to worry about patching the other guy up, Doc. He's going to a different department."

His grey-blue eyes studied me before he leaned forward. "As a physician I'm not supposed to be happy about that, but my father lost two brothers in the war, so I won't tear up anytime soon."

He squeezed my arm. "I'll check on your friend."

I slipped in and out until a nurse came in to fix me with an intravenous. Minutes later, I was out for good.

AN ANNOYING BEEPING woke me and through a fog, I took in my surroundings. It took a few minutes before my confused mind made out that I was in a hospital room. It took a little more time before I remembered the attack and my injury. I reached down and tenderly felt the bandages that were wrapped around my abdomen. Even that effort felt exhausting. On my right wrist was a black wrist-splint that left my hand mostly free.

Eventually, a nurse swept into the room. Seeing that I was awake, a friendly smile crossed her face.

"Welcome back, Mr. Wilson," she said. "You must be thirsty."

I nodded, running my thick tongue across the inside of my mouth.

She raised the bed, so I was sitting up, then held a little jug of water while positioning a straw for me. It was a blessing and after a cough, I felt better.

"Can you find my glasses?

From a side table that I hadn't seen, she retrieved my specs. After wiping them clean, she handed them to me, and I mashed them to my face.

"Thanks."

She smiled and pointed a button clipped to bedsheet. "If you need anything, just give me a buzz." With that, she left me to my thoughts.

I lay there for awhile staring at the ceiling when my oncologist entered the room. Last time I saw her she had told me I had months to live. Damn, it felt like such a long time ago.

"Hi Doc," I said with a smile. "How's it going?"

"Mr. Wilson," she said, her tone hinting surprise. She pulled my chart and looked up in shock. "Of course, I've followed your crusade with interest, but never suspected it involved you in the actual fighting."

"Careful Doc," I said, enjoying her discomfort. "You'll be infringing on my rights as a senior citizen."

"Make light of it, if you will, but as I explained to you a few months ago, you are pretty sick, Mr. Wilson. You should be in bed, not running around the country tilting at windmills."

"I don't run from a fight, and they weren't windmills. If my actions made even a little difference, then my life—or death—will be worth it, Doc. That has to be better than lying in a bed waiting to die."

She stared at me in disbelief.

The door opened again and cut our philosophical discussion short as the ER doctor entered. He nodded at my young oncologist.

"Mr. Wilson, your friend will be all right. She suffered a concussion, but after some time off her feet, she should be just fine. In fact, she was asking about you."

I smiled. "If either of you needs a tremendous nurse, catch her before they discharge her. I give her a five-star recommendation. There is no way I would have been able to accomplish what I have without her."

The two physicians exchanged a glance before turning back to me. My oncologist said, "To determine if that knife attack affected the cancer, we'd like to admit you for some tests. A knife wound isn't going to make your cancer 'worse', of course; but apparently, you've had some damage to tissues affected by the cancer, and we'd like to have a look at that."

I nodded. "I figured."

"How was the pain before the attack?" she asked.

I sighed and decided that the truth might be best. "It's been getting worse lately. Emily was going to bring me in for something stronger, so I guess I have to thank the little idiot that stuck me for that, at least."

The poor kid shook her head as if she was dealing with a nutcase, but the older guy saw my point and put a smile on his face. "I'll get the paperwork started for that," he said.

SUNLIGHT CROSSED THE floor, leaving the rest of my hospital room in shadow. I blinked at the light, realizing that I had slept since dawn which had made itself known a few hours ago. That was the last time I had wrestled with the bed-pan since they'd decided not to catheterize me. I was ready to wrestle again.

As I woke further, I allowed my eyes to cross the familiar-looking room. The hospital was a typical, institutional building with heavy walls and highly polished concrete floors that arched together into a graceful curve of baseboard six inches up the wall. Pale green walls. I was fortunate that I was in the old hospital and had been given a private room rather than being in the newer facilities that lumped everyone into an open-concept building that seemed to care little for noise or germ control. Just pack more bodies into the same space. All business; bigger bang for the buck.

I spied movement in the far corner and my heart about tripped over itself until I saw what seemed to be Simon's wide face grinning at me as he pulled himself out of a chair. But without my glasses, it could have been anyone's wide face grinning.

"*Boker tov*, my friend," he said in greeting. "I got you a private room." Definitely Simon after all.

"Good morning. How long have you been sitting there?" I found my glasses on the bedside table near a water carafe and put them on.

He glanced at the wall clock and shrugged. "About twenty minutes. You were sleeping soundly, and I didn't want to bother you."

I nodded my thanks.

"Mack will be in and out today, but he wanted you to know that his team is outside, and the entire floor should be clear. You should be safe here."

I nodded.

"He wanted to make sure you got the parcel he sent. You were asleep when he looked in last night."

I smiled and nodded. "Let him know that I found it during one of my pee breaks and that I appreciate it."

He looked like he wanted to ask what it was Mack brought for me but changed the topic.

"So, what's been happening?"

"The police identified the men who attacked the ranch house. They were Russell's comrades from the NMA's Atomwaffen Division. The police had warrants out for all of them, so your friends from the FBI were happy to close several open files."

"Remind me to send them a bill."

He chuckled.

"No sign of Russell, yet?"

He shook his head, frustration clear on his face. "You'd think with all the police looking for him and with him so badly injured that it would be a straightforward thing...?"

"With any luck, he's crawled into a hole and bled to death."

"I'd sleep much better if we could find him, dead or alive."

I nodded. "This open-ended story is getting tiresome," I said.

The silence that fell showed that he agreed. There would be no closure without a body.

"On a brighter note," he continued. "They'll discharge Emily later today. I'm flying her to Seattle, and she'll stay with her parents until she's ready to get back to work."

I nodded. "We talked a little last night. She's going to come see me before she goes. I'm going to miss her a lot."

My heart ached at the thought of kind-hearted Emily leaving me. But of course, I'd be leaving everyone sooner rather than later. Especially after what the tests had revealed.

"Simon," I said, feeling myself getting emotional. "Thank you for believing in me and for helping me accomplish all that we did. People have woken up and are demanding change."

"Donald, I may have greased the wheel, but it was your story and your resolve that moved things along. It happened because you cared so much for what you believed in."

"After what I saw in Germany, how could I do less?"

"Many have. You were not the only Allied soldier who saw the atrocities the Nazis performed not only against Jews, but all those who differed from them. Russians, Communists, Freemasons, and even German citizens. But of all those who knew, you were the only one to stand up to remind the world as the new ones came out of hiding."

"It might help for a while, Simon, but humans are their own worst enemy. Nazis aren't the only ones, either. Stalin killed millions of his own people, Chinese Communists killed hundreds of thousands of their own. Then there's Cambodia, Rwanda and Myanmar. When are we ever going to learn?"

Simon shook his head, his eyes looking dead. What had happened to the Jewish people was horrendous and evil, but genocide was ongoing. And unless the countries killing their own have something the world needs, like oil or the rare earths needed in microchips and solar panels, superpowers turned blind eyes.

He lifted his head and sighed. "Then, praise God, we must count our blessings when we win even a minor battle."

I nodded. "I just wish someone smarter than me can figure a way to do it without a repeat of the other day. There's been enough blood spilled."

"Amen."

He walked over to me and held out his hand. "Thank you again, my friend, on behalf of me—and my people."

I shook his hand, grimacing at the pain in my stomach.

"And don't worry, Mack and his team will be with you until Russell is found or..."

I nodded, biting my lip to control the overwhelming emotion. We'd shared a lot together.

With a tilt of his head, he turned and left me to my thoughts.

I WOKE WITH A START, gasping, as pain flared in my gut and was echoed in my pelvis. I was uncertain what woke me, but the room was completely dark, except for light in the bathroom. In the distance, I could hear the wail of an ambulance; and as I listened, I could tell it was inbound to the hospital. Someone was having the worst day in their life.

The closed curtain around my bed bowed inward as a breeze caressed it. I was cozy under crisp sheets, enjoying the warmth of a flannel heated blanket.

Then I heard the sound a second time, the one that had wakened me. This time, it was unmistakably the sound of a gunshot.

Joseph Russell.

I didn't need a crystal ball to know he was making his move. I was dying, and because he was too, he had no choice but to strike now or lose his chance forever.

Muffled yells of alarm and even a scream suddenly echoed through the thick door to my room. Muffled, but unmistakable in the quiet of the night.

The door to my room thumped open a few inches just as there was the sound of another gunshot, before falling closed again. In the distance, I could hear sirens approaching.

I tried to sit, but the hole in my stomach, the cancer and the cracked pelvis all protested together, and I fell back with a whimper, as pain, like anvil lightning, flashed across my whole being, making me blink repeatedly just to stay conscious.

As I watched, there was another report and the door slammed open wide. I watched, horrified, as Mateo pitched backwards, as if the noise had catapulted him, his right side slick with blood. He grunted as he hit the polished concrete floor, skidded to the far wall, and lay still. The door hissed closed again.

There was no sound for a heartbeat, but then the heavy wooden door swung slowly open again. A head poked through with eyes wild and wide as Russell's gun hand pushed the door fully open. He staggered into the room, panting with excitement, exertion and obvious pain. He let the door swing shut and leaned against it as it closed. With the barrel of the pistol, he hit the light switch and both of us blinked at the intensity of the fluorescents.

Russell wore hospital scrubs with an overcoat and surgical cap. The left sleeve of the overcoat hung empty, but the fabric was puddled with blood soaking through.

He took one look at me, cowering in the bed helplessly before tracking the gun out the door towards Mateo slumped against the far wall.

"No!" I screamed.

He glanced at me, and his mouth broke into a ragged, evil smile before returning his attention to the ex-soldier.

"You fucking coward!" I yelled. "It's me you want. Come and get *me*. You've been too chickenshit to meet me man to man. Now's your chance."

He leaned forward, shaking the pistol towards me. "Don't worry, you old piece of shit. You're next."

"And who's going to do your dirty work for you, you fucking coward?" I said in a frantic attempt to keep his attention towards me rather than my friend lying helpless and unmoving. "You always strike from your safe little hidey-hole. You let others take point, because you're too cowardly to stand up and fight. Just like Hitler hiding in his bunkers, and like all those losers you follow. You're all made of the same color of shit."

He snarled and turned towards the bed, waving a heavy, large-bored weapon at me. "I'm gonna make you suffer, you old fuck! You're going to die slow! If fact, I'm going to use this." As he spoke, he tucked his heavy revolver into a pocket of the coat and pulled out a blade. But it wasn't just any kind of knife. I had only seen its kind in the Commandant's quarters at Dachau. It was a real SS dagger, and I knew there would be an acid-cut engraving *Meine Ehre Heißt Treue* or 'My Honor is Loyalty' on the blade under a hilt marked with a swastika.

My eyes grew wide at the sight of the dagger. It looked authentic, and I wondered how Russell could have ever come across it. I knew it would be worth a small fortune.

"This blade was my grandfather's, and I will cut your heart out in his honor," he snarled, leaning threateningly towards me.

"I don't think so. Your grandfather was scum and so are you!" With that, I lifted the service pistol that Mack had delivered to me the night before to comfort me. I didn't bother to pull the sheet away, but simply raised the gun from where it lay beside me and fired at Russell's hate-filled face. The heavy 230 grain bullet cut through his skull and slammed his body back to the opposite wall. The kick from the pistol felt like it broke my wrist, and the sound of the shot deafened me.

I heard nothing for a while.

Chapter Forty-Five

"And you're sure that's all of it?" Torres said to me as he stood before my bed, a digital recorder sitting on the mobile table over my bed.

I nodded tiredly as both he and Nguyen waited patiently.

Mack sat at the back of the room, making sure that I wasn't being bullied by the irritated police detective.

"In that case, sign this form. It will be added to your statement once it is transcribed, so that it all legal."

> I, Donald S. Wilson, confirm this statement to be true under oath.
>
> I hereby state that the information above is true, to the best of my knowledge. I also confirm that the information here is both accurate and complete, and relevant information has not been omitted.

HE TURNED TO MACK. "Would you witness it for us?

I scratched my signature with my ruined right hand before pain took me away once more.

Epilogue

Mack watched as Donald's daughter, Gail, flinched at the harsh report of the honor guard's volley. Richard, her brother, had a hand on her shoulder to support her. Two more rounds echoed over the valley.

Benny hunched over his wife, Edith, who was crying, startled by the gunfire, having no clue what had happened. And Mack thought that might be a blessing since it would be a long time before he forgot Donald.

Bright sunshine belied the somberness of the afternoon ceremony.

Mack stood at attention, arm bent in a salute to a fellow soldier. Beside him, Christian Torres and Jamie Nguyen stood, heads bowed. Further back, two FBI officers stood rigid, faces emotionless behind dark glasses.

Mack's team was there, with the exception of Scott, shot a second time and resting by doctor's order. Mateo could not stand and was sitting, like Donald had, in a wheelchair because of the bullet wounds from Russell's Luger in the upper thigh and a lung. It would be months before either of the men would be ready to return to duty.

Two members of the National Guard, Honor Parade, marched forward, performing the flag presentation to the family and he could see both siblings weeping as they accepted the folded flag, a small gesture of the American people for one of their veterans.

As the ceremony ended, Simon walked over to Mack and extended his hand. "Mack, you need anything, ever, just holler. Use my name if you ever need an endorsement. You and your team went over and beyond."

Mack nodded as Simon moved towards the family.

He turned to Torres. "Are you going to be needing anything else from me or my team?"

The cop studied him before shaking his head. "Nah. We got Donald's sworn statement before he passed, and the prosecutor was not interested in perusing matters further. Donald admitted shooting Russell. But y'know, I'd still like to know why you brought him his service pistol?"

They'd been over this point a few times, but Torres was like a dog with a bone. He'd already threated to charge Mack with being an accessory, but the powers that be weren't interested in filing charges. They wanted the entire episode to go away. It had become a political dumpster fire.

"I told you. It was a dying man's last request. I was there when the doctor explained how bad off Donald really was. He had days, if not hours, left to live. The man wanted to die with a gun in his hand. It's no different from ancient warriors wanting to die with their sword in their hand. Who was I to deny him?"

"And you just happened to go for coffee and leave the side entrance of the hospital unguarded?"

Mack kept his expression neutral, glanced toward Mateo in his wheelchair, then dropped his eyes, and said, "Yeah, in hindsight, that was a big mistake on my part. But then again, it was a good thing Donald was armed, wouldn't you agree? After all, he saved Mateo and took down Russell."

The cop stared at him and then shook his head with disgust. He turned away and stalked off, Nguyen still chasing after him. Looking up, Mack could see the two FBI agents had left as well. He turned away from Donald's family so they could grieve in private. They deserved that, having missed Donald's last couple of months, other than their brief stay on the island.

He looked down at Mateo. "You ready?"

"Yeah boss. But next time, *you* take the shot, so the client can go out the hero." He grabbed his side as he helped Mack push the wheelchair. "This hurts like a bitch."

The big security consultant chuckled. "Deal."

The End

To the reader, I hope you enjoyed my story. For an author, reviews are like gold and can help the book we offer you become successful. Please consider taking the time to fill out a short review wherever you purchased the book or at www.goodreads.com

The Author

DAVE WICKENDEN HAS spent time in the Canadian Armed Forces before the Fire Service, so is as comfortable with a rocket launcher as a fire hose. He has brought six people back from the dead utilizing CPR and a defibrillator and has assisted in rescuing people in crisis. He has learnt to lead men and women in extreme environments. He loves to cook, read and draw and write. Dave ran his own home-based custom art business creating highly detailed wood and paper burnings called pyrography. One of his pictures of former Prime Minister Jean Chretien graces the walls of Rideau Hall in Ottawa.

After 31 years in the Fire Service and attaining the rank of Deputy Fire Chief, David took early retirement to write time. He is a member of the Writer's Union of Canada, The Crime Writers of Canada, the International Thriller Association, and the International Screenwriters Association. His short stories have appeared in several anthologies and literary magazines. He has adapted all his manuscripts into feature screenplays. Currently, Dave offers Professional Beta Reading Services for authors and is working on seventh novel, a political thriller.